The crac

The scream s...... him, his sinister face, lusting eyes, and sheer size. She screamed, dropped her keys and ran, realizing too late she was running toward the graveyard and wooded area just beyond. Stupid. Too late to run to Matt now. She gasped for breath, heart pounding in her ears.

Making it through the graveyard to the trees, Jessie ran along them, hoping she was headed back toward the church and the lighted parking lot. He was closing in fast. Tripping over a tree root, she pitched forward into the darkness, sliding sideways down a steep embankment, grabbing at the muddy grass. She chocked off a cry as she fell several feet to a ledge below, hitting her head on something hard.

She lay winded on her back, struggling for breath, looking up in the mesmerizing light show as a fork of lightning unfolded across the sky. On any other night it would have fascinated her, but now it was like a scene from a creepy movie. As she breathed deeply in and out her racing heart started to slow down.

"Jessie, sweet Jessie…" The man's mocking voice floated down to her. "I'll be back to play another day."

The Harvest Club

by

Iona Morrison

Bonnie Howler
Every moment is a gift
Iona Morrison

This is a work of fiction. Names, characters, places, and incidents are either the product of the author's imagination or are used fictitiously, and any resemblance to actual persons living or dead, business establishments, events, or locales, is entirely coincidental.

The Harvest Club

COPYRIGHT © 2014 by Iona Morrison

Cover Art by *Debbie Taylor*

The Wild Rose Press, Inc.
PO Box 708
Adams Basin, NY 14410-0708
Visit us at www.thewildrosepress.com

Publishing History
First Faery Rose Edition, 2014
Print ISBN 978-1-62830-521-0
Digital ISBN 978-1-62830-522-7

Published in the United States of America

Dedication

In memory of Linda Gross,
who inspired me with the story of a church ghost.
Also to Rob Morrison,
who encouraged me every step of the way.

Chapter One

She had escaped at last! Jessie glanced in the rear view mirror as the New York skyline sank beneath the horizon. There had been days over the past few months when she'd felt she would nearly burst out of her skin with restlessness. No more! She smiled and turned her attention back to the winding road. Any mistakes she made now were her own. At least it would be her life. The one she chose, not Dad's idea of Jessie's best life.

A Toyota with a dented fender cut her off with a blast of the horn as she speed dialed Katie on her cell. The driver gave her the finger. "Hi, it's me." She could barely contain her laughter. "I wanted to let you know I'm just leaving the city."

"What's so funny?"

"Just one of the locals sending me off in style."

Katie giggled. "I hate to tell you, but you'll find that wherever you go."

"I know, but New Yorkers do it with such flair."

"I can't wait until you get here." Katie was at a near-squeal pitch, a familiar Katie trait. "I'm already making plans for us."

"At least let me get settled in first."

"I will, but I won't let you become a recluse either. I've decided to make you my next project."

"That sounds a little scary." Jessie thought for a moment. "No matchmaking, Katie, I mean it!"

"Is your dad still mad?" Katie changed the subject.

"What do you think?" Jessie switched lanes, passing the driver of the Toyota who had slowed down to turn. She honked and waved. "He'll sulk for a while expecting me to come around and creep home with my tail between my legs."

"But you won't because you're just as stubborn as he is." Katie's grin was just about audible. Jessie smiled.

"True, I am my father's daughter. It took me long enough, but I finally discovered how to hold out against his guilt trips." Jessie chuckled. "I should be there in a couple of hours."

"I'll be waiting. Remember, turn left once you get off the highway on to the coastal road."

****

As Jessie rounded the headland on the coastal road she caught sight of a sailboat taking on the waves. Fascinated, she pulled over onto the shoulder and got out to watch. Wow, was the boat in trouble? The wind whipped her hair into her face, and she pulled it into a ponytail without taking her eyes off the boat. One minute the vessel seemed to struggle against the force of the waves, and on the next one, the wind caught its sails and glided effortlessly across the water. Whew. A sense of relief filled Jessie as she watched the small craft until it became a tiny dot on the horizon, off on some new adventure.

What an awesome welcome! Jessie took a deep breath and exhaled. She loved the smell of the sea air. As a matter of fact she loved everything about the ocean. The sound of the surf, the sunsets, and the summer breezes off the water—those were only some of the many reasons she was moving to Blue Cove. She wanted this to be a new beginning, a laid-back lifestyle filled with long runs on the beach, wave watching, hanging out with friends. And maybe, just maybe, someone special to share this perfect life with, please. She looked up toward the heavens.

Her ringing phone jolted her, and she fumbled it out of her pocket. "Hey, this is Jessie."

"Where are you?" Katie's cheerful voice sounded in her ear.

"Not too far away, but I'll probably take a look around town before I get to your place." Jessie got into her car and closed the door. "I'm so excited to finally be here that I've got to check it out."

"I can hardly wait to see you—so hurry!"

Jessie turned the key, and the engine hummed to life. She had missed Katie! She could still remember the first time they met. Katie was standing on the sidewalk outside of the school, big tears falling down her cheeks as her mom drove away. One of the big boys had pushed her, knocking her pencil box out of her hands. Jessie had rushed over so sure of herself. "I'll take care of you," she'd told Katie as they picked up the pencils. "I won't let that mean old boy push you again." As if she could have stopped him. A smile teased the corners of her mouth. From that moment on, they had been best friends.

Together again! Jessie took a deep breath. For the first time in a long time, she felt relaxed and excited about life. The last few miles seemed to fly by and soon enough Blue Cove came into view.

****

Driving slowly down Main Street, Jessie looked

around. How pretty! Beautiful old trees lined both sides of the street, and large ceramic pots filled with flowers decorated each corner and were spaced at intervals on the block. Most of the buildings had new facades, which added to the street's overall appeal. Old fashioned lampposts and the smell of the ocean gave it that wonderful New England feel. It would be stunning with the changing colors of fall, or a light dusting of snow in the winter.

Jessie spotted the Cove Book Store. Katie had mentioned it and that it was for sale. She still might buy it. Jessie filed the image of the brick storefront and weather beaten trim in her mind for later. A new name for sure. She frowned. Planters out front? Period hanging sign? Maybe some fresh paint on the trim…

She turned to look at the other side of the street. Yes, there it was just where Katie had said it would be, First Community Church, a pristine white building complete with a steeple, a bell, and an office with her name on it. She had liked it on the internet; it was even better for real.

A woman stood in front of the church staring at her. Jessie waved. The woman merely glared back and tapped her foot petulantly.

****

Wow, so much for all the locals being friendly. Whoever was late was going to get an earful it looked like. Jessie slipped her car into a space in front of Java Joe's, a cute little hole-in-the-wall coffee place. Definitely coffee time! Stepping inside she looked around. Nice, over-stuffed comfy couches, leather chairs, and modern art work. What a great place to hang out with friends. And it was right across the street from work.

"Can I help you?" A young woman walked out of the kitchen.

"Something smells wonderful!" Jessie looked up from the display case into a pair of deep brown eyes, accented by a garish dark green eye shadow.

"We just took some fresh lemon blueberry scones out of the oven. Would you like to have a taste?"

Jessie nodded and popped the piece of scone into her mouth. It was delicious, buttery, stuffed with blueberries and drizzled with lemon icing. She ordered two of them to go and a decaf coffee.

"Are you passing through or just visiting?" The girl smiled as she slipped the scones into a white bakery bag. "I don't remember seeing you before."

"Actually I'm moving here." She smiled back at her, noticing the girl's nose ring and multiple earrings.

"Oh, you must be Katie's friend. She's been telling everyone about you." The girl's eyes sparkled. "My name is Molly. Welcome to Blue Cove!" Molly handed her the bag of scones. "I'm afraid that after New York you'll find life here a little boring."

"I'm Jessie..." She reached for the bag. "Right now I have to admit boring sounds pretty good."

"Thanks for coming in." Molly's smile widened. "It's nice to meet you."

"I'm sure I'll see you again, Molly. My new job is across the street, and coffee is a necessity of life for me, even if it's decaf." Jessie dropped the change into the tip jar and turned to leave. As she stepped outside, the door closed behind her. The lady she had seen earlier was nowhere to be seen. Her friend must have finally showed up.

****

Jessie noticed a car in the church parking lot and made a U-turn, pulling her convertible into the space next to it. It had been a long time since she had attended church on a regular basis, much to her parents' chagrin, and here she was going to work at one. She might need to include a hard hat in her Monday attire, she smiled, just in case the roof fell in.

She sipped her coffee, pulled out her cell phone, sighed, and made the call she had been dreading. Instant relief filled her, Dad didn't answer, and she got his voicemail. Leaving him a quick message to let him know she had arrived safely, Jessie turned her phone off.

****

She got out of her car, stretching her legs, and strolled toward the church entrance. But it was the cemetery on the other side of the church that called to her. It was a gorgeous day, too nice to go inside just yet.

Katie, Jessie, and some of their friends used to go to the cemetery in their small town just to scare each other witless, especially on Halloween. The darker the night, the better!

She smiled as she strolled between the headstones, across neatly trimmed grass. Katie would get them all worked up ahead of time with stories of the dead who roamed restlessly among the graves. She had been the instigator of such outings, and Jessie always followed her. Jessie chuckled at the memory. Following Katie had gotten her into plenty of trouble.

Jessie paused to read some of the headstones. A few dated back almost a hundred years. Just ahead under the shade of huge maple tree she saw a new grave. Making her way there, careful to stay on the path, Jessie stopped in front of the grave so she could read the memorial on the stone.

Here lies the sunshine of our lives.
Beloved Wife, Mother, Daughter, and Friend
Gina Martin
Born June 5, 1982, Died March 15, 2012

It was a lovely area, well-manicured and maintained; fresh flowers filled the vases on each side of the headstone. A bench was placed directly across from the grave under the maple tree, and offered a view to the woods behind the church. Jessie sat down and sighed with pleasure.

As she sat, she calculated the years. Wow, this Gina was not quite thirty, only a few years older than herself. How had she died? Jessie frowned. Too young to die! She shook her head but couldn't stop the tears that trickled down her cheeks. Annoyed, she wiped them from her face.

"Every day is a gift, even though it's not wrapped with a bow. Live it fully!" Her grandma Sadie had told her often, and lived it by example. Looking at the new grave Jessie couldn't help but wonder about Gina Martin's short life. What had she been like?

Lifting her face, she saw a movement at the edge of the woods. The impatient woman she had seen earlier in the floral dress gazed directly at her, never taking her eyes off Jessie's face. Her curly short, brown hair framed her pretty face. She was surprised to see her again so soon. Her ride must have dropped her off here, after they'd gone wherever they were going.

"Hello." Jessie waved and smiled.

The woman didn't say a word but stood quiet and still, staring at her. Jessie looked away for a moment, and when she glanced back again, the woman was gone.

****

"How rude, I wonder what her problem is!" Jessie stood and shrugged, then walked through the cemetery back toward the church. Climbing the stairs, she opened the door. "Is anyone here?" She stepped inside.

"Can I help you?" A gray haired man shuffled across the foyer toward her, limping slightly. His smile was warm and genuine.

"I'm Jessie Reynolds, the new secretary. I saw your car in the parking lot and decided to come in and have a look around before Monday." She smiled back at him.

"Welcome, Jessie. I'm James Morris." He extended his hand. "Pastor Rick told the congregation we were getting a new secretary. I'd be happy to show you the church."

"That would be nice." She shook his hand.

Walking with James was a quick education in small town living. He seemed to know everyone and everything.

Jessie made a mental note to be careful what she said in front of him because his ability to recall details from years ago was incredible. He showed her the offices, the sanctuary, and the rest of the church. Bringing her back to the foyer, he stopped at a wall with several photographs.

"These are all the pastors who have served the church since it was built. This one here was the founding pastor; of course I wasn't around yet." He laughed. "I would have to be older than I already am." He pointed to a painting and then went on to point out the photos of those pastors he had known personally. He told her a story about how each them had made their way to First Community. When he came to the smiling face of a pretty, young woman with dark curly hair, he paused. "This is Pastor Gina Martin. She was such a sweet young thing. She's dead, you know, murdered right outside the church a few months ago. They still don't know who did it." He shifted his weight to his good leg and leaned against the wall.

Startled, she looked at James. "I just saw her grave." Jessie turned back to the picture, feeling a little light headed. "She was a pastor here?" It…it looked a little like the lady she had seen in the woods. Not possible. She gave her head a tiny shake. A sister? Maybe just her vivid imagination at it again.

"Yes," he answered. "Gina was our Assistant Pastor and we all miss her something terrible."

She could feel those pesky tears gathering again. "How many children did she have? Any…any siblings? She wiped an errant tear from her cheek.

"Two children," he said. "A boy and a little girl. They live with Gina's parents at Rocky Pointe until the custody battle with their stepfather is settled. No siblings that I can recall, at least none that I ever met. Are you all right?"

"Yes." She cleared her throat and managed a smile. Why this deep sadness? She'd never met this woman. Tired, she decided. She was just tired.

"James, I think I'd better get on my way. I still have to get settled in." She offered her hand once again. "Thanks for the tour. The church is lovely." She turned and walked briskly toward the front doors.

Striving to keep up with her, he made it to the door in time to hold it open for her to walk through and then followed her out. He pointed to the tree where Gina's body had been discovered. "She had several gunshot wounds, real messy, if you know what I mean. It's a sad business, and the church is still trying to recover." He paused. "I hope you'll enjoy working here and this won't scare you off."

She mumbled a goodbye, bolted across the parking lot and got into her car as fast as her feet would carry her. Wanting to speed away from the church, Jessie calmed herself first. She started her car, going over Katie's directions in her mind. Why hadn't Katie told her about the murder at the church? Was it a random killing? Or had Gina been a target? And who in the heck was the woman? Not a ghost, that's for sure. She'd looked way too real. There was a story to be uncovered here for sure!

She drove a little way and then pulled over on the shoulder, needing to get hold of herself before she saw Katie. She would want the scoop, and Jessie wasn't ready to tell anybody about how Gina's grave and murder had impacted her. At least not right now.

A car pulled in behind her. In her mirror she watched a neatly dressed man approaching her car. He leaned down to see her better; brown eyes with gold flecks looked inquiringly into hers. "Are you all right? Do you need any help?" He straightened up and continued to look at her curiously.

"Everything is fine." She gazed up at him. "I'm new in town—I just arrived from New York and needed to get my bearings."

"You must be Jessie, Katie Donovan's friend. She told me you were on your way and to keep a look out for you. My name is Dylan Mitchel." He smiled at her. "I'm one of the police officers in town. Welcome to Blue Cove."

"Thanks." She smiled. "I'd better get on my way before Katie sends out the militia." She laughed and started her car, shifting it into gear.

"Your turn off is just up the road. Katie has one of the prettiest places you'll ever lay eyes on. I know I'll be seeing you around." She nodded and he headed back to his car.

****

Making the turn onto Blue Iris Lane, which was obviously named for the inn, she slowed down to take it all in. She was going to enjoy the moment in spite of murders and ghosts!

Irises and lilac bushes lined the roadway filling the air with a fragrant floral scent. At the end of the road was the inn just like its magazine picture, yellow clapboard siding and pristine white trim, accented with shutters and several pairs of French doors leading out onto a beautiful large wraparound porch. No wonder the Blue Iris Inn had been given a five star rating in the *Beautiful Inns of America Magazine*. It was special, with its charming gardens and spectacular ocean views. Jessie pinched herself, smiling, to make sure she wasn't dreaming.

Katie was waiting on the porch. Her coppery hair was ablaze in the sunlight as she posed like a model among the white wicker furniture. The moment Katie saw her, a smile lit up her face she waved excitedly, jumping up and down. Jessie grinned.

"Jessie, Jessie." Katie ran down the steps toward her. She opened the car door, grabbed Jessie, and wrapped her in a big hug as she climbed out of the car. "I'm so glad you're here. Dylan called and told me you were on your way. We've so much to catch up on." Pausing only to take a breath, Katie hugged her again. "Ooh, I like your hair long. Everything about you is long!" She stepped back with a stunned look on her face.

"What?" Jessie laughed

"Oh, my gosh, you look great! New York was good for you. You'll be like manna to the single guys in town."

"I'm not sure how to take that, but thanks, I think, and hi back at you." Jessie chuckled, as Katie's green eyes twinkled with mischief, just as she remembered.

"Have you always been this tall?" Katie looked up at Jessie, gesturing for drama. "I don't remember being this short next to you. I feel like a monkey next to a gazelle." They both giggled.

"Oh, how I've missed you…and missed laughing. I don't think I've hardly laughed at all the past several years except for when you called."

"Seriously…we'll remedy that as soon as possible." Katie grabbed Jessie's purse from the car and closed the door. "Just as soon as we get you settled we're going to dinner to celebrate your arrival." She hugged Jessie again.

"Sounds good…I can't wait to see my place. Did everything get here okay?"

"It's all there waiting for you to put it away." Katie took her hand and pulled her down the path.

****

The cottage was perfect, away from the main inn, down a path through the beautiful gardens and set on the property in such a way as to have a breathtaking view of the ocean. It was a place she could only imagine in her dreams, but she was standing in it.

Katie left her to do some immediate unpacking and freshen up. From the cozy living room she stared out at the distant horizon, the sun now high in the sky, turning the cove a deep blue hue. "Thank you, my dear friend," she whispered.

If it hadn't been for Katie she would still be in New York City, living in a tiny flat with two other girls from work.

She had arrived there, a very naïve twenty-one-year-old fresh out of college, and had been hired as an intern by a family friend, to write for a cable news company. After several promotions, Jessie's salary was great, but with each passing year she felt more unsettled and restless. She wasn't one of those people who thrived in the city.

The news industry had become extremely competitive, with everyone after the credit for the next big story. Jessie had started the job wanting to make a difference, but that wasn't what it was all about. Well, she still wanted that—to make a difference.

This past year she had made a decision to look for something different. Every weekend she used her one pricey purchase, called fondly her sanity keeper, a fully restored 1964 red Mustang convertible, to explore the coastal Northeast. It had all seemed like a pipe dream until a couple of months ago. Then the call had come from Katie.

"Jessie, guess what?" It had been a wet, chilly

evening after a disappointing day at work. Katie's voice on the phone was as impatient as ever. "Oh, you'll never guess. I've inherited an inn at Blue Cove from my uncle Robert. I'll be moving there, in a couple of weeks. It's called the Blue Iris Inn."

"Perfect! I can't wait to see it. Just think, Katie, it'll be like old times. We haven't lived this close in years. I'll actually get to see you once in a while."

"I've been thinking." Katie paused. "You're always telling me you want to get out of the city; you could come and help me out, or find a job. I have a cottage on the property you could rent. I'll give you a great deal. Give it some thought, okay?"

"I'll do it." She had decided on the spot, a rush of relief washing through her. "It sounds too good to be true. Not only getting out of the city, but to be with my best friend as well. It might be hard to pass up."

"I'm hoping so and one more thing to tempt you… it has a spectacular view of the ocean. I'll let you know when I get there and in the meantime, you can check it out on the internet. Oh, and, I heard about a job opening at First Community Church. They're in need of a secretary."

She had checked it out, applied for the job, did two phone interviews and was hired. Just like that. When she turned in her two week notice, her boss, Neil Dempsey, had asked her if she would consider doing some freelance news stories, to which she readily agreed and, voilà, here she was.

Jessie sighed and turned away from the window. In her new kitchen, she unpacked the box sitting on the counter. Distracted, she put things away without her usual planning.

She couldn't explain what had happened to her today, but her intuition told her it was more than being tired. There was something for her to find here. In the meantime, Jessie loved it, the town, the inn, and her cottage by the sea. She was home.

Chapter Two

Finished…Jessie smiled and stepped back to survey her handiwork. She liked it! The soft blue gray of the walls, gleaming white trim, sun-washed floral chairs, and white couch with floral pillows; the bones had been there, but now it was her room. Her books and family photos were on the built-in bookcases on each side of the fireplace. Grandma Sadie's painting hung on the wall, her laptop was on the writing desk, and scented candles and knickknacks decorated the end tables. The kitchen had her small appliances on the counter, and she had filled her favorite vase with flowers from the garden and placed it on the table. The room looked and felt like home.

All of it done with a few minutes to spare. She ran the brush through her hair, changed her shirt, and put on lip gloss. Grabbing her purse, she locked the door. It was girls' night out.

She strolled through the gardens back to the inn inhaling the perfume of honeysuckle that filled the early evening air. Everywhere she looked the flowers were in full bloom, a rainbow of vivid color and beauty. This was going to be a great place to live!

She waved at an older man wearing a large brimmed hat, who was working in the vegetable and herb garden that filled the space behind the inn's kitchen. He waved back. "It looks like we're in for a beautiful sunset." She smiled at him.

"It looks that way. Are you Ms. Donovan's friend?" He stooped to pick up a basket filled with green onions.

"I am. I just moved into the cottage today. Would you like me to take that to the kitchen for you? I'm on my way there."

"Yes, if you don't mind." He handed her the basket.

"No problem. I'm Jessie by the way."

"You can call me Mr. Yamamoto." He grinned. "Believe me it's easier than trying to pronounce my first name."

Jessie wondered which of Katie's creations these green onions would find their way into. Katie was an amazing cook, and she'd enjoyed being her guinea pig over the years. There had been a few disasters in the beginning, but Katie's culinary skills had grown with time. Jessie slipped quietly into the kitchen, placed the basket on the counter, and waited for Katie to finish what she was doing at her desk.

"I'll be right with you, Jessie. I'm going to take you on the grand driving tour of Blue Cove. Which should take all of about fifteen minutes, and then we can eat."

"Take your time. I can wait."

"I'm all done." She laid down the pen. She picked up her purse and opened the back door. "I can't believe I'll be able to see you every day, if I want to." They walked out to the car together. "How do you like your place?"

"What's not to like!" Jessie fastened her seatbelt and looked at Katie. "Okay, Ms. Donovan, it's time to impress me with your wealth of knowledge about Blue Cove." Jessie laughed.

****

Katie drove down Main Street. "Here's where our tour begins." She smiled lifting her nose up in the air.

"My, aren't we uppity."

"Shush…" Katie put her finger to her mouth. "I'm leading a tour here." She proceeded with an English accent. "A major revitalization project was just completed in several areas of town. The idea, of course, is to attract more tourists. Doesn't it look nice?"

"Pretty sweet…Main Street looks picture perfect." She got into the spirit of the conversation. "Does tourism play a big role in the town's economy?"

Katie nodded. "The town almost triples in size during the summer months. The season officially kicks off with a concert in the park a week from Friday night. From what I've heard, people bring a picnic supper and stay to enjoy the live music. There's also a concert on July Fourth with fireworks at the end."

"That sounds great! I like the idea of community gatherings." Jessie brows furrowed. "This is only a hypothetical question; if I were to buy a business here, how would it survive in the off season?"

"The local people keep the economy going, of course, but there isn't much of an off season." Katie stopped at the stop sign.

"What do you mean?"

"The fall bus tours are filled with folks who like to spend time here, and they shop. And as I've so aptly pointed out in my grand tour we have several Christmas shops; we also have an Old Town Christmas." Katie's eyes sparkled. "In past years the inn has been full and they had a sleigh that brought guests to the park for the lighting of the town Christmas tree. It will be my first year to continue the tradition, and I'm really looking forward to it." Katie's enthusiasm brought a smile to Jessie's face.

"You sound a little like a brochure for Blue Cove." Jessie looked at Katie and smiled.

"Don't I know it! I had to learn all of it, so I could tell my guests. There is something to do almost all year round."

"How do you like being an innkeeper?"

"I love it." Katie smiled. "The people are fantastic, most of them anyway." She scrunched her face. "I enjoy being able to live here, and I already have several wedding parties booked for the summer."

"It's a beautiful inn and the gardens are perfect for an outdoor wedding. Your uncle was kind to leave it to you."

Katie's expression softened. "I know. I couldn't have written a better script for my life. Plus with the outstanding staff and the landscape genius I have working for me, I can take a night off every now and then."

"By the way…" Jessie glanced at Katie. "I love the way you cut your hair. It makes your eyes stand out and you look happy, really happy."

"I am. I finally feel like I found my place in this big old world."

Jessie's stomach grumbled. "Not to change the subject, but where are we going for dinner?"

"I thought we would go to Angelo's tonight, if that's okay with you." Katie slowed for one of the few stop lights on the main street. "They make a really great pizza."

"Angelo's it is." Jessie nodded. "I hope someday soon I can figure out what my place is." She sighed.

****

The minute she stepped through the door she could smell the Italian spices and baking pizza. It smelled delicious. Her stomach grumbled again as she followed the hostess to their table.

Jessie liked what she saw, red and white tablecloths, white linen napkins, and drippy candles in wine bottles on each table. It was the perfect touch for a place called Angelo's. They decided on the Blue Cove Special, with sausage, onions, green peppers and extra cheese; salads and drinks finished off their order.

"Look Jessie, there's Dylan." Katie pointed to a table. "I wonder who's with him. I can only see his back." She smiled and waved.

Jessie looked where Katie's finger was pointing and waved too. "Katie, I've got to ask you something." Her fingers drummed on the table.

"You sound so serious." Katie turned around quickly to look at her.

"Why didn't you tell me about the murder at the church?" She frowned at Katie.

"Do you want the truth?" Katie met her stare.

"Of course I do!"

"I thought if I told you, you might back out of coming. Besides, I just learned about it a few weeks ago myself." Katie shrugged. "How'd you hear about it so soon?"

"I stopped at the church, before I came to your place. James Morris showed me around and told me about it." Jessie shivered. "He was one of the people who saw the murder scene."

"You don't need to worry. It wasn't random—the police believe she was the intended victim."

"I have to admit that at first it really bothered me." Jessie shifted in her chair.

"What about now?" Katie prompted.

"I can see the potential for a great story. Murders don't happen every day at a church, you know. A young woman's life was cut short, a mystery has yet to be solved, and I think it might make a good story to send Neil."

"Just be careful, Jessie. There's a murderer out there, and this is a small town."

"Meaning…" Jessie lifted her brows.

"Everyone knows each other's business. It wouldn't take much for someone to find out you're poking around and asking questions," Katie whispered.

"What are you two up to?" Dylan's voice startled them "You girls were so deep in conversation you didn't even see us coming." A flicker of amusement lit the other man's dark blue eyes. "Jessie, this is Matt Parker, a good friend of mine."

She met Matt's smiling eyes. "It's nice to meet you."

"Sure, same here." He inclined his head. "Dylan told me you're from New York City."

"It's been home for the past several years."

"How long do you think you'll be able to handle our small town? Won't you miss the shopping or whatever it is that you girls like to do?"

"I think I'll manage just fine." Her answer was curt, her chin edged up a notch. Shop indeed, as if that's all she did!

She enjoyed listening to the conversation that followed. It gave her a chance to study the two men. Dylan was handsome and refined, tall with brown eyes and impeccable manners. She could tell Katie was interested in him. Her eyes and face lit up every time he said something to her.

Matt was such a contrast to Dylan, every bit as tall but a little on the scruffy side. A five o'clock shadow darkened his face. He had dark hair and blue eyes so deep they appeared almost navy. His answers were abrupt, and he spent most of the evening scowling at her. Dylan's face broke into a smile often. Matt had a lopsided grin. As crazy as it seemed, of the two, she was drawn to Matt—which bugged her. He was good-looking, but a little too tough guy for her taste. Maybe she was in the market for a good fight; she didn't even know Matt, but she didn't like him. She frowned and could hear Grandma Sadie scolding her. "Give the poor man a chance." Maybe what she needed was to sleep and to start all over tomorrow.

Several times, she caught Matt staring at her with a puzzled expression on his face. She got the distinct feeling he didn't like her either. Boy, was she glad when the guys left and dinner was finally finished. Rubbing her eyes, she thought bed sounded more inviting all the time.

"Matt couldn't take his eyes off you." Katie nudged her as they walked to the car.

"If glaring counts, I guess that's true. I don't think he liked me much, and I don't feel overly fond of him either." She opened the car door.

"Matt's a nice guy. I'm sure you were just reading him wrong. He's also a police officer and probably could answer some of your questions about the murder." Katie paused. "By the way what do you think of Dylan?"

"He's a nice guy, but a better question might be what do *you* think of Dylan?" Jessie fluttered her eyelashes flirtatiously.

"Am I that obvious?" Katie started her engine.

"Pretty much." Jessie laughed.

****

Once back in her cozy cottage, Jessie shut off the lights, climbed into bed, and stretched out. This had been one crazy day. A long drive, some kind of hallucination, or who knows what, she learned there was a murder at the church, and then had met a man who glared at her the whole evening. She was still avoiding her dad. If it wasn't for this lovely little house she would be crazy not to get back in her car and head right back to New York.

Oh well, tomorrow is another day. Face it, girl, you're not going anywhere. Monday you start work, and you know you're itching to find out more details about Gina's murder.

****

Jessie arrived at work on Monday, wearing her new navy blue pant suit and no hard hat. She walked through the church doors with a smile.

"Good morning, you must be Jessie. Finally I can put a face to the name. It's nice to meet you." Pastor Rick extended his hand as he met her in the foyer.

"You too, Pastor." She shook his hand, wanting to pull it back immediately. He reminded her of a car salesman or one of those TV evangelists, every hair in place and little too slick.

"Are you getting settled in okay?" He glanced at his watch.

"I am. The town is great, my place is perfect, and living near my best friend is an extra bonus."

"Good to hear." He sounded bored. "Before you start your day, I'll show you around and give you a set of keys to unlock all of the doors." He started to walk.

"Sounds like a good plan!" She quickly followed him.

Nearing the end of the tour, he stopped in the foyer and looked at his watch again. "I have an appointment, so I'll let you get to work." He was brusque.

As she walked to her office, Jessie found it strange that he had never once mentioned Pastor Gina's murder during the tour. She frowned as she thought about him. She didn't like him. He made her feel uncomfortable. What had she gotten herself into? She opened the office door. Was there something in the drinking water in this town? Between Matt and her boss she wasn't sure what to expect next. Sitting down at her desk, she took out a note pad and scribbled *Try to keep an open mind!* Which might be easier said than done.

The previous secretary had left her a list of things that needed to be done. Most of the job was routine, including answering the phone. Several church members stopped by to introduce themselves, giving her nice breaks throughout the day. All in all, she thought it was a good first day on the job.

By Friday she was puzzled; not one person had talked to her about Gina. Her name was never mentioned. She was hoping to have some details by now, but not wanting to be insensitive, she didn't mention Gina. Next week she would have to put out some feelers to see if she got any response. Startled by a loud bang in the hall, Jessie jumped up to look.

The woman's frizzy, red curly hair was pulled on top of her head in a haphazard updo, which was threatening with every movement to spring loose of its confinement. Her clothes were wrinkled, her eyes still puffy from sleep, but it was her gravelly voice that brought a smile to Jessie's face.

"Sorry, I didn't mean to scare you. I dropped my bucket of cleaning supplies. I'm having a blonde moment. I can't for the life of me remember where I put my keys." The lady tapped her forehead.

"Can I help you?" Jessie struggled to hide her amusement as she sat back down.

"Not unless you know where I left my keys."

"You can borrow mine if you need to." Jessie nudged them toward her.

"I'm Melinda, the custodian, and I have to empty the trash can in Pastor's office. Is he there?"

"No, it's his day off."

"Right, I forgot. I think I'll sit for a minute. Maybe I'll remember where I put the darn things." She peered at Jessie, her faded hazel eyes bright with curiosity. "You're our new secretary, aren't you?"

"Yes, I'm Jessie."

"I'm a little rattled at the moment. I saw her again." She drummed her fingers on the chair, while her foot bounced back and forth under the chair.

"Who'd you see?"

"I forgot you're new, and you wouldn't know what I'm talking about. You must think I'm nuts. Sometimes this place really freaks me." She scratched her head. "It was Pastor Gina that I saw, walking in the hall. She was

murdered, you know." Melinda's eyebrows arched.
"Several people in the church have seen her, although
most of them don't want to talk about it. Reba Thomas
is keeping track of all the sightings. So tell her if you
see Gina."

Jessie nodded at her. "I heard there was a murder
here, and I saw the picture of her." Jessie pricked up her
ears. "What was she like?"

"She was pretty cool. Everybody here liked her."
Melinda shifted in the chair. "She was totally better
than the one we've got now. I guess I probably
shouldn't say that. It could get me fired. You won't tell,
will you?"

Jessie shook her head no.

"My mouth always gets me into trouble. Still I
miss her."

"It must be hard on her family and the church."
Jessie gave her a sympathetic glance.

"Devastated is the word. It's even harder when
Pastor Rick won't acknowledge her in any way. He
thinks it's better for the church to just move on. But, we
all still need to talk about her." Melinda took her
glasses off her head and put them on.

"You said others have seen her. Are all the
sightings in the same place?" Jessie's heart beat rapidly.
Had she seen her? Was she the woman watching her
from the woods?

"Oh heavens no, she seems to be at home all
around the church and outside it for that matter." She
sniffed. "One day James heard her arguing with
someone in the fellowship hall. On several occasions
I've heard her singing. We'd like to believe she's
looking out for us, just like she did when she was

alive." Melinda heaved herself to her feet. "I guess I'll borrow your keys, and then I'll look for mine."

There had to be a logical explanation. Jessie wondered if a grief counselor had been called in to talk with the congregation. Her eyebrows furrowed. Still, she had to admit she felt a bit unsettled over the conversation with Melinda because she was still reasoning out her own experience in the cemetery.

A few minutes later Melinda flew around the corner. "I found my keys. I must be losing my mind; they were in my pocket all along." She put Jessie's keys back on her desk and headed for the door.

"One question..." Jessie's voice stopped Melinda. "Do the police have any idea who the murderer is?"

"No, there is plenty of speculation, but nothing firm. Matt Parker is heading up the investigation. He could probably tell you more. I'd better be getting back to work." She walked out into the hall. "I'll be seeing you around."

Matt Parker, now wasn't that just great. She was sure he'd be real happy to tell her more. He'd be even happier not to have to deal with her at all. Jessie pursed her lips. Well, he'd better get over it!

Jessie finished up her day, locked up the office and started down the hall. When she reached the foyer she felt someone watching her. A cold shiver ran down her back. She was afraid to look. She hurried out the doors, and ended her first week at work.

****

Her last stop before home was the police station to see if Matt Parker was in. She rehearsed over and over again in her mind what she would ask him. She would have to be the one to approach him if she ever wanted to learn more about Gina. He certainly wouldn't offer the information willingly.

All her rehearsing was for nothing. Matt was in a meeting, and so she set up an appointment for Monday morning. She had the weekend to think about it and would approach him at the start of a new week.

Chapter Three

By Sunday evening, Jessie was feeling restless. She laced her running shoes and headed out on the walking path between the inn and the marina. It was a good ten mile run there and back. With the moonlight over the ocean and the sound of the gentle waves coming ashore, it was a night made for running. She loved it. She felt totally in touch with her body, the rhythm and the sound of her feet striking the ground, and the sweat trickling down her back as she pushed herself to go farther and faster. It felt almost sensual to her. She smiled.

She turned around in the parking lot of the marina and headed back. Each mile seemed better than the one before, and she ran the last mile in under ten minutes. In no time, she was back at the cottage. She showered, relaxed with a book, and then slept like a baby.

****

The ringing phone woke her before her alarm went off in the morning. "Good morning, sweet girl." Sadie's cheery voice greeted her.

"Hi, Grams, are you okay?" She rubbed the sleep from her eyes.

"I don't want to keep you long, but I wanted to tell you not to let your dad's anger bother you. Your dad still tries to tell me what to do. I constantly have to remind him I'm of age, and I can decide for myself."

"Oh, Grams, you're such a hoot!" Jessie laughed.

"There's something for you to do there, I can feel it. Drop me an email from time to time, and let me know what's new."

"I will. I only wish I knew what it was." She sat up in bed.

"Get moving and discover it! I need a new adventure in my life. It has been a little boring lately."

"I'll do it, Grams. Talk to you later."

Going through her closet she picked out today's outfit with care, wanting to look feminine but not overly so, assertive but not too much. She tried on and cast aside six outfits before she settled on a gray pencil skirt, gray jacket and her favorite pink shirt. She looked in the mirror and decided she would pass.

The morning air had a slight chill to it. She stepped out the door with a coffee mug in hand, got into her car and was off. Katie waved at her as she drove by the inn. She smiled and waved back.

"Mr. Parker, I do believe I'm ready for you." She smiled.

****

She walked into the newly remodeled police station in the Old Town Square complex. It was almost pleasant in comparison to the precincts she had been in during her days in New York. The floors were highly polished, the cream colored paint was a nice change from the normal prison gray and several paintings of the area hung on the walls.

She stopped in front of the reception desk where a young red-haired officer leaned over a computer. She cleared her throat. "I'm here to see Officer Parker. I have an appointment with him. My name is Jessie

Reynolds."

"I'll check to see if he's ready for you." His green eyes gave her the once-over. He picked up the phone and pushed Matt's extension. "Hey, Matt, there's a Jessie Reynolds here to see you. Okay, I'll send her back." He hung up the phone. "He'll see you now. It's down the hall, third door on the left." He pointed the way.

"Good morning, Miss Reynolds." Matt stood up as she reached his open door. "Please be seated." He sat when she did his voice chillingly polite. "Tell me how I can help you."

So that's how it's going to play out. Her chin lifted slightly. "Officer Parker." She smiled at him. "As you may have heard, I'm working at First Community Church. I was told this past week about the murder of Gina Martin. It was also said that you're the one in charge of the investigation. I was wondering what you could tell me about the case."

"It's an active investigation. We have a few people of interest, but no suspects as of yet. However, we do know it wasn't a random act, that Gina was the intended target." His stare was icy. "I have just shared with you all that I'm prepared to share since you are not a relative or close family friend."

And the gloves were off. "I see." Her back straightened. "I had hoped that maybe I could be of help to you because people often come by my office to talk to me about Gina. I thought maybe you could tell me something I might be listening for." She started to stand.

"You may have been an important writer in New York, Miss Reynolds, but you're not in New York now."

"If you don't want my help…fine!" she snapped.

"You'll stay out of it." His tone was flat. "Do I make myself clear?"

She stood up, bent over his desk, leaning on her hands to meet his stare. "Clear, yes, I would say I'm seeing it very clearly. I've had to deal with men like you all my professional career, men who resented me as a woman for the promotions I earned, and men who tried to keep me in my place." She swallowed hard. Her mouth went dry. It was hard for to her to remain focused the way he was looking at her. "Do you know what I did?" He shook his head, grinning at her. "I simply worked harder and smarter and earned every promotion that I got." She stood up wanting to retreat. "I will leave you to your work now, but know this—I will do a story about Gina, and I won't need your help to do it." She turned her back on him. "Good day to you, Officer Parker," she said over her shoulder. She walked out the door pushing passed an open-mouthed Dylan who was standing in the doorway.

****

"What the hell was that, Matt? She had fire in her eyes. I've never known you to treat a woman like that." Dylan glared at Matt.

"She gets under my skin." Matt ran his hand through his hair.

"You don't even know her—you know what I think?"

"No, and I don't give a damn." He crossed his arms.

"You're going to hear it anyway." Dylan leaned a shoulder against the door jamb, grinning. You're attracted to her, and you don't want to be. She's a strong woman, no pushover, and it scares the hell out of you. You wouldn't be able to run roughshod over her."

"I don't know her well enough to be attracted to her, but she does bother me." He shrugged, irritably.

"So you won't mind if I try my luck with her." Dylan was grinning.

"She's not your type, but by all means, give it your best shot." Matt scowled at him.

"How do you possibly know my type?" Dylan smirked. "When I look at her smile and those blue eyes, I feel afflicted."

"You'll get over it. Can we change the subject?" Matt frowned at him.

Dylan stared at Matt with a silly grin on his face. "You've got it bad, and you're lying to yourself. I hope you wake up before someone else comes along. Although, I have to admit I would so like to be around to see you fall." Dylan walked back to his office laughing.

Matt was left to his thoughts. Tapping his pencil on the desk he knew he had acted badly both times he talked with her. He'd sworn he would never let another woman get to him. But she had rattled him with her fearless, sassy attitude.

It was a small town, and he would probably see her again, even if he didn't want to. He was simply going to have to find a way to be nice. Who did he think he was fooling? He wanted to see her again. Dylan was right—he was attracted to her, but he didn't want to be. She was just too damn pretty. The total package—he didn't stand a chance.

****

Jessie was livid the entire drive to the church. More than once she had to slow down. Speeding was out of the question. Matt would be more than happy to write her a ticket, and she didn't want to give him the pleasure. And what was that look all about? She exhaled. It didn't make any sense at all.

She stopped at Java Joe's to get her coffee mug filled and hoped to calm down before she went into work. Between her dad and some of the guys she had worked with, she had gotten thoroughly sick of being told what she could or couldn't do. Writing a story about Gina was a real possibility. She wanted to do it because the story had captured her, and not out of spite because Matt was being a jerk.

Still fuming and going over conversations she would like to have with Matt, she parked and headed for the church door. She was met by Melinda; whose rumpled appearance brought an instant smile to her face.

"Hi, Blondie, I heard from Pastor you were a writer in New York. If you ever want to write about the things going on here I can tell you some stories." She raised her eyebrows for emphasis and then turned around to dust the display area.

"You can stop by and talk anytime you want. I'd enjoy hearing some of your stories." Jessie continued down the hall toward her office.

"Jessie, I opened your office to clean earlier," Melinda called after her. "Reba Thomas is there. She wanted to meet you."

Jessie walked into her office to find an impeccably dressed woman sitting in the chair in front of the desk, ankles primly crossed. "Hello." She dropped her purse on the desk.

"Good morning. Could this be the famous Jessie Reynolds? Are we to meet at last?" Reba motioned to the chair beside her and patted it.

"I plead guilty, I'm her." She sat down next to the attractive older woman. Jessie loved the twinkle in her brown eyes and the way her silver gray hair was pulled into a neat chignon.

"I've heard such stories of you through the church grapevine; you're a famous writer from New York, so kind to everyone and almost perfect in every way, a paragon, first class." Her eyes sparkled with amusement. "I've come to see for myself."

"I'll try hard not to disappoint." Jessie laughed. "I'm afraid I might though since I'm not famous or perfect, but hopefully I'm kind; it's only been a week though."

"I'm Reba Thomas, by the way." She sat forward in her chair reaching for Jessie's hand.

"It's a pleasure to meet you."

"Melinda told me that she's been telling you about our elusive guest who seems to appear especially to those who are touched by her plight." Reba's brown eyes scrutinized Jessie's face.

"I've only begun to hear about her the last few days." Jessie nodded.

"You will no doubt have a visit or two from her, since you're just the kind of gentle soul she looks for." Reba saw Jessie's worried expression. "I've caused you concern." She patted Jessie's hand. "Don't be afraid. Gina would never do you any harm. She wants to be free, but something or someone is holding her here."

Jessie took a slow breath. "I'm not sure what to say

or if I believe any of this."

"It has nothing at all to do with your belief. It just is. She is trapped here and wants out. We have to find out what will free her." Reba paused. "I've said enough. The church grapevine didn't do you justice, Jessie, dear." She rose gracefully. "I know I'll see you again. We will need to talk more."

Bizarre was the only word Jessie could find to describe her meeting with Reba Thomas. She shook her head as Reba let herself out. She was deliciously eccentric. She probably would be talking to Reba again if for no other reason than she liked the woman. Her day had definitely taken a turn for the better.

The ringing phone started her work day. "First Community Church, this is Jessie, may I help you."

"Jessie, this is Matt Parker. Say look, umm, I'm sorry for being so rough on you a while ago. No excuses."

Jessie's jaw dropped. "Sure."

"Talk to you later then."

"Okay, goodbye." She hung up the phone.

She managed to keep busy the rest of the morning, not giving herself time to dwell on her conversation with Matt. Jessie had just finished lunch when Pastor Rick walked into the reception area and sat down. "Have I had any calls, or is there anything I need to handle?" His foot shook back and forth the whole time he talked to her.

"I placed some messages in your box. One was from a Mr. Campbell. He wanted you to know his wife was admitted to the hospital." She shuffled her papers on the desk to take another look at the message book.

"I'll do a hospital visit later." He took his messages

from the box and looked them over. "You've been working here a week. Do you have any questions?"

"So far, so good, everything is pretty straightforward." She smiled up at him. "I'm getting to know more of the congregation, and I hope my work is satisfactory."

He cleared his throat. "I've heard only positive comments about your work. The congregation seems to like you. It's obvious that you know how to work with people because you fit right in." He jumped up and started to pace. She watched him fascinated.

"Jessie, I was wondering if on Wednesday you could stay for a few extra hours to lock up after the town book club meets. They change meeting sites each week, and I forgot this was our week to host it. I scheduled something else on the same night."

"I'd be happy too. Is it okay if I go have dinner during their meeting time and then come back to lock up afterwards?"

"That's fine. They arrive about 5:30 and are usually done no later than 8:00. They bring their own sack dinner, so Melinda will have everything set up for them. All you have to do is lock up when they leave." He walked back to his office and shut the door.

Strange...She looked at the closed door. Why was he so nervous? He'd never been that way before. If anything, he was so self-assured, almost arrogant. She made a note to watch him the next few days to see if the trend continued.

****

On Wednesday, Jessie had arranged for Katie to meet her at Patterson's Pub at six. She could watch the church doors and parking lot from the windows at the front of Patterson's where she got their table.

Patterson's had the worn look of an old Irish pup, with dark paneling and trim. Billiard tables and dart boards were in the back room. She liked that it was the locals' place to hang out. They're the best. A long bar was the center of attraction in the main dining area and the small stage hosted live music every weekend. The owner was a little grumpy, but she would win him over from the dark side. She loved a good challenge.

"How is work?" Katie sat down across from Jessie and picked up a menu.

"It's good. Not the stress level that I'm used to, at least not yet anyway, but I'm only in my second week and everyone still likes me." She laughed. "Ask me again in a couple of weeks."

"So what's new?" Katie peered over the menu at her.

"On Monday I went to talk to Matt Parker about Gina's murder." Jessie paused at the waitress's approach. "I'll tell you more in a minute."

"The Rueben is huge and really good. Do you want to split one?"

"Sounds great and I'll take an iced tea."

"Now what were you saying about going to see Matt?" Katie's eyebrow arched.

"We ended up having a shouting match. When I left his office, I was so angry. I felt just like I did when I was the newbie in the newsroom in New York, and the good old boys club fought me every step of the way." Jessie zoned thinking about it.

"What happened?" Katie tapped Jessie's hand to get her attention. "I want details, all the juicy details."

"He told me to keep my nose out of it, basically. If

I remember correctly at that point I got eye to eye with him and went off."

"You didn't?" She laughed.

"Oh yes, I did." Jessie felt herself blushing. "I'm not proud of it, but I told him I was writing a story about Gina without his help and to spite him."

"Are you crazy?" Katie eyes twinkled with amusement.

"I believe I am." Jessie laughed. "But in my defense, he started it and certainly gave as good as he got."

"Who was there to witness your free fall?" Katie was shaking her head.

"Dylan was standing in the doorway dumbstruck, and whether anyone else heard, who knows? I'm not exactly quiet when I get wound up."

"Jessie, you are such a hothead when any guy challenges you." Katie rolled her eyes. "Didn't your mama ever teach you anything? Sweetie, you can catch more flies with honey than vinegar." She laughed.

The waitress set their food in front of them, and the girls were quiet for few minutes until she left.

"Do you want to know what happened next?" Jessie's face lit up.

"You mean there's more?" Katie choked back her laughter.

"I'm glad you are being entertained by my hardships." It was Jessie's turn to roll her eyes."

"You have to admit it's pretty funny." Katie's eyes sparkled.

"Now, yes, then, not so much. A little later, someone called me. Any guesses who it was?" She held up three fingers.

"Matt?"

"Yes." Jessie nodded her voice dropping to a whisper.

"No way!"

"Yes way! He called with a lame apology. I shouldn't say that, but he annoys me."

"At least he apologized." Katie shrugged. "What did you say?"

"I was so stunned." Jessie laughed. "I said sure and goodbye."

Both girls found her words hilarious.

After they finished dinner, Jessie stood up. "I'll be back in a few minutes. I have to go lock up the church. I see the book club is leaving a little early."

"Do you want to share a dessert?"

"Sure." She smiled and Katie giggled. Jessie waved on her way out the door to Dylan and Matt who were just coming in.

****

"Are you finished or can we join you?" Matt asked Katie.

"Have a seat. I'm waiting for Jessie to get back." She nodded to the open chairs.

"I'll be right back. I see someone I need to talk to." Dylan walked over to another table.

"So tell me about Jessie." Matt sat down in chair across from Katie.

"What do you want to know? We've been friends since we were little girls. She's pretty, huh?" Katie grinned.

"That's obvious." He would use the word stunning. "What's she doing here?

"Why to live near me, of course." Katie smiled.

"Actually, she was tired of the city. We were raised in a town smaller than this."

"Why didn't she move back home?"

"She wanted to stay near the ocean, me, and away from her dad. He's a little bit of a tyrant when it comes to her. He's pretty overprotective, but not abusive or anything." Katie clarified.

"How she'd hear about the job at the church?" Matt leaned back in the chair folding his arms.

"I told her about it. It seemed like a perfect fit. That was before I knew of the Pastor's murder of course."

"Naturally. What else can you tell me?"

"She's very organized when it comes to her work. She has goals ten years out." Katie smiled at his expression. "I know, crazy, huh?" He nodded.

"Does she have anyone steady in her life?" He couldn't believe he asked it and regretted it the minute he had. He knew Katie would tell her and probably anyone else who'd listen.

"Do you mean like a guy?" Amusement lit her eyes.

"Yeah…Some guy in the city maybe?"

"No, there isn't anyone in particular, but there are plenty who would like to be." She tilted her head and looked at him. "I have a theory that I'm working on. Someday remind me to tell you about it."

"I'll hold you to that." Matt couldn't believe there was no boyfriend.

"Jessie has this plan, you know, things she wants to do. It's rare for her to deviate from her goals." She looked at Matt. "I think it's going to take something out of the ordinary, like falling in love, to get her to be even a little spontaneous."

"Is that so?" He lifted his brow in challenge.

"Are you interested?"

"Only professionally." He turned his head and was happy to see Dylan on his way back.

****

Jessie walked up the church steps stopping to chat with the people who were leaving. She went first to the fellowship hall to make sure the lights were off and then checked the side door, which led to the parking lot. On her way back to the foyer, she heard the piano in the sanctuary and someone singing. Her voice was lovely.

She went to check on it, intending to ask whoever it was to lock the doors when they left. The closer she got to the sanctuary, the more apprehension she felt. Mumbling something about listening to people's crazy ghost stories, she pushed the door open just as the last note was played. The hair on her neck stood up, and a shiver went down her spine. The lights were off, and no one was there. Jessie knew what she had heard was real. She laughed uneasily, trying to shake off the strange feeling. She turned on her heels to walk out, and a cool rush of wind whished past her. Fear paralyzed her; she stood motionless, heart pounding in her chest—swish, it brushed her other side, and then she ran. She turned off the lights in the foyer and locked the church doors. Standing outside, looking in through the window beside the door, she saw the woman in the floral dress standing and staring at her mouthing a word. *Help*!

She paused to get her emotions under control and walked slowly back to Patterson's, breathing deeply, trying to calm her racing heart. Who was that woman, and how could she help? Panic subsiding, she found herself once again fighting back those pesky tears.

Katie looked up at Jessie as she made her way through the restaurant to their table. "Are you okay? You're as pale as a ghost."

How ironic…"I'm fine, and I'm looking forward to dessert." Her voice sounded shaky even to her.

"Are you sure you're all right? You're so white." They all stared at her.

"Yes!" Just let it go, Katie, she pleaded with her eyes. She leaned over to whisper in her ear. "I'll explain later."

Jessie pushed the dessert around the plate without taking a bite. The rest of the night was uneventful, except for every time she looked his way Matt was watching her. She was the new piece of evidence under observation. The room seemed to close in on her, and she needed to get away from his watchful eyes.

Matt stood up and bent down close to her ear so only she could hear. "Something happened to you when you were at the church, and I want to know what." He walked into the back room.

Like that was ever going to happen. All she needed was for him to think she was crazy, too. It was her cue, time to go.

"Hey, guys, I'm a little tired. I'm going to leave." She put her money on the table.

"At least you've got your color back. I'll talk to you tomorrow." Katie eyed her critically.

"Okay." Jessie nodded. "Goodbye, Dylan, and tell Matt I said goodbye."

"Will do…" Dylan lifted his coffee mug in a salute. "See you around!"

****

Matt got her number from Katie when he came

43

back to the table. Thought she could duck him, did she? On his way home, stopping for a light, Matt called her. "Are you going to tell me what happened at the church?" He spoke the minute she said hello.

"I wasn't planning on it."

"I know something happened to you when you went to the church. You were clearly distressed when you came back, and I want to hear about it. You got that?" he added more calmly. "Maybe I can help."

"Have me committed to an institution is more like it."

"What's that supposed to mean?" He was clearly irritated.

"Just what I said."

"Where do you live? I'm coming over."

"There is really no need for you to come, and I don't want you to."

"I'm not asking, I'm telling you." The light changed and he accelerated. "If you don't tell me, I'll find out where you live and be there with or without your permission."

"I live in the first cottage down from the inn."

"I'll be there in ten minutes, and you'd better be prepared to talk."

"Okay." She sounded amazingly meek.

"What, no lip? I was kind of looking forward to it." He smiled.

****

After Matt's call Jessie stopped pacing in her living room and sat down on the floral chair, drawing her legs up under her. She forced herself to relax taking deep breaths. She tried to make sense of what had just happened to her at the church. Was it a ghost, a person or possibly both? How could she ever explain it to anyone? No more being afraid, she was no weakling! She would find out who the woman was, ghost or human, and what she wanted. It was time for her to get control over her life. She made a list of the people she needed to talk to and some of the questions she needed to answer. Reba Thomas was number one on the list.

Chapter Four

Jessie went to answer the knock at her door. Before she got there, Matt walked in.

"You really should lock your door. Anyone could just walk in."

"He just did." She frowned at him. "Didn't your mother ever teach you to wait until the door is opened before you barge in?"

"Nice place you've got here." He found a chair and stretched out his legs as he sat down.

"Would you like a glass of water or some tea?" She turned her back on him and walked into the kitchen.

"Iced tea sounds great," he called after her.

She handed him his glass and had barely got seated when his deep voice cut through the awkward silence in the room. "So what happened at the church, Jess?" He studied her. "I know you saw a lot working in New York. What rattled you?"

"My name is Jessie, by the way." She paused pressing her lips together thoughtfully. "I probably need to tell you about the first day I came to town. I saw a woman pacing in front of the church. The strangest thing was she was glaring at me like I had kept her waiting or something. I went into Java Joe's, and when I came out she was gone."

"She probably wasn't even looking at you." He shrugged.

"At the time I didn't think so either. I thought she was waiting for a friend." Jessie frowned and described seeing her again while in the cemetery. She leaned forward in the chair and made eye contact with him. "I could've dismissed it all except for James telling me the picture I was looking at was of Gina Martin, their murdered pastor; I hadn't even heard there was a murder at the church. No one including Katie had told me about it." Jessie frowned. "To see Gina's picture inside the church after seeing her grave was bad enough but add to that a strange woman glaring at me. A woman who looked a lot like Gina, I should add. Well, it blew my mind to say the least."

"Crazy." He scratched his jaw thoughtfully. "That's a little tough to explain. There are a lot of things that happen for which there are no tidy explanations." He leaned back in the chair. "I wonder, though, how you ever made it in New York, seeing as you're such a bundle of contradictions."

"Just what do you mean by that?" She started to stand.

"Don't get all flustered. You're an anomaly to me; you cry at the grave of someone you don't know one moment and the next you can look me fearlessly in the eye and let me have it. You're hard to figure out." He raked his fingers through his hair.

She relaxed and sat back in the chair. "Tonight I saw the strange woman again, but not before I had my wits scared out of me." Her face paled as she told him about it. "The woman who glared at me and the woman I saw tonight was Gina Martin or an identical twin which nobody knows about. Don't ask me how that's possible. I have no idea." She shook her head.

"At least I understand your statement earlier about having you committed." He grinned.

"I've never thought about this kind of stuff before." She twisted a strand of hair around her finger. "So I have no logical answer. But others at the church have told me about seeing her."

"I'll have to think about this a little while. It's way out of my experience as a police officer. I know you believe what you saw was real."

"It was real!" She flushed. "And I've had enough too. I'm through being afraid; I'm going to find out who she is and what she wants, so that maybe she can rest in peace or I can. You can call me crazy if you want, but that's what I'm going to do." She stood up.

"Okay, well, that's my signal to go." His smile faded. "No helpless female here. I know one thing for sure; once you make up your mind I won't be able to stop you."

"We've been at each other's throats from the first day we meant. There is one thing you need to know about me, Mr. Parker." Her back straightened and her chin nudged up. "I don't need to be lectured or told what to do. I have a mind and every day when I wake up my mind starts working. It's funny like that. You're right, I'm not a helpless female, and I wouldn't have it any other way. I won't try to do your job, and I expect you not to tell me how to do mine."

As he stood up to leave, he touched his finger to her lips. Slowly he traced the curve of her lips to her chin, lifting her gaze up to his. "Use your head, Jess. Someone killed Gina. And now you're going to snoop around." His hand dropped, he turned on his heel and walked out the door. Breathless, she locked it behind him. He'd done it again. She leaned her shoulder against the door, eyes closed. He called her Jess.

Her dreams that night were filled with images of Gina. Some were carefree and laughing, and some were tortured and frightening. At one point in the dream she saw Gina standing in front of her saying, "Help me, you can help me." Jessie thrashed about in the night, and when she awoke the sheets and comforter were in a hopeless tangle.

****

Her phone beeped and she read a text from Katie reminding her of the concert in the park tomorrow night. Jessie returned a message. *Looking forward to it.*

Putting the last touches on her face, she grabbed her keys and left for work. She tried to make sense out of something that made no sense at all. What had she really seen? And Matt, just when she thought she could write him off, he had surprised her.

When she got to the church, she walked down the hall to the offices. As she put her key in the door, a shiver ran down her back. Someone was watching her. She could feel it. Running wasn't an option even though she wanted to. She stood her ground and spoke out loud. "I can help you if you want me to."

Not that she expected to hear a voice or anything. She wasn't sure what would happen. She hadn't gotten that far in her plan. A simple sense of relief washed over her. Gina must have liked what she heard.

Several times in the morning, she felt those eyes watching her. Who would ever believe her if she told them that Pastor Gina shared the same space with her. Jessie decided it was time to do the first thing on her list. She got out the church directory, found Reba's number, and gave her a call.

"Good morning, Reba."

"Jessie, I was waiting for your call this morning."

"How did you know I would call?" She frowned at the phone.

"I know many things, Jessie girl. My mother was the same. I set lunch time aside, will that work for you?"

"Yes, that's perfect. We could meet for a salad at Java Joe's."

"I will be there at noon, and Jessie, you've made the right decision."

"I've made the right decision about what?" Jessie wasn't sure if she wanted Reba to answer her or not.

"Why, helping Gina, of course."

"I only just decided. How could you have possibly known?" Jessie was perplexed.

"Don't struggle with it, Jessie, dear. It is what it is."

Jessie got to work on the newsletter and Sunday's bulletin. When she finished with the newsletter and looked up at the clock, she still had about thirty minutes until lunch.

"Excuse me, miss," a man's voice startled her. "I didn't mean to frighten you."

Jessie looked at the face of an older distinguished man with silver gray hair standing at the door. "Hello." She smiled at him. "You're Pastor Robertson, aren't you? I saw your photo upstairs."

"Yes, and who are you?" He tilted his head and smiled slightly.

"I'm Jessie Reynolds, the new secretary." She stood to greet him.

"I'm here to pick up my son. We're going to lunch." He sat down in the reception area.

"He's been out for most the morning, but I expect him at any time." She sat down in the chair beside him.

"Do you like working here?" He smiled at her. "I know I always did, until a few months ago, that is." His brows creased.

"I was sorry to hear about Pastor Gina. It must have been so hard for you." She patted his hand.

"It was. I'm the only one that knows most of the real story."

Jessie stood up when she heard Pastor Rick's voice in the foyer. She wondered what he had meant by the real story. He was definitely going on her list.

"Dad, are you bothering my secretary?" the pastor asked sharply.

Jessie was startled by the gruffness of his voice, and replied back to him. "Actually, I was the one bothering him. We were having a nice chat and getting to know one another." She smiled at John.

"Let's go, Dad. I don't have all day." Pastor Rick was already walking down the hall.

"It was nice to meet you, Jessie, and I'll be back to talk with you sometime when my son will be gone all day." He winked at her.

****

At noon, Jessie walked across the street to meet Reba at Java Joe's. After ordering an organic oriental chicken salad and cinnamon spice muffin, she joined Reba who had already ordered and was sitting at the table.

"Jessie, I forgot to get your drink order." Molly came to the table.

"A glass of water with lemon would be great." Jessie thanked her.

"So you've seen our Gina. I can tell." Reba reached for Jessie's hand. "Tell me where and when."

Jessie explained about the first day she had seen the woman walking in front of the church and then again at the cemetery. "Until last night at the church, I thought the woman I was seeing was a living person." She straightened in her chair. "The thing is I had the feeling the woman standing in front of the church was waiting for me. I know that must sound strange."

"Not really dear." Reba patted Jessie's hand. "We've all been talking about the new secretary from New York coming to work at the church for weeks now. There was anticipation in the air, and Gina must have gotten wind of it."

"You talk like she knows what is happening around here. That's just a little much for me. There must be a more logical answer."

"You believe what you must to cope, dear." A flicker of amusement lit Reba's eyes.

After their lunch arrived, Jessie picked up the story by telling Reba about last night at the church. "It was then that I realized the woman I had seen was Gina Martin." She sipped her water and added any other pertinent information.

"It seems you are the one she has chosen to entrust with this job. There's a lot at stake for her children. I believe if this was an open and shut case, she wouldn't be here at all." Reba proceeded carefully. "Sometimes folks get stuck, if something is left unfinished in life, especially when their lives are taken suddenly. Oh, I know people think I'm strange, but there are a lot of spiritual things in this life that we don't understand at all."

"But, why me, I wonder? I've never been open to this kind of stuff. In fact I'm still skeptical."

"You're a strong woman, but you also have a tender heart. It seems to me I read somewhere that as a writer you were tenacious about getting the facts right. You're absolutely the perfect woman for the job!" Reba's expression became thoughtful. "I do have a word of warning, Jessie. Be very careful. Once it is known that you are asking questions, you could become the next target. In fact you will be challenged in the near future."

****

As if a ghost wasn't enough, Reba's warning left her apprehensive. She didn't want to become anyone's target. Not now, not ever!

Right now, she had to take care of the second thing on her list. Using her cell phone, she called Rocky Pointe. "Hello, may I speak to Mrs. Bradley?"

"This is her."

"My name is Jessie Reynolds. I know you don't know me, but I'm working at the church where your daughter was a pastor. I'm also a journalist and would like your permission to do a human interest story about your daughter."

"What good would it do but dredge up some very hurtful stuff?" The woman's tone was cold.

"First of all, it would keep the unsolved murder in the news, before people, which could spark someone to remember a small detail that might be helpful to the police. And, besides that, I have been touched so much by her story I would like to see it told."

"I'm not sure. I would need to talk to my husband first. My grandkids have been through so much already. I just don't know if it would be right."

"I can understand your hesitancy, and I have a suggestion that you can accept or decline. I could come and meet you and your husband. I will explain to you why I want to do the story, and you can decide. If you tell me no, I'll walk away and leave you alone."

"I have your number from your call, so I'll call you back and let you know."

"Thanks for considering it. I know this has been a hard time for your family."

Who knew what would come of that, but she had to try. Sensing she wasn't alone, Jessie whispered, "Gina, you're going to have to work on your mother if you want me to do this. I'll keep trying."

At five, she turned off her computer, unplugged the coffee, and went back to Pastor Rick's office to let him know she was leaving for the day. Before she knocked on his closed door, she could hear his angry muffled voice speaking on the phone. Pastor Rick didn't sound too happy. She turned to leave, but then retraced her steps and knocked on the door.

"Just a minute, I'll be right with you. I've got to go, and don't call me here again," she heard him say. "You can come in now." He motioned for her to be seated.

"I thought I should tell you that I'm leaving for the day." She sat down on the edge of the chair. "Everything is done for the week. Is there something you would like me to do extra, tomorrow?"

"I can't think of anything." He looked at her. "Will you be going to the concert?"

"Yes, I'm going with a friend."

"Good, I'm sure I'll see you there." He smiled at her.

The way he was staring at her was unnerving. She stood up before he could say anything else. "I'll look for you tomorrow." She walked out of his office, got her belongings, and left the church.

On the way home, she tried to figure out why Pastor Rick made her so uncomfortable. She couldn't put her finger on the exact reason. The whole package just seemed to bother her, and for a moment there, she had a feeling he had wanted to ask her out. That was so not a good idea on so many levels.

What in the world was wrong with the men here? Matt was sort of a jerk, and yet she found him intriguing. Rick was a little too slick, and there was something else. Dylan was nice, but Katie was pretty gone on him.

She had just turned on Blue Iris Lane when her phone rang. She pulled over and answered it. "Hi, this is Jessie."

"Jessie, this Mrs. Bradley. My husband and I would like to meet with you on Saturday. The kids will be gone at lunch time. Would that work for you?"

"That would be great. I appreciate having a chance to talk with you both. I'll see you Saturday at noon."

How was she ever going to tell Gina's parents that Gina was the one orchestrating all of this?

****

So many questions and very few answers. She changed into her running clothes and hit the path to the marina. *Hello Mr. and Mrs. Bradley, I'm not a crazy person, really.* She smiled. *Your dead daughter is*

*coming to me for help. Strange, you've got that right!
No, please, don't call the police. I'm actually sane.*
Jessie nodded at several other runners along the path.
Running usually helped to clear her mind. She hoped in
worked tonight.

There had to be a reason Matt wouldn't tell her
much about the murder. She had searched the public
record and news articles earlier and hadn't found much
information. Something more was going on, and
instinct told her to keep searching, for the second story
beyond the story. How many layers would she find?
One thing she knew for sure. This was not a simple
murder case.

Chapter Five

It was the day of the concert, and Jessie hoped the day would go fast. No such luck. She waited for someone, anyone to stop by so she could ask questions about Gina, but there was no one. Not Melinda, not even Gina. She tapped her pencil on the desk to a catchy tune in her head. She doodled on her note pad and watched the clock. Lunch came, went, and still no one stopped by. She talked to Katie, cleaned out her files, and reorganized her drawers. Could there be a slower day? Her eyes glanced over and over at the slow moving hands on the clock. The silence in the building was almost maddening. Where was everyone today? Probably at the park already, but here she sat. Finally, when it was almost five, she jumped out of her chair tidying the office. Another glance, it was five straight up and she was done. Jessie changed into her favorite jeans and T-shirt, locked the church, and walked out to her car. With the top down and tunes playing in the background, she made the turn onto Blue Cove Drive, around the curve. She passed the village shops, the cove and marina, and made the left turn toward the old town square.

It was hard to believe she had been here only few weeks. All the strange incidents had completely taken her out of her normal routine. Telling Katie about Gina was a no-brainer. She needed to tell someone and maybe Katie could help her make sense of it. If not, at least they could have a good laugh.

Making her way to the public parking across from the town square, she slipped her car into a parking space, put up the top, and locked it as she got out. With a couple of hours yet to go until the concert, a pretty large crowd had already gathered. The park was filled with activity, bringing a smile to her face as she crossed the street.

An animated volleyball game was in the works with intermittent cheers and high fives. On the other side of the park, a loud rowdy group of guys played flag football, punctuated by some colorful language and coarse remarks. So that's what it would be like to have brothers. She grinned.

The grassy area in front of the stage was filled with people on lawn chairs and blankets, already staking their claims for a choice spot. It was obvious that the town showed up in force to celebrate the coming of summer. Jessie loved it.

Standing at the park's entrance, she glanced back and forth through the gathering crowd, looking for Katie. Jessie spied her in a perfect spot, not too far from the stage with her blanket spread and picnic basket beside her. As she made her way toward Katie, Molly stopped her.

"Hey, Jessie, I want you to meet my boyfriend, Kenny." Molly's eyes lit up as she introduced him.

"Hi, Kenny, it's nice to meet you." Jessie extended her hand and smiled.

"Molly told me you're the new secretary at the church where the young pastor was murdered." He grabbed her hand in his, pumping it, his blue eyes lighting up his face. "How do you like working there?

"I'm enjoying it so far." She shifted her weight to the other leg. Jessie liked him instantly, punk hair and all. She could tell by the way he looked at Molly that he was in love with her.

"Molly told me it gives her the creeps just thinking about it. She could never work there." He smiled showing off two big dimples.

"Gina used to come into Joe's almost every day. She was such a sweet lady." She gave Kenny a playful push. "I was so sad when they found her murdered, that's the real reason I couldn't ever work there. Plus, I've heard stories about people seeing her around the church and cemetery. I think that's a little creepy, although I've never seen her. Have you?"

"I actually like working there. The people are nice. The writer in me likes the strange and unusual that comes with a good story." She evaded the question and before they could ask her more, she added, "I need to find Katie. It was great seeing you, Molly. Enjoy the concert." She waved as she walked away.

She had thought Molly had a lot of ink and piercings, but Kenny might actually have more. In some weird way they made a cute couple.

Winding her way through the crowd, she heard someone calling her name. She traced the sound to Reba who was waving Jessie over in her direction. Sitting on her lawn chair, dressed in a floral sundress, she looked like a queen holding court. Next to her was her prince, a very handsome, distinguished man with a head of salt and pepper hair. He had a kind face, smiling eyes that never stopped watching Reba as she spoke to Jessie.

"Hi, Jessie, dear, this lovely man is Lawrence. He's been the man in my life since I was fifteen." She patted his hand and smiled at him.

He stood to meet Jessie. "It's a pleasure to meet you, Mr. Thomas."

"Lawrence, please, and the pleasure is all mine. My wife has told me so much about you, and you're just as she described. You have nothing to fret about, young lady, for she told me only good things about you." He smiled at her.

"I told him you reminded me of myself when I was younger. I was ahead of my time you know. I was a strong, independent woman, working my way in a man's world and having to fight every step of the way."

Jessie thought Reba sounded just like her Grandma Sadie.

"She's always been one feisty woman, which has kept me at her side for all these years." He leaned over and kissed her cheek.

"We won't keep you, Jessie, but I wanted you to meet Lawrence, and I wanted him to see our famous Jessie who lights up a room and showers everyone with kindness."

"The rumor is you can walk on water." Lawrence winked at her as he sat back down in his chair.

Jessie laughed and continued to smile as she walked toward Katie.

"What's got you smiling?" Katie asked as she patted the ground beside her for Jessie to sit down.

"I spent a few minutes with Reba and Lawrence Thomas. She always cheers me up."

"Don't you think she's a little weird? It's like she knows what you're going to say before you say it."

"Eccentric maybe, but she's definitely not weird. I think they're a very handsome couple." Jessie sat down and watched the crowd around her.

Everywhere she looked she saw smiling, happy faces, people greeting each other, and picnic baskets on blankets. This was how you were meant to spend an early summer's evening.

Not one black rain cloud loomed as a threat to what had to be the perfect summer night. The band was setting up, doing microphone checks, and tuning their instruments; children were running around the blankets with laughs and giggles intermingled with a few cries. She could get used to this lifestyle.

"I invited Dylan and Matt to come by during their break and get something to eat." Katie started unpacking the bag with the condiments in it. "They both have to work tonight. I hope you don't mind. You and Matt are always at odds."

"I don't mind. I can be civil if I work hard at it." Jessie laughed and threw the salt shaker at Katie. "Nice catch."

"I know how your devious mind works. I've learned to expect the unexpected when I'm with you." Katie laughed. "By the way, I've waited long enough for you to tell me what had you so upset the other night. You did say you would tell me later if I let up, which I did, so fess up." Katie grabbed Jessie's shoulder and shook her playfully.

"Don't interrupt like you usually do and let me get through the whole story first, and then you can ask any questions you have." Jessie cleared her throat and retold the story about all her sightings of Gina.

"Wow, I didn't see that coming." Katie put her

hand to her face and pushed her hair behind her ear. "You don't believe in ghosts, do you? I guess that's a stupid question in light of everything you've experienced since you've moved here. It's a wonder you haven't moved back to New York already."

"I don't know what I believe, but I can't just dismiss it as though nothing has happened. I now know the woman staring at me as if she was waiting for me, the woman at the edge of the woods, and the one who I saw in the church was Gina Martin. For some reason she has come to me and wants my help, so I'm going to do it." Jessie saw Katie's puzzled look. "I know, crazy, huh? I'll attempt to tell her story and hopefully in the process find out who killed her."

"I don't know what to say. I've never heard anything like this before."

"Wow, now this is a first, you speechless." Jessie laughed. "Seriously, I'm going to write a story about Gina, but some of what I might find out will have to be kept secret."

"Are you kidding me?" Her eyebrows rose. "Of course I'll keep what you tell me secret. There is still a murderer out there. Aren't you just a little bit afraid you'll stir up trouble and get in over your head? Remember I told you this is a small town. Everyone knows everyone's business."

"I'm already in over my head by no choice of my own." She frowned. "I have a ghost hanging around me, which is unusual even for me." Jessie opened the lid on the picnic basket. "What did you bring for dinner?"

"Oh, no, you don't!" Katie snapped the lid down. "It's the same thing I packed in the box dinners for the guests at the inn."

"Which is?"

Katie never answered her because they were interrupted by Pastor Rick and a friend who strolled over.

Rick looked at the man beside him. "This is my new secretary, Jessie." Rick smiled at her. "Jessie, this is Brad Martin."

Chills went down her spine when she heard Brad's name. "Hi." She paused. "I hope you're enjoying the evening." She managed a forced smile. He greeted her with a barely an audible hi back, his face showing no visible emotion at all.

"Brad was married to Gina and is still grieving, so I thought I would get him out among people tonight." His eyes shifted to Katie and then back to Jessie.

"Pastor Rick, this is my friend Katie."

"Hi." He locked eyes with Katie. "How long did you have to twist Jessie's arm to get her out of New York to this insignificant town?" He gestured around him and smirked. "I thank you." He saluted her.

"We've been friends a long time. Believe me, no amount of convincing on my part would have brought her here if she hadn't wanted to come." Katie turned her face to hide the anger in her eyes.

"I was hoping for a chance to see you tonight, Jessie!" He paused, giving her a long insolent look. "Enjoy the music. I'm going to introduce Brad to some other folks. See you around." He turned his back and walked away.

Jessie felt almost sick as she watched Brad and Rick walk away. The two of them together didn't seem right. Neither was the way the Pastor had been looking at her.

"Your boss is nice looking but a little too—I don't know, what's the word I'm looking for?"

"Too slick, polished, maybe too much like a used car salesman?" Jessie overemphasized each word.

"Too forward. Truthfully he gives me the creeps, and he made me angry."

"I could tell. You had fire in your eyes, and I fully expected for you to blow smoke out your nostrils." Jessie laughed.

"No, I didn't."

"Oh please, yes, you so did! Now it's your turn to fess up. What's for dinner?" Jessie reached for the picnic basket and looked inside. "Oh, man does this ever smell good."

"On the menu for tonight is a baked chicken breast on a bed of salad greens with asparagus, topped with honey mustard dressing, a slice of banana walnut bread with cream cheese, and a lovely chocolate raspberry torte for dessert." She took two boxes out of the basket and handed one to Jessie.

"Do you always eat like this? If so, I'm coming up to the inn every night."

"I treat my guests well. I must if I want to keep them coming back year after year."

After they ate, Katie and Jessie stretched out on the blanket to listen to the music. The concert headlined two groups, one that played folk music and an alternative rock group. Jessie liked the first band's sound.

"I have a confession to make." Katie looked at Jessie.

"Oh, no, what did you do to me, now?"

"I might have talked to Matt the other night about your crazy goals, among other things."

"Katie, how could you? He gives me a hard enough time as it is."

"You need help, my friend, and I only gave him a small nudge."

"I told you no matchmaking. When I'm ready, I'll take care of it myself. Please, please don't try to set me up." She pleaded with her eyes. "It'll just turn out like it did that time in college the last time you interfered, a real mess." Both of them started to giggle.

"Every time we get near you two you're laughing." Matt sat down followed by Dylan.

Katie looked at them. "Your dinner is in the basket." She sat up. "Everything should be in the boxes, including your utensils and napkins."

"This tastes great." Dylan took a big bite.

The second band's music was too loud to have a decent conversation, so the guys ate and the girls stretched back out. Dylan tapped Katie's shoulder when they were done. "We have to get back on duty. Thanks for a great meal."

"You're welcome. See you around." Katie waved and so did Jessie.

"Well, that passed without another round of tug-of-war between you two."

"Just remember to keep loud music playing so no conversation can take place when we are in the same vicinity. As long as we don't open our mouths, I think the two of us could grow to be very good friends."

"Do you know what I think?"

Jessie rolled her eyes. "I shudder to think!"

"You really like him, and all of this is some weird

mating ritual." Katie gestured wildly with her hands.

"You're crazy." Jessie rolled her eyes. "I hardly know the man well enough to form an opinion. However, I do believe if we could get past the fact that we are completely at odds and opposites in every way, we could have a professional, working relationship." She laughed.

"You have to admit he's good-looking." Katie playfully swooned.

"He sure is, that is if you like the strong, silent type, unless of course he is lecturing me. I don't need another man to tell me what to do, I have Dad." She looked at Katie. "No match-making."

"Who me? I would never do that." Katie crossed her fingers behind her back.

****

Later, Matt was watching the departing crowd and thinking about how smoothly things had gone. Dylan came from the other side of the park and stood beside him.

"Matt, I've been watching Brad Martin and Rick for some time. They moved their chairs close to Jessie and Katie and were staring at them all night."

"As far as I know there's no law against looking at a pretty woman. If that were true, every guy on earth would be in jail. I imagine many of the upstanding citizens of Blue Cove looked at Jessie tonight." He chuckled. "She looked fine in those jeans. Besides, I was keeping an eye on them, too. The pastor has a thing for her, but he's not the one I'm concerned about."

"Brad sure doesn't look like a grieving husband to me." Dylan waved as someone said goodnight to them.

"It's the pastor's relationship to Brad that's got me

thinking." He frowned after the departing pastor.

"Maybe I should walk the girls to their cars. I see Brad and Rick walking behind them. Do you want to come along?"

"You're on your own. I have some work I want to catch up on before my shift is over, and besides I can handle Jessie better at a distance." He grinned and shrugged.

"I thought you said Jessie looked fine tonight." Dylan slapped Matt on the back and laughed.

"I did, but some things are just better to look at and never touch. It's like my relationship to spicy food. It smells good, looks even better, but it gives me indigestion. She might give me indigestion, but I'm not blind." Matt smiled and walked toward the station and turned to watch until Dylan caught up with the ladies.

The park was clear of people except for a few stragglers when he finally opened the door to the station and walked in. Matt noticed the newest member of the force siting at the desk. He looked so young, with his dark hair and his head bent over a book. Matt wondered if he had ever looked that young or had been as nice as this kid was.

"Hi, Matt, how was the concert?" Joe Collins looked up from his book. "It's been a real snoozer here, nothing much going on."

"It was pretty quiet in the park. We had only a few minor skirmishes, not bad for the size of the crowd. How's your wife and baby girl?" Matt smiled taking inventory of the dark smudges under Joe's eyes, his disheveled uniform, and his hair standing on end.

"Both my wife and I would be great if only our new little sweetheart would sleep at night." His hand propped up his head.

"If anyone needs me I'll be in my office. I'm off duty in about an hour." Matt started down the hall.

"Okay, Matt." Joe watched him walk away.

Matt turned on the light and pulled Gina's case file. He looked over the list of suspects and wrote on the margin next to Brad Martin's name *Pastor Rick* and then circled it.

"What is the connection between these two?" His brows furrowed. "It's not pastoral in nature, I'm sure. I'd even stake some money on that." He tapped his pencil on the desk.

He wrote a new column in the file and put the pastor's name at the top.

He started to make notes of observations, and what he personally knew about the man.

"Pastor, there are some things I would like to know about you. I'll find out. You won't be able to hide much longer." Concentration etched lines in his face.

For the next hour, he pored over the time line and made notations in the case file. There was something nagging at him in the back of his mind, but he couldn't put his finger on it.

"Hey, Matt, you're still here?" Dylan's voice startled him.

"I was going over Gina's case file. Seeing Brad and the pastor has stirred up something, but I can't figure it out. I know I'm missing something." Matt rubbed his temples.

"You'll put it together. Something's got to break soon," Dylan encouraged him.

"I wish I felt as positive as you. These guys were professional; they didn't leave a trace of evidence other than a note with no fingerprints or handwriting."

"They'll slip up eventually. Bad guys always do." Dylan changed the subject. "As soon as I caught up with the ladies, Brad and Rick veered off in another direction."

"Stands to reason they wouldn't want to be observed by you." Matt closed the case file and a second file he'd opened. He picked up the second file to take with him.

"Say, are you about to call it a night?"

Matt nodded.

"Give me ten and I'll walk out with you." Dylan turned to walk to his office.

They said goodnight to Joe on their way out the door. "You want to stop for a beer?" Dylan asked.

"Not tonight. My mind is still going over the case, and I think I just want to keep my focus for a while."

Dylan got into his new Ford pickup and Matt went to his vehicle, his pride and joy, a cherry red '53 Chevy pickup, fully restored, by his truly, in mint condition.

Stopped at a red light on the drive home, he thought about calling Jessie to tell her about his decision, but it was too late.

He'd known for a while that he needed a fresh pair of eyes to look at some of the evidence in the case. Jessie might be that pair. After he did a background check on her and talked it over with the police chief, his mind was made up.

Anderson had asked Matt about Jessie. He had heard of her reputation. When Matt told him what he had learned in his background check on her, the chief advised Matt to use her as part of his team. "You can keep an eye on her since she's new in town and make sure she doesn't mess up your investigation."

It was actually Thomas O'Malley, the last New York homicide investigator he had talked to, that had sealed the deal.

"Jessie is a smart and trusted journalist," O'Malley had said. "Her research is impeccable. If we asked her to withhold information for the sake of the investigation, she could be trusted to do what we asked."

"How did she help and work with your department?" He explained to O'Malley that he was thinking of bringing Jessie into his case.

"On several occasions she obtained information during her research or interviews that she shared with us. We solved a few cases because of it. One look at those blue eyes of hers, and people simply told all." He laughed. "She's a sweetheart. There isn't an officer in this precinct who wouldn't trust her with vital information. That's saying a lot." He chuckled. "We don't particularly like newspeople."

"I hear you," Matt responded.

"She'd have made one hell of a cop. But to tell you the truth, she's more effective being an outsider. People just seem to open up to her. We were all sorry to see her go—she brought class to this joint. By the way, what's she doing now?"

"She's working as a church secretary."

"I'll be damned, if that's not the perfect cover for her."

Matt remembered Thomas's parting words to him. "Treat her good, you hear, or you'll answer to me and a few others here at the precinct. Her research is sound. The way she puts it together will make your head spin, but she's tenacious and gets to the truth, thinking like a woman would."

Hell, she had already messed with his head, but his mind was settled. He would take her to dinner and ask for her help, a truce of sorts—nothing more. Truth was he wanted a whole lot more.

Chapter Six

Jessie's mind was a whirl of activity as she drove to Rocky Pointe. She didn't exactly know how to approach Gina's parents. Hopefully they would say something during the introductions and small talk that would give her the opening she needed.

Rocky Pointe was beautiful. There were no beaches, just rocky bluffs which were quite majestic looking. Clouds were building over the ocean, and the waves were slamming the rocky shore line. It was totally awesome, and Jessie had to pull over and take pictures.

She loved the old Victorian and Cape Cod houses that made up the older section of the town, built along the rocky cliffs overlooking the ocean. Some of them were private homes, but others had become inns or small shops.

She followed the Bradleys' directions, and before long, she found herself parking in front of their home. They lived in the newer section of Rocky Pointe in a well maintained modest house on the far edge of town.

She felt a little nervous, but she was in too deep to turn back now. She walked up the sidewalk to the front door. It was time to peel back a layer. Perhaps she could secretly help Matt without him knowing. Impossible, absolutely improbable, there was no way; he would just have to accept her help and like it. This was not a simple murder case.

She listened to the three-note chime of the doorbell. The door was opened by a pretty brunette with dark brown eyes. Jessie knew the minute she saw her where Gina got her looks. Mrs. Bradley was an attractive, petite woman with a smile just like her daughter's.

"You must be Jessie Reynolds." She opened the screen to let her in.

"Yes, I am. Thank you for agreeing to talk to me." Jessie smiled at her.

"Please be seated." She motioned to a chair. "My name is Pam, and this is my husband Don."

Jessie acknowledged the introduction and continued cautiously. "As I told you on the phone, I wanted the opportunity to explain to you why I want to do this story. Then it's up to you. I don't want to intrude on what must be a very hard time for you both." Jessie paused, gathering courage. "I don't want you to think I'm weird, because nothing like this has ever happened to me before."

She proceeded to tell them all that had happened to her since moving to Blue Cove. "So you see, I didn't know your daughter or that she had been murdered when I took the job. Until I saw her picture hanging in the church and James Morris told me she had been murdered, I thought I was seeing a living person."

Gina's parents showed very little reaction to all she had said. Jessie could only imagine what they must be thinking. "The dream was the turning point for me. The expression on Gina's face when she asked for my help got to me. When I told her I would help her, it felt like the right thing to do." Jessie paused, and heard only the sound of the refrigerator running.

After a few minutes Pam's soft voice broke through the heavy silence. "Gina loved that floral dress, and it sounds like something she would do to get help for her kids if she could. You must be overwhelmed, Jessie. It's strange even to think of it as a possibility." Pam looked at Jessie, her eyes moist with unshed tears. "Gina was a wonderful daughter, not perfect by any means, but caring and a very good mother. Whatever else she was, she was first and foremost a great mother."

"Her kids miss her something awful." Don straightened in his chair. "We are trying to help them find a new kind of normal, but it's not easy with the custody battle hanging over their heads. They're not even Brad's kids. He's just doing it to make it look like he cares and give the impression he's a loving father. The kids don't want to be with him, but Brad had started the process of adoption before Gina was killed."

"Who's their real father, if you don't mind me asking?" Jessie looked at Don as she asked the question.

"His name is Bill Johnson, but he's had nothing do with the kids for years. He's in prison for drugs and armed robbery."

"Is there anything you can tell me that might lead to the person or persons who murdered your daughter?" Jessie threw out the loaded question.

Don looked at his wife and clearly made a decision. "We are going to tell you what we know because I believe, however strange your story seems, Gina is trying to help us find her killer."

Pam leaned forward. "Ever since I can remember

Gina wanted to be a pastor. She was assigned her first church, when Bill Jr. was little and Gina had just found out she was pregnant again. Bill resented her time at the church and became overly protective and jealous of her. He called her nonstop, wanting to know where she was and who she was with. Pastor Scott, the senior pastor, was trying to help Gina; he could see the problem escalating so he sent her to another pastor friend in the next town for counseling." Pam stopped to collect herself.

"Bill was becoming very abusive. To make a long story short, Bill followed Gina one day and caught her in an innocent embrace with her counselor and almost beat her to death." Pam wiped the tears rolling down her cheeks. "To this day I don't know how she didn't have a miscarriage."

"Bill was arrested, and before his case went to trial, high on drugs, he robbed a liquor store and threatened the clerk with a gun. After he was convicted and sent to prison, Gina divorced him."

Pam continued. "After counseling, she seemed to be doing better. It was during this time she met Brad Martin, who fell head over heels in love with her. He left the priesthood to marry her. I'm not sure she felt the same way, but she saw it as a way to survive. Gina was assigned to the church here almost three years ago. Excuse me, my throat's a little dry. I'll be right back." Pam went into the kitchen to get some water and brought Jessie a glass, also.

"Thank you, Pam." Jessie took a sip.

Don took up the story. "Everything seemed to be going well, at least we thought it was. Then we started to notice bruises on Gina's arms that were only visible if a sleeve slipped up. Bill and Sarah seemed to be fussy and always wanting to stay here. And then right before Gina was killed, she told us she had found out something and was going to leave Brad. When we asked her what it was, she wouldn't tell us. She told us it was too dangerous, if we knew it could get us killed. It must have been what got her killed." Don walked across the room to the desk and pulled out a piece of paper. He gave it to Jessie to read. It was a copy of a typed note: *Now, dear Gina, you can no longer see anything.* He wiped his forehead with the back of his hand. "Did you know that when they found the body her eyes had been removed? The public wasn't given that information. The police wanted to keep it under wraps. She was shot after she died. The body was staged, and her blood was everywhere." His voice trembled as he sat back down. "We still wonder how much she suffered."

Jessie felt sick. "I didn't know." Her voice was barely a whisper.

"My daughter's eyes were beautiful, so full of mischief and life." Pam was openly crying and looked at Jessie. "They took her beautiful eyes. I get so enraged just thinking of it."

Don's hands tightened into a fist. "When you described Gina to us the way you saw her. It gave me comfort to know you saw her with her pretty brown eyes again. I wish someone could tell me—how we can ever get over this? I know in my heart that Brad had something to do with it. He was abusing her, and no matter what his alibi is, that bastard is somehow connected to this." Don turned away, breathing hard. "He's alive, fighting to get my daughter's children, and she's dead and has no say, at least until now." His voice broke. "Maybe you can give her a voice."

"I'm certainly going to try." Jessie stood. "Here is my phone number. You can call me anytime you think of something no matter how small you think it is; something as little as a deposit slip or a phone number can sometimes break a case wide open. " She reached for Pam's hand, and held it. "Before I leave, could you please tell me some of your happiest memories of your daughter? Anything from when she was young and recent stories would be great, too."

She couldn't imagine the pain they felt every time they thought about what had happened to their daughter. Don and Pam's stories gave her a better idea about who Gina was before she hit the troubled times in her life. Gina had been a kind, generous person who was outgoing and very talented. She was a good mother, but maybe a little naïve when it came to men. But then there was probably at least one bad relationship in every girl's life, Jessie reflected.

"Thank you for sharing your daughter's life with me. It sounds like she was a lovely person. I hope in some small way this will help the police solve her murder." She walked toward the door. "I will stay in touch and send you a copy of Gina's story before I send it to my boss. You can read and approve or disapprove it." She stepped onto the porch and turned to leave.

****

When Jessie got in her car, she checked her phone and noticed a message from Matt. He wanted her to give him a call.

Interesting…She called before starting the car. "Hi Matt, this is Jessie, what's up?"

"Where are you? I've been trying to reach you all morning."

"I've been in Rocky Pointe visiting Gina's parents." She took a quick breath. "Before you go ballistic on me, I did tell you I was going to do a story, and I was very careful not to upset them."

"Could you meet me for dinner tonight at the Chowder House?" He sounded amazingly calm. "You could tell me about your visit, and we can talk about some other things I wanted to discuss with you."

Jessie couldn't tell from his voice if he was angry or not. "Are you all right? You're not mad or anything?" She was puzzled.

"We can talk about it tonight."

"Only if you promise you're not going to yell. I don't want a scene in public." She wondered if he was frowning.

"I'm not going to yell, but I should ask for the same promise from you. You haven't always been sweet and civil."

"Touché!" Was he smiling? "What time? I'm leaving Rocky Pointe now."

"Does 6:30 give you enough time?"

"I'll see you then."

Now what's he up to? Her mind went through several scenarios on the drive home, most of them not pleasant. She arrived back in Blue Cove with just enough time to change and get to the Chowder House without being late.

Spraying her favorite perfume behind her ear, she checked her appearance in the mirror. Her blue floral sundress looked good with her black strappy heels. She didn't know why she was dressing up. Jeans and a flannel shirt were more his style. She grabbed her sweater and headed for the door. Admit it. She was intrigued. Matt was full of surprises.

Chapter Seven

When she pulled into the parking lot, she saw him standing next to a fully restored beautiful old pickup. He looked like a male model from a cologne ad. Dressed in jeans, a blue dress shirt, and jacket, his long muscled frame leaned against the truck. He actually looked a little sexy.

Before she could stop herself, it flew out of her mouth. "You clean up nice."

"Well, now, aren't you a pretty shade of red?" He smiled at her. "You clean up pretty nice yourself." He motioned toward the restaurant placing his hand in the small of her back. He glanced back over his shoulder. "Sweet car, by the way. '64 was a good year for the Mustang."

Jessie loved the restaurant's décor, a charming blend of New England and old English country inn. The Chowder House was set on the waterfront in a recently remodeled building; it had a fantastic view of the sun over the ocean. Matt had reserved a table by the window, so they could see the sunset and it looked like it was going to be spectacular. There were enough high, thin clouds from the earlier storm for the sun's color to paint a stunning picture of pink and orange. Matt pulled out Jessie's chair, taking her completely by surprise.

After they were seated, an older man approached the table. He was carrying a couple of menus. A broad smile on his face crinkled the corners at his eyes until his whole face seemed to light up.

"How are you tonight, Matt?" He looked over at Jessie. "Who is your lovely companion?"

"I'm fine, Roger." He turned toward her. "Jessie, this old womanizer is Roger Blackman. You'd do well to stay clear of him." He chuckled.

"Don't believe a word he says. I've been married to the same woman for almost forty years. You have nothing to fear from me." He handed her a menu. "I've never seen you before. Are you new to the area?"

"I moved here two weeks ago today." She smiled at him. "I've already learned to take what Matt tells me with a grain of salt."

"So you see, Matt, this lady is intelligent. She's too smart to believe everything you say. It could spell trouble for you, my friend." He waved for the waiter. "Peter will take good care of you tonight. I recommend the filet mignon and lobster."

Matt went with the steak and lobster and Jessie settled on a large salad, with grilled chicken, apples, walnuts and gorgonzola. Roger sent over a complimentary bottle of wine and two glasses. Peter poured the Merlot into each glass.

Jessie sipped her wine and waited for Matt to explain the real reason they were out to dinner. She knew this wasn't a date. Be patient. She waited for him to begin.

"I have a proposition for you." His deep voice intruded into her thoughts. "This is a truce of sorts. You and I both know we have strong opinions about each other. We are hardly together for a minute, and I say something that raises your hackles, and you get in my face. However, I thought it only fair to start this evening by telling you I did do a background check on you."

"What, are you kidding me?" She started to stand up. "And you think that's a truce?"

"Sit down," he said curtly. "I acted within my boundaries as a professional, and I make no apologies for it. Be honest. If our roles were reversed, wouldn't you do the same thing?"

"I suppose I would." She frowned at him.

"I know you would." A flicker of amusement lit his blue eyes. "I found out a lot about you from Neil Dempsey and Lieutenant O'Malley."

"And what was that?"

"You are well-liked, respected, and came highly recommended. I was also duly warned that if I didn't treat you right, I would have to answer to several people in New York. The question is now, are you going to tell on me?" His lips quirked into a half smile.

"I guess it depends on how vengeful I'm feeling." She smiled. "So what's this all about?" She motioned around the restaurant.

"This is my peace offering and a set-up of sorts before I make a request of you. I'm not smooth enough to ask it without help from the Chowder House, and I figured you won't make a scene in public."

"Cut the bull." Her lips twitched. "The one thing I know about you is you're not too shy to tell me what you're really thinking."

"I'll just spell it out then. What I learned about you tells me we could have a professional relationship. It will have to be incognito for now. No one besides you, the chief, and I can know about it. Not Katie, Dylan, or anyone. The more people who know, well, it could put your life in jeopardy. That could change in the future, but is necessary for now." He looked at her, his expression serious.

"I want to bring your eyes, ears, and research in on Gina's case. For everyone else, you must be the sweet little church secretary writing a freelance story about Gina. On this point, we must totally agree. We can continue our public dislike of each other, which shouldn't be hard. Whatever you do has to be discreet because every question puts your life at risk, and these guys are real professionals who will let nothing or no one stop them."

"Won't this little scene change all that?"

"No, because you can get mad and walk out on me after dinner." He smiled.

"It should be easy enough to do with very little acting on my part." She chuckled.

"Ok, sweetheart, now that's just mean and personal." He clutched his heart. "Seriously though, how did it go with Gina's parents?" He nixed the flirtatious banter.

"They're great people, and I learned a lot about Gina. It's hard for them, especially the way Gina was murdered, and the fact that her eyes were missing."

"They told you? It was pretty awful to be sure." His voice trailed off, and he seemed lost in thought.

The silence gave her time to watch him as he leaned back in his chair, turning the stem of his wine glass slowly in a circle, an indescribable expression on his rugged features. "Can I ask you something?" she asked him.

He lifted his brows. "Sure."

"How do you do it? I mean examining the crime scene for evidence, seeing the victims in gruesome reality, and telling their families? I could hardly stand to see the pain on the Bradley's faces."

He frowned briefly. "In the beginning it used to twist my insides into knots. Eventually, I disconnected my work from my life. It's a job. Some might think I'm hard, but in truth I'm trying not to feel anything." He paused to watch her for a moment. "I do have a certain sense of satisfaction when a case is solved and another bad guy is off the streets. I imagine it's something a little like what you must feel when a story you've labored over is published or read on a newscast somewhere." His face closed down suddenly. He was done sharing.

"You guys see some of the worst parts of humanity." She shook her head.

For the next hour, as they ate, she told him what she had learned from Pam and Don Bradley, the people at the church, and how oddly Pastor Rick had been acting. She was able to fill in some information that he hadn't gotten in his interviews. She gave him her email address so he could send her information from Gina's file. Earlier, he had mentioned to her that he wanted her to draw her own conclusions and do her own research. To let him know what she was thinking. She liked that idea. She already had an angle working in her head.

"How did you end up in New York?" He put off the inevitable clash.

"My father's good friend Neil Dempsey, as you now know, offered me an internship when I graduated from college. It was a great start for me. I learned so much from him. In the beginning, I did his research.

Neil demanded excellence, and legitimate sources. Everything had to be corroborated. I was given opportunities to advance based on real merit. In other words, I had to work for it. My favorite area was investigative work. I worked with some of the best in the field." She smiled not quite believing they were actually talking normally.

"Why didn't you go home if you wanted to leave New York?" He tried to hide his grin.

Her chin lifted in reaction to the way he had phrased his question until she saw his smile. "I had thought about it, but I'm an only child and my dad has a hard time not interfering in everything that has to do with me. Plus, I wanted to stay by the ocean— something my hometown doesn't have. And of course, then there is Katie, my best friend since childhood. When she came here, it was perfect. It made it easy for me to decide this was where I wanted to be."

"I hope you won't be sorry for leaving your great job behind."

"I'm still doing work for Neil and, to tell you the truth, I'm happy to be out of the hectic pace of life." Her expression softened.

"Ok, Jess." He touched her hand and winked. "It's time for you to get upset and walk out on me. Before you do, I want you to know I've learned a few new things from you, today. Lieutenant O'Malley was right when he told me people naturally trust you and open up to you in a way they won't with the police. They consider you safe. So don't listen to me, keep on being exactly who you are." Had he actually complimented her?

He handed her a card with his email address and

cell phone number. "If anything comes up, let me know. If you feel afraid or think someone is watching you, let me know. You got it?" He leaned forward in his chair. "Now, sister, remember what a damn pain in the ass I can be and let me have it." He frowned.

Jessie jumped up and in her haste knocked over the chair so everyone in the restaurant looked at them. "Well, I never, don't even think of getting up. I'll see myself home!" As she snapped at him, loudly, she felt the familiar heat rising up from her neck and knew her face was red again. Jessie turned her back on him and stormed out playing the scene to perfection.

****

Roger walked over to Matt. "It looks like it didn't go so well with your pretty lady. I've never known you to treat a woman bad. What gives?" He studied Matt's face.

"I'm not sure." He gave Roger a sheepish look. "She seems to bring out the worst in me. I've only met her a few times, and every time we get into some kind of argument."

"That's too bad, my friend. She seemed real nice. You've been a bachelor too long. Maybe you don't know how to treat a woman anymore. I could give you a few lessons." He laughed.

"Just give me the bill, and I'll get out of here," Matt said briskly.

By the time Matt got out to his truck, Jessie was already gone. He couldn't have had the little scene at the end play out any better. It had actually been a pleasant evening, and he hated that Jessie was about to experience small town living at its worst. She was game. He would give her that.

He wondered what angle she was working on, because he knew she had one. She was smart, and there wasn't a doubt in his mind she would figure some of the details out on her own. All in all, the night had worked out just like he had hoped. By morning, Blue Cove would know they'd had dinner together but that she'd walked out on him.

Now, if only he could control this insane attraction he had for her as easily, he might actually solve this case. It was those damn blue eyes. He could forget his next sentence when she looked at him. Working with her would either cure him or drive him crazy.

Chapter Eight

Jessie drove home with a smile on her face. It had been a great evening. She had actually gotten what she wanted. The big plus was she got to yell at Matt to boot. Although, she had to admit he was almost likeable tonight. She had enjoyed their conversation, and he wasn't bad to look at either.

After meeting Gina's parents, it was important to her to be a part of this case. No matter how unorthodox the reason was that got her involved, she wanted to be there to see it solved.

She was stoked. When she got home, she sent off some emails to family and friends. The only other person other than Katie she told about her experience with Gina was Grandma Sadie. Jessie knew she would understand.

Next, she wrote a rough beginning to her story about Gina and then made a list of the things she needed to do. Tomorrow was Sunday. She would go to church. Maybe if she begged, Katie would go with her. She needed to get to know some of the people who might be able to fill in some more details for her. She was especially hoping to see John Robertson.

She looked at the clock; it was still early enough to call.

"Hi, and where have you been all day?" Katie blurted out the question.

"I went to Rocky Pointe for a drive and to see where Gina's parents live. Call it rash, but I wanted to meet her parents, run the idea of doing a story about their daughter by them, and begin my research. There are some things about a person you can only learn from family."

"I heard you went to dinner with Matt and you walked out on him. Tell me it's not true."

"No can do. It made for a great evening." Jessie laughed. She knew Katie was irritated.

"What were you doing at dinner with him?"

"He asked me, and it was supposed to be a peace offering by him, which was short-lived. It's a good thing we don't have to negotiate a real peace agreement for others. It would be an awful disaster. Don't worry, my friend. I think we both have concluded, we can't get along when it's just us. It's a requirement now. We have to be with others to be civil."

"Jessie, this is no laughing matter. I don't want you to ruin a good thing with him. He asked me questions about you the other night. He said he was interested professionally. I think it's more than that."

"Don't go there. Look, Katie, you need to let it drop. For whatever reason, we don't hit it off. I can live with that, and so can he. Anyway, I want to ask you something but before I do..." Her voice trailed off. "How did you hear about me walking out on Matt? Good grief, it happened only a couple hours ago."

"It's a small town. You keep forgetting that fact." Katie laughed. "News travels fast. What did you want to ask me?"

"Remind me not to do anything in public that I will regret." She paused. "Do you want to go to church with me tomorrow? I wanted to meet some of the people who could give me the details of Gina's time at the church."

"Sure, I'll go. Someone has to keep an eye on you."

Jessie rolled her eyes.

For the next couple of hours, Jessie did research. She began to put some odd connections together when it came to Pastor Rick and Brad Martin. She made a list of questions to ask Pastor John, Rick's dad. She needed some confirmation or insight from somewhere else.

Putting it all aside, she went to bed. Sleep was not long in coming after her head hit the pillow.

****

Sitting in a pew the next morning, Jessie noticed people were in various stages of attentiveness. Her mind was doing the same thing. She wondered what they were thinking about this morning beside the sermon.

"Wouldn't it be fun to see what was going on in all their heads?" Jessie said under her breath.

"No, because maybe they could see what's going on in mine." Katie frowned. "Man, is this guy long winded," Katie whispered. "I wish he'd wrap it up."

"Shush, you're worse than a little kid." Jessie gave Katie the look her mother used to give her.

"I'm hungry, and I want to get out of here. What a way to spend my day off."

"I'll buy your lunch if you'll just behave," Jessie promised.

"You've got a deal." She grabbed Jessie's hand. "You have to admit he does go on and on."

Jessie nodded and put her finger up to her mouth.

"Don't tell me to be quiet," Katie whispered when someone looked at her. "I see several of the men nodding off which sounds like a pretty good idea to me. Wake me when he's done." Katie smiled closing her eyes.

As soon as the final prayer was said, Katie jumped up and headed out into the foyer. Jessie was hot on her trail seeing Pastor Rick bearing down on her. Thank goodness, Reba Thompson headed him off and started bending his ear.

In the foyer, the commotion came at Jessie like a whirlwind, her red frizzy hair pulled precariously into a ponytail of sorts on the top of her head.

"How's it going, Blondie?" Melinda's voice yelled out.

"Not bad, Red. How about you?" Jessie laughed

"I think I'm going to survive. Have you had the joy of seeing you know who yet?" She pointed at Gina's picture.

"Do you mind if I to talk to you about that later?" Melinda nodded. "I need to talk to Pastor John before he leaves." Jessie walked fast to catch up with him.

"Hi, do you remember me?" She smiled at him.

"I sure do, and I haven't forgotten we are going to have lunch together. I'll call the office this week and set up a time as soon as I know Rick's schedule. Feel free to just call me John. I'm retired." He smiled at her. "I'm also hungry, thanks to my long-winded son." He winked at her and walked away.

Jessie stopped before walking out the door when a cold chill made her shiver. She looked around expecting to see Gina. Instead, she saw a pretty young woman standing near Gina's picture looking directly at her. Jessie walked toward her and introduced herself.

"I've heard you're writing a story about Gina. My name is Andria, and I was her best friend. No one else knows that because we tried to keep our relationship quiet. She needed someone to talk to. Is it possible we could get together away from here one day and talk?"

"Of course, I'd love to. We could do coffee on Saturday morning if that works for you?" Jessie nodded.

"How does Java Joe's sound? Would 9:00 work for you?" She reached down to pick up her little girl who had latched onto her leg.

Jessie nodded. "I'll see you then." She walked over to Katie.

"Now, may we please leave?" Katie took her arm and pulled her out the door.

"Where are we headed for lunch?" Jessie tried to pull her arm away from Katie's tight grip.

"Oh, no, you don't. You'll go back in there and try to have another boring conversation with someone." Katie held her arm tighter. She refused to let go until they were getting into the car.

"Have you lost your mind?" Jessie laughed and rubbed her arm where it had started to turn red. "I actually met two people who might be helpful."

"I'm hungry, and even you have to admit that was a boring sermon. He went on and on."

"Okay, you win." She threw her hands up. "It was awful. Sometimes, I wonder if he is really meant to be a pastor. Now, where are we headed?"

"There's a great place in Seaside Village called the Captain's Table. They have a wonderful brunch. You'll like it, trust me."

After lunch, she dropped Katie off at the inn and headed to her little slice of heaven by the sea. It was too pretty to stay inside. She decided to change her clothes, grab a book and some iced tea, and read outside for a while.

Instead, she checked her email and found one from Grandma Sadie who said she would call sometime during the week, one from her parents, and Gina's case file from Matt. Once she got into reading the file, it hooked her. She couldn't put it aside. She was at her computer until both her neck and back were stiff.

She stood up and walked around rubbing her neck, thinking about what she'd just read. All of it was tied to what Gina had found out about Brad's dealings. Jessie knew that much, but how was she to find out what Gina had learned? It had gone with her to the grave. Or maybe not...

She changed her clothes, tied her shoes, and headed out the door. Down the path toward the marina her feet pounded against the pavement, her ponytail swished back and forth slapping her neck, long even strides mile after mile. *Gina, we need to talk. What did you learn? What was it that tipped you off? It had to be something easy for you to see once you started paying attention.* An idea hit her. She needed to get home and research it. Jessie looked at the beautiful cove and felt euphoric as she started back the way she'd come.

For the next several hours at her computer, she followed one rabbit trail after another. She was about to quit and go watch the sunset. She jotted off a quick email to a friend, who owed her big time, and the reply was instantaneous; he must have been on line. The email gave her links and the codes she needed that would help her access some private information. A half hour later, she found her first connection for Brad and Pastor Rick.

"Well, well, pastor!" She eyed the numbers on her screen. "I know you don't make that kind of money from your church. I wonder what you and Brad have been up too. You've been naughty boys indeed." Jessie stood up excited, she reached for her phone. She punched in Matt's number and was surprised when he actually picked up.

"Hi, this is Jessie."

"I know, what's up?"

"I found my first connection between Rick and Brad. They both have big offshore accounts. I called in a favor from a friend to get this information. If Gina had found out there was an offshore account, she would have wanted to know where Brad was getting the money." She took a breath. "Their regular checking accounts are nice and cushy, but nothing to tip anybody off. But the offshore accounts have huge deposits up to a hundred thousand dollars. Obviously, Rick doesn't get this kind of money from pastoring a church. I'll send the links to the site, to your email. It won't be easy but I'm going to try to establish a money trail."

"What made you think of an off shore bank?" Matt asked.

"I was running and having a little talk in my head with Gina. I tried to think like a wife. What would tip me off and cause me enough concern to think my husband was doing something illegal. The first thing I thought was if he was spending lots of money, money I knew wasn't in our account and that we shouldn't spend. Maybe he would say he was paid in cash. You get the picture I'm sure."

"I can see now that's been one of my problems—I don't know how to think like a wife." He laughed. "You've made a great find. Follow the trail, but Jess, be extra careful."

"I will and check your email. I just sent you the information."

Jessie stretched and went to the window. The first stars were appearing in the early evening sky. Where did they get the money? Who paid them and why? Most people put money in offshore banks to hide it. She wondered what these two were up to and how many others were involved. It was bad—it had to be or Gina would still be alive. Her mind was filled with so many questions, she needed to take a break and let it go for a few minutes.

She started to close the curtains, but the fluttering leaves on the trees changed her mind. She watched as the wind sent waves of motion coursing through the flowers and bushes. What was that? She saw something move, caught in the light for a second, before the moon was veiled by the clouds. Was Gina out there walking in the night? Her eyes tried to focus hoping to see it again. Was it her? *If you are there Gina, I'm asking for your help. I want to find your killer, but I have so little to go on.* She shivered, rubbed her eyes, but whatever she had seen was gone.

Chapter Nine

The next couple of days at work were slow. The phone hardly rang and no one stopped by to chat. Pastor Rick came to work, but went right into his office, muttering something on his way. He only came out when he was leaving for the day. He didn't say much to her, which she didn't mind. He was totally preoccupied.

By Wednesday, she was bored. She was ready to climb the walls. Pastor Rick had just whisked by her for the umpteenth time mumbling that he would be back as he raced out the door. She was doodling on her note pad, and daydreaming when the ringing phone jolted her back to the present.

"First Community Church, may I help you?"

"Jessie, this is Neil. Say, the outline you sent me about Gina looks real promising. Even if you don't go any farther with it, it's a great human interest story. What are you thinking?"

"This story is a lot broader than I imagined." She kept her voice down. "And if it goes where I think it is heading, you'll have a big scoop. I'm following some trails and speculating now. There are some things that can't be shared because the case is still under investigation."

"Okay, keep me in the loop, and we'll talk later."

"I will."

Jessie was just getting over the surprise of talking

to her old boss when the phone rang again. She answered to find Pastor Rick's father on the phone.

"Hi, John, did you want to talk to your son?"

"No, I called to set up our lunch date. Rick is leaving Sunday for a mission trip to India. So how about on Monday we have lunch?"

"Sounds great." She didn't have the heart to tell him she knew nothing about the trip.

"I'll meet you at Patterson's at noon, how's that?"

"I'll be there." She wrote the date and time down on her personal calendar.

When she hung up the phone, she was baffled as to why the Pastor hadn't told her he was leaving for India. She wondered if it was really a mission trip or something a little more sinister than that.

Jessie was finishing up the calendar of church events when Pastor Rick came rushing back into the office and suddenly stopped by her desk. "I'm sorry I've been so distracted lately. I'm trying to get ready for a mission trip to India with some pastor friends and civic leaders. I should have told you sooner." He grabbed the messages from his box. "I'll be gone all next week and won't be back in the office until the following Wednesday. Reverend Peterson at the Baptist Church and my dad are on call if any emergencies come up. I've written out the numbers."

"Is there anything you would like me to do while you're gone?" She took out her notepad.

"I'll put a few things on a list for you. You'll need to send the guest speaker a copy of the finished bulletin so he'll know the order of service. He'll email you his sermon title and the scriptures he'll be using."

"Okay." She tapped her pencil on her notepad.

"When do you leave?"

"I'm leaving after service, Sunday." He started to walk away and then turned to look at her. "Oh, and Jessie, when I get back we need to have dinner together." He walked swiftly to his office.

Secretly, Jessie hoped he would forget the dinner altogether, but on the other hand, it might be a good way to get some information. She wondered who these friends of his were. How could she find out? Maybe the airline would have the information she needed. It looked like more research was in order, and coffee with Andria might also provide some useful information.

****

On Saturday morning, Jessie found Andria already at Java Joe's when she arrived. Molly wasn't working so she got her coffee and sat down at the table with Andria.

"I'm so glad you're doing a story about Gina. I don't want people to forget her. "Andria leaned forward, her expression fixed. "She was a good friend. Usually she would come to my house, and we spent hours talking and laughing. I miss her so much it hurts. She was the sister I never had." She paused when a big man walked by their table. He sat down at table in the corner his back to Jessie.

"When was the last time you saw Gina?"

"I saw her a few days before the murder. She wasn't her normal self, and I kept asking her what was wrong." Andria looked around to see if anyone might be listening. "She told me she was afraid for her life. I asked if Brad was hurting her, and she told me she was more afraid of his friends and the people he was doing business with."

"So Brad wasn't hurting her?"

"He had grabbed her roughly, there were some bruises above her wrist, but believe it or not, he was in love with Gina. He had told her to let him take care of the business and begged her not to get involved because he couldn't control some of his associates. He kept telling her they, whoever they were, wouldn't let anyone out of the organization once in because they knew too much and everyone involved was getting rich. Brad also told her he was in too deep and couldn't get out. If he tried, his life was worth nothing."

"I wanted to blame Brad for her death, so it could be solved right here and now."

Jessie sipped her coffee. "Did she believe Brad?"

"I think she did. She said the only way to protect her life and her kids was to get away. She was saving money and had accepted a position in a church on the West Coast. She was going to move in a few weeks."

"Did Brad know she was trying to leave him?"

"I don't think so. She hadn't told anyone but Pastor John who actually helped to arrange it."

Jessie's mind took off at that point. If Gina had told John, and he'd mentioned it to his son, well, then, Brad would have known. No doubt about it. But if he didn't kill her, then who did and why? Who was calling the shots, and was Pastor Rick's life in jeopardy?

"You've given me a lot to think about, Andria. Do you know the name of the organization?"

"All Brad told Gina was that it was a civic group. She found the initials HC on some of his notes. I hope this will help catch her murderer. You are free to tell the police. I was never questioned because they didn't realize I was her friend. I was nervous even thinking about talking to them, but I trust you. If they want to question me now, I would like you to be with me." She paused, reached into her handbag and took out a sealed envelope. "Gina gave this to me the last time I saw her. She said to keep it safe; there was someone who should have it, and I would know when it was right to give it to them. The minute I saw you, today, I knew you were the one. Gina wants you to have this." She stood up, pushed in her chair, and turned to leave. "I need to go. We'll talk again soon."

Jessie's eyes followed Andria all the way out to her car. She didn't know what to think, but she wasn't about to read the letter here. Whatever was in it could have been the very thing that got Gina murdered. She stood up to leave and said goodbye to the young man behind the counter, leaving a tip at the table. She noticed the man in the corner had changed seats and was looking over the top of his paper at her. Something about him bothered her.

How did Andria know to give the note to her? This case was getting stranger by the minute. She was in the center of a murder, a cover-up, or what exactly? Armed with the pastor's airline and flight numbers, she would check the passenger list for familiar names.

****

She walked through the door, kicked off her shoes, and carefully read the contents of the envelope. Her heart was racing before she had even finished it. Matt needed to read this.

She put in a call to him hoping he would pick up. She got his answering machine.

"Hi Matt, this is Jessie. Could you call me back as soon as possible. I really need to talk to you. It's an emergency." Jessie paced back forth across the room, waiting impatiently for a call back. Maybe she could find out where he lived and run by there.

She grabbed her purse, put her shoes on, and was headed for the door when the call came.

"Sorry, I was talking to someone. What's up?"

"I was given something today that you need to see. We have to meet. Is there someplace secret we can go?"

"I'm on duty today. Why don't you just swing by the office. Never mind, that's not a good idea. Too many people will have too many questions. Do you remember passing Ted's place about fifteen miles outside of Blue Cove on your way here?"

"I'll meet you there in fifteen minutes." She snapped her phone off and was out the door before he had even replied.

It seemed to take forever to get there. Matt must have raced there with his lights flashing because he was sitting in the parking lot in his car. As soon as she got out of the car, he rolled down his window. "Get in."

She couldn't tell if he was upset and proceeded cautiously. "I know you didn't want us to be seen together, and I wouldn't have bothered you if I didn't think this was really important." She peered over at him warily.

"Jess, you can contact me anytime you need to. I'm only concerned because you sounded afraid on the phone. I'm trying to keep you safe, which is why I hesitated to get you in the middle of this to begin with. So let's have it." He rubbed his temple. Shifting the car into gear, he started driving toward a scenic overlook and picnic area about twenty miles out of town.

Quickly, Jessie filled him in on her conversation

with Andria.

"Why didn't she come forward when we were conducting interviews at the church?"

"She's shy, but she told me she would come in and talk if I would go with her. Anyway, I asked her if Brad was hurting Gina."

"What did she say?"

"She said Brad loved Gina. He said there was too much money involved and even he was in too deep to get out now. His life wouldn't be worth anything." When Matt pulled into the picnic area and parked, she took her seatbelt off and turned in the seat so she could face him.

"I wonder what he got himself into and how the pastor is involved?" His brows furrowed. "You mentioned you had something for me to read."

She pulled the envelope out of her purse and proceeded to explain what Andria had told her about Gina telling her to keep it safe and she would know the person she was supposed to give it to when the time came. "Don't you think that's strange?"

"It's odd, but a lot of things about this case are strange." He started to read.

> *To Whom It May Concern:*
>
> *If you are reading this, then I am probably gone or dead. I'm hoping it's because I'm gone, but I fear it's because I'm dead. Lately I've noticed someone following me. I'd say it was my imagination, but I've noticed this guy too often for it to be coincidence.*
>
> *My husband is involved in something and I don't believe it can*

be legal. I found some information about several offshore accounts that he has in the Caymans. Huge deposits of money were made consistently, and he refuses to tell me where he's getting it. He's also traveling a lot but will not tell me where or with whom. He mentioned a civic organization. I found the letters HC in some of his notes which might be the letters in the group's name, but I'm not sure. Enclosed is a copy of a bank record I printed out from his computer.

He became angry when I confronted him and told me to keep my nose out of what was not my business or someone else might cut it off. I believe he was more afraid for me than I was. He told me there was no way he could get out of what he was into or he would have to be erased because he knew too much about the operations. He said his associates would never let anyone interfere, and they could make people disappear without a trace.

Pastor John has worked with me to get a new job on the West Coast— hopefully I'll be here until next week when I fly with my children to the new life that awaits us. I told John I was leaving Brad because he was abusive and there was no hope for our marriage. Really I'm leaving to save our lives.

You have this letter because I can trust you to someday set the record straight for me. Please, if I'm dead let my kids know how much I loved them and was trying to do everything I could to get them somewhere safe, a place where just the three of us could have been a family without some crazy man to mess it up. I don't know how I seem to attract all these bad boys. I'm sure it's a weakness in me.

Brad was good to us for a couple of years, and I'm afraid for his life. He'll either die or be in prison. Tell Matt Parker to keep an eye on Brad's coming and goings.

Please think kindly of me and say nice things about me after I'm gone. I should be more positive, but I don't believe there is any way to prevent the inevitable.

Pastor Gina Martin

"Damn, this is what I've been concerned about all along. This is something big and not just a simple domestic issue." He folded the letter, put it back in the envelope, and looked at her. "How am I going to keep you safe?"

"You don't need to worry about that. I'll be careful." She reached over and touched his hand.

He turned his palm up, linking their fingers. "The

hell I don't. I invited you into this mess."

"I was in it from the first day I saw and heard about Gina. This letter confirms it was meant to be."

"Aren't you being a little too cavalier about all of this?"

She shook her head. "I think you're overreacting and a tad too concerned."

"The hell I am." He frowned.

"Look, Matt, I'm in it whether I want to be or not. I work with Pastor Rick, who might be involved. Gina has come to me in the church and in my dreams. I'm in it." Her voice softened trying to put him at ease.

"That's another thing bothering me, that so called pastor you work with looks at you the wrong way. You shouldn't have to put up with that crap. Why don't you go back to New York?"

"Are you wanting me gone, for me or for you? What are we talking about?" Her back straightened as her chin inched up.

"Before you get mad, how am I supposed to keep you safe? I have one unsolved murder. I don't want you to be another one."

"I'll keep myself safe and call you only if I need you." She yanked her hand from his and turned to look out the window.

"Like hell you will." He reached across the seat and pulled her hand back. "I'm going to be your shadow. I want to know where you're going and who you'll be with. You got that? If you feel threatened or notice someone following you, I want to hear about it, the very first time."

"I will." She lost her train of thought when he looked at her that way. "I'll make you a daily schedule, if it involves something other than working in the office." She tried to free her hand. He held tight. "While I'm thinking of it, Pastor Rick is leaving for India on Sunday, after church. I have his flight numbers and airlines. I'm going to check the passenger list to see who is going with him."

"Look into it and let me know what you find." He studied her. "I'm sorry I acted that way; I'm just not sure how far reaching this is, who is involved in it, and what's involved. Trust no one, Jess. Be careful what you say and who you ask questions."

"Pastor Rick mentioned he was going to India with some other pastors and civic leaders. It makes me wonder if their smuggling some kind of contraband. The question is what?"

"I'm working on a theory that could involve a lot of money." His thumb stroked her hand.

She felt weak in the knees. "I have Jeremy looking into something for me right now. I'll let you know when I hear from him." She doubted Matt was even aware of what he was doing to her. But, boy oh boy, she was. "Rick asked me to go to dinner when he gets back into town."

"You don't have to go out with him at all, ever." He was frowning.

"I know, but it might be a good chance to get information."

"I don't want you alone with that man until we know what his involvement in all this is."

"You're not thinking like a cop." She arched an eyebrow. "I work alone with him almost every day. I can't avoid him. Besides one dinner doesn't constitute a date. I never date co-workers or my boss. It's my policy."

"Are you serious?" He grinned. "That seals our fate because I'm your boss and co-worker. You never dated the men you worked with in New York?" He let go of her hand.

"That would be correct." She nodded

"I never thought I see the day—a respected journalist and one with principles." He chuckled, started the car, and headed back to her car at Ted's Place.

"I'm glad you can find something to laugh about in all of this. I find it all a strange welcome to a new town." She gave a rueful chuckle. "I was hoping to come here and live at a slower pace, build a circle of friends, and enjoy the ocean. I was not counting on meeting a ghost, or working for a pastor that may not be a pastor at all. It adds up to a few strange weeks. I'm happy to give you something to laugh at." She mocked his grin and laugh.

"Nothing personal, sweetheart, in this job you have to find your laughs where you can."

Once back at Ted's Place she opened the door to get out of the car. "Why didn't you tell me before I walked out on you the other night everyone would be asking me about it for the next several days?" She closed the door before he could answer.

He rolled down the window. "Welcome to the nice quiet lifestyle of Blue Cove." He smirked. "By the way, I think I'll be doing a little undercover work at the airport tomorrow. Email me the airline and times. I'll let you know what I find."

Chapter Ten

As he drove away, his first thought was this was bigger than this small town police force could handle. He put a call into Chief Anderson to ask about getting some county or state help.

"Matt, give me any information and evidence you have on Monday, and I will see if it's enough to get some extra help. If your instinct is right, then we're dealing with some influential people from several areas." The chief sounded concerned. "With the kind of money you say is being deposited into these accounts, there's something major happening. How did you get the information?"

"Jessie got it. By the way, I'm going to do some undercover work at the airport tomorrow. I want to see who some of these people are: names, towns, and how we can connect them to a source."

"I told you this was your investigation to do with as you see fit. So I trust you to stay on it and work it from every angle."

His next thought was how to keep Jessie safe. This case needed his concentration, which he found hard to do when she was around. He wanted her involved because the situation was fluid, and he could only be in one place at a time. Hell, she had gotten the letter from a friend that the police didn't even know existed. Pastor Rick so far didn't have clue, but if people continued to talk to Jessie, it wouldn't take long for him to realize something was up. He hated the fact Rick was Jessie's boss. She worked in the church alone with him. She was vulnerable. He was jealous. Just like some damn teenage boy.

Jessie was driving him nuts. He was having a hard time keeping his hands off her. She had no clue, and he didn't want her to. He should try to put some distance between them, but he already wanted to see her again. He was the one boss she would have to date. His mind was made up.

****

Matt simply didn't make sense.

They had a case to concentrate on. After tomorrow, they could know more about some of the players. Now all they needed was the connection. Who were the people pulling the strings? What were they were smuggling, and who had killed Gina?

"Gina, it's slowly coming together. I hope we'll have an answer soon for your family." She smiled, talking to a ghost now.

She needed to do something routine today. The case went on the back burner, and a clean house, laundry, and grocery shopping took its place, anything that could make her life seem normal. A few hours away from it all would do her a world of good.

She stopped at the store on her way back into Blue Cove and did her grocery shopping. With that taken care of, she headed home to do her other chores.

Listening to the washing machine fill with water, she watched as the detergent turned to suds. Absentmindedly, she placed her clothes in the water, realizing for the first time that her life could be in jeopardy.

Gina was murdered because she found out something that was beyond her and Brad, and now Jessie had walked right into the same situation. She had been so smug when she told Matt he didn't need to worry about her.

"Well, somebody had better." She slammed the lid down on the washer.

Jotting a quick email to Matt with the airline information, she wandered aimlessly around her cottage, pacing like a caged cat until the music on her phone startled her.

"Hi, baby girl, how are you doing?" Grandma Sadie's voice came over the line.

"I'm doing okay." She felt her eyes tear up. "It's great to hear your friendly voice, Grams."

"Your email has shaken me, Jessie. I know what happened to you is real. You're far too sensible a girl to be taken in by someone trying to scare you. How are you holding up?"

"Up to a few minutes ago, I was doing pretty well considering the crazy few weeks I've had. Today I realized it's much bigger than just a simple murder. There are two kids whose security and custody are at stake. People who you should be able to trust, you can't trust at all. I wonder if my life might be in jeopardy writing the story about Gina."

"Does anyone there have your back?"

"Matt Parker, the cop in charge of the investigation does. But we seem to fight every time we get within a few feet of each other."

"You're no quitter, I know that well enough. I wouldn't blame you if you headed back to New York.

Although, I know my girl, and you'd never do that."

"No, I'm going to do this story, but I realized today I do need to think about safety and being smart about what I do."

"When I first met your grandpa, we fought every time we got within a few feet of each other. I can tell you, it wasn't love at first sight. The thing was, we were both strong people and neither of us wanted to give up control. It took years for us to realize we didn't have to, and that's when we knew we were in love. I'm not saying that is your situation now, but two strong, opinionated people can learn to work together. If you're in real danger, Jessie—trust him enough to tell him."

"I will, Grams."

"You know, I'm only a call or email away. Stay in touch. Oh, and like you asked I won't mention any of this to your parents. Your dad would be there on the next plane to drag you back here. You'd miss a great adventure, and I wouldn't be able to live vicariously through you." Sadie chuckled.

Jessie smiled. "I love you, Grams. Your voice was the one I needed to hear."

"I love you, too, sweetheart. Talk to you soon."

Jessie put her clothes in the drier, picked up the novel she was reading, got a glass of iced tea, and went outside.

The view was breathtaking, and the floral scent of the garden was rich with honeysuckle, lilac, and the irises next to her porch. Jessie could see Mr. Yamamoto busy at work. She smiled at him, and he stopped to chat with her for a few minutes.

A young couple, who were guests at the inn, said hello as they strolled by hand in hand. She returned the greeting, thinking all the while, when things calmed down this could be a really nice life. She would eventually meet that special someone to enjoy life with.

Was Matt in her future?

Chapter Eleven

Matt got to La Guardia about two on Sunday afternoon and found a strategic spot at one of the gates where he could watch the people who walked by. He figured if their flight left at eight, they would be there by three or four since it was an overseas flight. His paper in hand, he kept a close eye on those making their way to the gate for the flight to India. It wasn't lost on him that he was in Jessie's old stomping ground.

He'd called yesterday and set up an appointment to have coffee with Lt. O'Malley earlier in the day. It had been well worth the time. Not only did he learn more about Jessie, but he got another perspective on this case. O'Malley had a few suggestions about what Brad and Rick might be dealing in for the kind of money Jessie had found in their accounts. But Matt needed some real evidence before he said anything to anyone.

He could never live here, he thought, too crowded, too smoggy, and people were in too damn big a hurry to enjoy anything. But, if he was honest, he had to admit that most women in Jessie's place would think this was a piece of cake compared to what she had experienced of peaceful, quiet, small town living so far.

"Now this is interesting," he muttered under his breath. He watched Pastor Rick and city councilman, Ed Jones walk by together. Not far behind them were Brad and the mayor of Blue Cove. Several other men joined the group, some of whom he recognized as council members, clergy, and even a state senator. He watched them until they boarded the plane. Jason Cummings, he knew from high school. Matt went to the police academy after college graduation, and Jason went into law, wanting to get into politics. He'd been mayor for a couple of years now.

Maybe this was just a goodwill mission trip, like Pastor Rick had said, but why would Brad be going? Matt leaned back in the uncomfortable plastic chair, trying to make sense of what he was seeing. He wondered if all of these boys had offshore accounts. It was something they needed to check out. But he'd need warrants, which would take some time. Meanwhile, Jessie could do some snooping around.

As the plane taxied out for takeoff, he headed for the exit, armed with some new avenues to follow. Better get Jessie involved in the research sooner than later. She had the nose for this. Once in his car he gave her a call.

"Hey, Jess, this is Matt. Are you busy?"

"Not really. I take it you saw you what you went to see."

"Probably more than I wanted to. I've started on my way back, but I wanted to get you going on something. Did you get the flight list?"

"Yes."

"Will you check and see if there is a rabbi, and Episcopal priest listed and if you find names, check for an offshore account along with Blue Cove's mayor, Jason Cummings, and city councilman Ed Jones."

"Sure, I'll take care of it. Is that all?"

"There were several guys I recognized, but I would

have to look at the list to see if I can put names to their faces. We're talking about some other councilmen and a senator. Oh, and Brad Martin was in the group."

"I'll get started and email you the list so that you'll have it when you get back. I wasn't doing anything but reading and waiting to hear news from you."

"Let me know, Jess, when you find out."

"I think you do that on purpose."

"What?" He tried to sound innocent.

"Call me Jess, when you know my name is Jessie."

"You make it so easy." He laughed. "Talk to you later."

****

Jessie chuckled. She seemed to walk into every trap Matt put out there. At least he got a lot of laughs at her expense. He was like a splinter in her finger, nothing major, but annoying.

She spent the next few hours at her computer. Both of the men Matt had talked about also had offshore accounts in the same bank. Huge deposits had been made on or around the same time as the deposits into Brad's and Rick's accounts. She spent the next few hours trying to follow the money trail, but the accounts were well protected. She needed the help of Jeremy who could get through anything. His skills on the computer were something legends were made of.

She sent an email off to him and told him what she needed. If anyone could find it, he could. Now she would just have to wait to hear back. In the meantime, she began to think about what she wanted to ask Pastor John tomorrow at lunch.

She had doubts that Pastor Rick was a real pastor. He might have studied for it, but his heart wasn't in it.

She wondered if it was a cover for his illegal activities.

She emailed Matt the flight list and what she'd learned so far.

"That's it for me. I've had enough sitting at the computer for one day." She stepped out her front door, looked up into the starlit sky, and with the sounds of the breaking waves in the distance, sighed. She looked around the garden, the paths lit softly with small lights. It was a beautiful evening. As she stood there, she caught sight of a shadowy figure standing beside a tree about fifty feet away. When he saw her looking that way, he dodged quickly behind the tree, and she saw him walk away toward the shoreline path.

It was probably nothing—maybe a guest at the lodge—still, hadn't she just told herself she needed to think about her safety and take nothing for granted? She would keep her eyes open, lock her doors even in the day, and deadbolt them at night.

She rubbed her arms trying to rid herself of the sudden chill she felt then hurried inside, locking up everything nice and tight. Even from a distance, she could tell he was a very big man.

Chapter Twelve

Jessie's night was restless. She had awakened several times thinking she had heard a noise. Straining, she listened to all the sounds in the night. Work was calling now, but what she really wanted was sleep, at least a couple of hours more.

She felt a little better after a shower and her morning coffee. Still, a lingering fear lurked at the back of her mind. She should probably tell Matt about the man watching her, and she would if she saw someone watching her again.

She honked and waved at Katie as she passed by the inn. Oh, how Jessie wished she could stop and unburden herself to her best friend, but that was not in the cards, at least not until Matt told her she could.

Another slow work day, a ticking clock that never seemed to move, a phone that refused to ring, and a deathly quiet building all made her fidgety. Suddenly something fell in the hall, and Jessie jumped up to see what it was.

"Sorry, Blondie, did I startle you?" Melinda picked up the broom she'd dropped.

"Just a little. It's been so quiet here all morning."

"I bet you thought it was our church ghost." She cackled. "I know you've had to have seen her by now. You want to hear what happened to me last night?"

"Sure, Red, tell me."

"I think someone was in the building when I came in to straighten and do some cleaning. I always like to come in at night or early morning so I don't bother the various groups having meetings. The ladies' circle is meeting today, and I wanted to set up. Anyway, I thought I saw the office door open, and I started down the hall, but then I heard heels clicking across the tile in the lobby, but no one was there when I went to check. When I came back down the hall the door was shut, but then I heard the side door of the church shut. You know what I think?" She paused to look at Jessie shaking her head. "I think Gina was looking after me. I came in afterward and looked around, but didn't see anything missing. What do you think?"

"You're probably right," Jessie stammered.

"I tell you, Blondie, sometimes this church is downright scary at night when no one else is in the building. I think I'm going to start working when you're here."

"Sounds like a plan to me." Jessie opened one of her drawers to get a paper clip. There, on top of her office supplies, was an envelope with her name on it. She started to open it, and then the phone rang. It was one of the church groups, wanting to schedule some time in the meeting room. She slipped the letter beneath some papers waiting for her attention as the phone rang. She'd get to it later.

Melinda caught her eye and waved as she headed for the lobby. "I'll talk to you later. I need to make sure I set up right for the women's group."

The next time Jessie looked up at the clock, it was time to meet Pastor John. She grabbed her purse and headed to Patterson's.

****

She found Pastor John sitting in a booth in the main dining area of the restaurant, head bent as he looked over the menu.

"Hi, I hope you didn't have to wait long." She smiled and waved at Patterson as she sat down. He nodded back. Was that a hint of a smile she saw? "It was quiet all morning. Just before it was time to leave, I had several phone calls, and Melinda came by to talk to me."

"No problem." He looked up and smiled at her. "I've only been here about five minutes. I just started to look at the menu—although by now I should know it by heart."

"How do you like being retired?"

"To tell you the truth, I miss the church and the people." He gave her a wan smile. "After Gina died, I was so saddened I let my son talk me in to retiring. But there are days, I would love to be back at the helm, helping people walk through all of this mess. For some reason Rick has got in his head that not mentioning Gina will make it all go away. I think people need to talk about it."

"I agree with you. Several people have talked to me about needing an outlet for their emotions." She paused and then pushed on. "Was Rick trained to be a pastor?"

"If you mean did he go to school, the answer is yes, but if you want to know if he is called—it was never on his radar until a little over a year ago. He wanted the church to hire him, but Gina had been hired the year before and people loved her. The church turned down his proposal. I told him I could help find him a church somewhere else, but he said it had to be here."

After they gave the waitress their order, Jessie waded in just a little bit deeper, not wanting to cross a line and upset him.

"Did Rick pressure you to retire so he could have the church?" She tried to gage his reaction. "You don't have to answer if you don't want to."

"In fairness to Rick, and where I was at the time, my first response would be no. But having said that, when I look back, I would have to say it was a first rate job he did on me." He fiddled with his water glass. "I've never known my son to be like he is now. He's tense, seems nervous, and I don't personally like being around him. As far as how he's doing as a pastor, he's doing an awful job." His mouth tightened, and he paused as the waitress set down their orders. "I'm about to call the district office to get involved. I can't talk to him at all. He refuses to listen to me or to the church board, and he reacts to almost everything said to him. I hope I haven't shocked you, but you heard how he treated me in the office that day." He leaned forward, his eyes on her face. "You're working with him, what do you think?"

Jessie measured her words carefully. This was her boss they were talking about. "I think he's appeared tenser lately, getting ready for the trip and all."

"I realize I'm putting you on the spot. He's your boss, and I know you want to be careful. I'm speculating now. I have no facts to back this up, but he's using the church to cover up something."

"What makes you think that?" She sipped her iced tea.

"He's had a lot of strange phone calls. I've

overheard some of them, and he seems to have an unlimited amount of money to travel. I have no clue where he's getting it." He took a bite of his sandwich, chewed and swallowed, before speaking again. "Some of the people in the congregation have asked if he was using the church's money. They're getting suspicious, too. When I asked Rick, we had a major fight."

She looked at John's worried face and tried to think of something that would put his mind at ease. "It's possible he found a side business to supplement his income."

"It can't be legal. I know of very few things where you can make the kind of money I'm watching him spend." John suddenly grabbed her hand and looked into her face. "I'm not going to tell him we talked. It's our secret, but I need you to tell me what you really think."

"Okay." She spoke quietly. "You should tell Matt Parker what you've told me. There's no doubt in my mind your son is acting strangely. There seems to be a general disconnect between him and the work at the church. I can't help but think, like you, that his work at the church is a cover up for something else he's doing." She patted his hand.

"I'll stop by the police on my way home." He struggled. "I never thought I would have to talk to the police about my son. I also want to warn you that Rick is interested in you. It scares me. You're just the kind of girl I always had hoped for my son, but I wouldn't wish him on you the way he is now."

"Rick has told me a couple of times that we need to go out, but I've changed the subject every time. I will tell him if he asks again that I have a firm policy about

not dating someone I work with, especially my boss."
She folded her hands.

"That's a good idea. Thank you for talking to me. I
thought I was going off the deep end thinking about my
own son like this. I've heard, through the grapevine,
you're doing a personal interest story on Gina. I wanted
to meet with you originally to talk about her. I know
you need to get back to work, so I'll call you after I talk
to Matt and fill you in on what I know. How's that
sound?" He picked up the bill and laid down his credit
card. "This is my treat. Thanks for being a listening
ear."

"Thanks for lunch." She stood and smiled at him.
"By the way, I think the church misses you as much as
you miss them. Maybe you should consider coming out
of retirement." She said her goodbyes and walked back
to the church.

On her way back to her office, she stopped to chat
with the ladies' group which was just breaking up, and
Reba told her she would be down to see her in a few
minutes. So Jessie headed back to her desk.

She sent a quick email to Matt telling him John
was on his way to see him and passed on Melinda's
news about the office intruder. She had several days
until Pastor Rick was back, and she decided to use this
time to work on Gina's story. One point of concern to
her was that John had heard she was doing a story
already. If he had heard, she was sure others had as
well.

"Did you have a nice lunch, my dear?" Reba's
cultured voice asked.

"Yes, I did. I spent a little time with Pastor John.
He's such a nice man."

"I dearly wish that he was still our pastor. No offense to his son, but he just doesn't have the same regard for the congregation as his father, and there's a troubled aura about him." She walked into the office and sat down. "How is your story coming along? By now, I figure you're learning more about the mystery and unraveling the many layers. I never thought it was a simple murder or that Gina wouldn't still be roaming here."

"Gina was well-liked, generous, and by all accounts a great mother." Jessie evaded the question with a smile. "Her parents and children miss her dearly. I learned that she was a pretty terrific human being and maybe got too close to someone's ugly secret, which we'll mostly likely never know about because she took it with her to her grave."

"Secrets have a way of being found out, my dear, so keep looking." Reba glanced at her watch.

"I will, but I don't hold out much hope."

"I wanted to tell you something that concerns me, but I don't want to scare you. I just want you to be careful. I had a dream about you. A large dark shadow was spying on you and following you around. This was not of the ghostly variety, but human. So watch your back, my dear, and I'm going to tell that Officer Parker to do the same. Someone considers you a risk. You must be getting close to the truth." She stood up to leave. "I believe you'll be okay, but it will get worse before it gets better."

Worse, before it gets better. That doesn't sound good. "Have a nice day, Reba." Jessie smiled at her.

"You too, dear." She walked out the door.

What should she do with that? Why did everyone

keep coming to her with all this information? Sure, she had asked a few questions, but not that many. A large dark shadow? Hadn't she'd seen him the other night? Matt needed to know that, too.

"Gina, you must have been terrified," she whispered. *No wonder you wanted to get your children and yourself to safety. I've walked the streets of New York and never come up against what you had to face in this small town. I wish there had been someone you could have trusted to protect you."*

The phone's ring shook her out of her pensive thoughts.

"First Community Church, this is Jessie. May I help you?"

"Jessie, this is John. I'm glad I talked to Matt. Thanks for the suggestion."

"You're welcome."

"Matt told me I should be careful not to meet with you too often in case someone is watching. It might put you in jeopardy. It sounds like my son is messed up in something very serious."

"It could be, but maybe he's an outsider." She tried to give him hope she didn't feel.

"He also gave me your email address, so I'll be sending you the information I was originally going to tell you." He hesitated for a moment. "I'll check on you by phone every now and then. I'm sorry you came here to be drawn into this mess. Hang in there, and let others help watch out for you, okay?"

"Okay, and thanks for your concern."

Chapter Thirteen

Matt gave his report to Anderson when he got to work, and he called the sheriff's department in the county seat for some assistance. A meeting was scheduled for the next morning to go over the evidence with Sheriff Taylor who had friends at the state level as well. Anderson agreed with Matt. They needed more manpower, and they had a little over a week to get a plan of action and key people in place to do surveillance.

Anderson looked at Matt sitting across from him. "This case is all yours, Matt. I'm going to take a back seat on this one. You're in charge. I'll be here to help if you need it, but only if you ask." He took a sip of his coffee. "I'm grooming you for when I retire. Just keep me clued in on what's happening." He looked Matt in the eyes. "You've done a damn fine job with it so far."

"What does that mean? Can I work in some protection for Jessie?" Matt asked him.

"It's all your call, Matt, but you'll have to judge it by the manpower. You don't want to overextend your men in the field." He sat back in his chair. "You could run your command center from her house, which would keep someone near her," he suggested. "I want you to run all the meetings, deal with the law enforcement coordination, and see to the search and arrest warrants."

"Yes, sir. Is there anything else?

"I'm going to recommend the council hire you as my replacement when it's time." Anderson put a hand on his shoulder. "The letter is already written, and you've more than earned it."

"I appreciate your confidence in me, sir." Matt smiled at him and stood.

"Hell, you're the son I never had and always wanted. I know you'll do a great job and run it with integrity." Anderson stood and shook Matt's hand. He watched Matt walk out of his office.

Matt was anxious to get some help. He could see the case starting to gain momentum. He had no doubt someone had been in her office probably searching her computer, checking notes, and looking for anything they could find to use against her. Checking the clock on the wall, he put a call in to the church to check up on her. He waited impatiently as the phone rang once, twice, three times. Finally, on the fourth ring she picked it up.

"First Community Church, this is Jessie. May I help you?"

"Hey, Jess, I called to say thanks for sending John over my way. He filled in quite a few blanks concerning his son." He paused with relief at hearing her voice. "What more can you tell me about the intruder?"

"Only what I told you in the email. Nothing was missing or seemed out of place."

"Is any of your research there?" He waited for her reply.

"No, I would never keep anything here. It's all on a computer at home, protected by some pretty heavy duty firewalls and passwords. A friend I know set it up for me. He can get around just about everything out there, so he's in the know. He's one of the best. Even if someone broke in and stole my computer, they would be hard pressed to get anything. I always send a copy of my notes to Jeremy for safe keeping and to my boss, which in this case is you, so I sent it to you in a special file entitled AS-THE." She waited for a response. When none came she said, "The letters stand for '*As Seen Through Her Eyes.*'"

"Catchy!" He breathed a sigh of relief. "It's good to know."

"You mean about the file? I'm always very careful with information."

"A safe file is good news. The fact you see me as your boss is the best news of all. I like hearing it from your own lips." He grinned, imagining her expression. "I'll hold you to that when you want to argue with me about something."

"It's only good for work related issues." She chuckled. "When it comes to my life personally, you have no say."

"For a while, I imagine everything will be about this case. Is there anything else you need to tell me?"

"It's probably nothing, but the other night I stepped outside in the evening, and I noticed a shadowy figure in the distance. When he saw me looking his way, he hid behind the tree and then moved down the path toward the marina. He was a pretty big man. Needless to say, I didn't sleep well after that. I'm locking up pretty tight at night and even keeping my doors locked when I'm there in the day."

"Why didn't you tell me this before?" His knuckles whitened on the phone.

"I dismissed it as a guest at the inn until Melinda told me about the intruder."

"The chief and I made calls to the county and state and talked to them about getting some assistance for our small department, seeing as we have some players that are from other counties. I also want to get you some protection on the clock."

"I don't need or want protection."

He could hear the tension in her voice over the phone.

"The hell you don't, and just so you remember, I'm the boss. I'm calling the shots."

"I'll think about it."

"No, you won't. It's a done deal."

She abruptly changed the subject. "I sent out an email to the church folks about doing a story on Pastor Gina's life. Several people responded, and so I've arranged to do several interviews while Pastor Rick is gone. You know, a human interest story with all the feelings and emotions of people's sense of loss. The church people want and need to talk about Gina. I was thinking maybe I should leave a benign story where it's easy to find to throw our intruder off the track." There was still tension in her voice even though she had changed subjects.

"Sounds good, but I can't believe you gave up so easily."

"I'm choosing to pick my battles and live to fight another day. Hey, it's time to leave. I need to lock up. See you around."

"Goodbye, Jess." He could hear her mumble something under her breath.

He wouldn't tell her, but he was sending officers

on the night shift to patrol the church a few times. He would sit outside her house, walk the area, the gardens, and the path toward the marina.

****

Jessie was a little concerned that she had forgotten something significant, but couldn't for the life of her remember what it was. She was just happy to be home. She changed into her favorite shorts and T-shirt and was ready to chill in her cozy, peaceful space. Every time she walked through the rooms, she marveled that this was her home.

The sun was getting low in the sky, and it wouldn't be too long before it set over the ocean. Sunset watching was her nightly ritual. She sighed, and walked into the kitchen to take something from the freezer to make for dinner.

Her feelings were all jumbled up inside, twisting her into knots. Shadowy figures, ghosts, intruders, police protection were things she had never worried about before. She hadn't chosen this case, it had chosen her, and she wasn't about to let worry rule her life. She wondered how that was even possible and went to her computer to check her emails.

There was something from Jeremy. He gave her a few things to check out. Up-line, he told her, there were some pretty strong firewalls, but he was working at getting around them. He'd found several major hospitals in the chain, but didn't know how they fit in. Some pretty influential people were in the mix, he wrote, and quite a few people were getting money from the same stream. He hadn't found the source of the stream, but he was as hooked as she was. Jessie knew he would keep searching just like she would. She copied Jeremy's note to her special file, forwarded it on to Matt, and deleted it from her emails.

She decided to run before it got dark. She didn't relish the thought of being taken by surprise. The slightly cooler temperature had brought out several runners to use the path, so she was in good company. She should be safe. The steady pace she set meant she wasn't overtiring and would have a reserve just in case. She was thinking and planning, going over several eventualities and what ifs.

She needed to run a different path. I'm so predictable that anyone could easily follow me. I probably should run in the morning and change my times up, she thought. Be smarter, pay attention, keep your enemy guessing, isn't that what she had learned in her self-defense class? She should have listened more intently. Who would have known that one day she might actually need it?

Her phone vibrated in her pocket. She looked at the name and answered it.

"Hey, stranger, where are you? Are you okay? You sound out of breath?"

"Hi, Mom, I'm running."

"That explains it. Why don't you call back later on when you're ready to chat? It must be hard to run and talk at the same talk."

"Okay, I'll call you back."

She had just rounded the curve toward home. There were a lot more runners on the trail, here. Out of the corner of her eye she saw a big guy on one of the benches along the path. Though his face was partially covered by a newspaper, something about him seemed familiar.

It could be her imagination, but she felt his eyes on her, following her, until she no longer was in his sight. She picked up her pace and kept moving. Never in her life had she been so happy to get home and lock the door behind her. She didn't want to think about the fact that one good kick by him could probably knock the door off its hinges.

"I'm getting paranoid," she said softly.

Jessie made dinner for herself and sat down to eat and watch one of her favorite programs. She didn't want or need anything exciting for the rest of the evening.

She called her mom back and fell asleep curled up on the couch with the lights on.

Jessie's dreams were filled with awful images of Gina without her eyes. Near the end of the dream, Gina's eyes became like a two-way mirror. Jessie could see the image of a huge man with a cruel look on his face reflected in Gina's eyes. She awakened in a cold sweat, disorientated. Her heart felt as though it would pound out of her chest. She knew she had seen that man. He had been sitting on the bench watching her earlier tonight. She glanced over her shoulder at the clock; it was only 11:30.

She picked up her phone and pushed her speed dial.

"Jess are you okay?" Matt answered instantly, his voice filled with concern.

"I hope I didn't wake you, but I need to talk with somebody, and I can't talk to anybody about the case but you. Where are you?"

"I'm sitting in my patrol car right next to your car. Now I'm getting out of my car, I'm walking up to your back door, and I'll be knocking right about now."

She went to the door, opened it, and motioned him in. "I hate to admit it, but I'm glad you're here."

He looked her over and grinned making Jessie wonder about her appearance; curly hair must be going in every direction, she was still in her running clothes, and she had rubbed her eyes. Her mascara was probably smudged. Concern grew on his face. "What's up?"

"I had a terrible nightmare, but before I tell you about that, did you see the email I sent you earlier?"

"No, I was doing a little surveillance work at a friend's house." He grinned.

"Do you mean me? Why didn't you tell me earlier?"

"I didn't want to let you know how uneasy I was and mess with your head."

"I need to show you this email I got from Jeremy." She opened the file on her computer.

"It looks like his thinking and mine might be running on the same track. What happened that has you so upset?"

"Earlier, I went running and on my way back I passed a big man sitting on a bench along the path. The thing is, he seemed to be staring at me. He appeared familiar, but I thought, maybe I was letting my imagination run away with me. Then I had this dream about Gina. It was a nightmare actually. Toward the end of the dream, I saw a man in the reflection of her eyes. He had a cruel, sinister look on his face, and he was the same man who was sitting on the bench. I think…I think he was also at Joe's when I was there on Saturday." She pushed her hair back away from her face. "I never used to have to worry about anything like this before. What have I walked into?"

"It's a damn mess for sure, and you're in the center of it all." He took her gently by the arms pulling her in to his chest. His chin rested on her head. His hands rubbed up and down her back. "Always go with your gut, your instinct. It'll keep you alive. That's why I'm sitting outside until I have others to help shadow you as much as possible."

"I'm afraid to close my eyes." She shivered. "I don't want to see anything else. I'm more than a little freaked." She liked his strong arms around her, but pulled away. "Can I get you something to eat or drink?"

"You don't need to wait on me. Just take care of yourself." He looked amused.

"I never could have imagined a few weeks ago I would have so many strange experiences living here in this little piece of paradise."

"Hair raising experiences might be a better analogy." He grinned at her. "Have you seen your hair, lately?"

"Are you trying to tell me my hair is a mess or I look messy in general?"

"I'm taking the fifth. That's a loaded question." He chuckled.

She went to look in the mirror in her room. Matt heard her moan and then mutter something under her breath.

"Jess…" he called out. "Why don't you try to get some sleep? I'll stay here on your couch. If I fall asleep, I'm a light sleeper and will hear anything. Is that okay with you?" He paused. "I'll get whatever for myself and watch a little TV. I'll keep it low so you can sleep, and I'll be close by if you have another dream."

Walking back in the living room, she gave him a grateful smile. "Thanks. I have work tomorrow, and I don't want to be a complete zombie." She laughed cynically. "I can remember when such a statement was just a joke. I've always prided myself about planning and being in control. Since I've moved to Blue Cove the joke's on me. It makes me long for the peace of New York."

She left the living area and headed for her bedroom again. With her grooming taken care of, night clothes and robe on, she passed him on the way to the kitchen to get a glass of water.

"I was wondering what Katie will think seeing your car here all night." She made a face.

"Probably nothing…I stopped by to tell her I would be in the area most of the night because we had a report of a suspicious prowler. She thinks I'm on a stakeout for work. I told her I'd be in my car and walking the area between here and the marina."

"Looks like you covered all the bases then." She felt relieved. "Goodnight and thanks."

"Goodnight, Jessie, and you're welcome." He smiled.

"I was beginning to think you would never call me by my name."

"Sweetheart, you make it too easy for me." His smile widened to a grin. "I love teasing."

Chapter Fourteen

When Jessie got up Matt was already gone. He'd left a note. *Hey Jess, I left before the sun came up. You were sleeping soundly, snoring like a trooper, and I didn't want to disturb you. Hang in there. Dylan has been briefed, and we'll be taking turns looking out for you until the back-up arrives.*

"Snoring, humph. I don't snore!" she shouted at no one in particular.

Jessie left the house wearing her bright multicolored skirt with a fuchsia top. She was happy Matt had stayed the night. Of course, she would never tell him that.

The first stop on her agenda was Java Joe's for coffee and a bagel, or maybe she'd splurge and have a cinnamon roll, or better yet, one of their delightful scones. Molly's friendly face greeted her the minute she walked through the door.

"Hi, Jessie, you're looking good. That's a perfect color for you."

"Thanks, Molly." Jessie looked at the sign that posted the specials for the day. "I want a medium hazelnut coffee, and a chicken salad sandwich to go. I'll eat it at lunch."

"If you can wait a couple minutes, I have some killer cranberry scones that just came out of the oven; they need to cool just a little in order to bag them."

Molly handed the coffee to her and started on the sandwich. "Do you want chips or a salad with the lunch special?"

"I shouldn't, but I'm going to have the chips." Jessie stirred cream into her coffee.

"Kenny asked me to marry him last night. Isn't that cool?" Molly's face glowed. "We're looking at a late November or early December wedding." She stuck her ring finger out for Jessie's admiration.

Jessie looked at Molly's gorgeous solitaire diamond. "Congratulations to you both! Kenny has great taste. Your ring is beautiful."

"Isn't it though? He picked it out all by himself and surprised me. I wouldn't have chosen anything so amazing. It must have set him back a pretty penny." She held her finger out, staring at the ring. "See how it sparkles?"

"It's beautiful." Jessie smiled at her enthusiasm.

"I'll get your scone so you can get to work. I asked Katie, too, and was wondering, even though we are new friends, would you consider being in my wedding? Think about it, okay?" Molly placed the warm cranberry scone drizzled with a vanilla icing in a box, placed it in a bag followed by her lunch, and handed it to Jessie.

"Molly, I'm honored you would even think of me to be a part of your special day. I would love to." Jessie paid, put a tip in the jar, took the bag, and thanked Molly again.

"Since it's almost July, I'll let you know as soon as our date is finalized. I know we don't look the part, but we are going to have a beautiful wedding."

"I know you will." Jessie's smile widened. "And,

Molly, you are uniquely you. My grandma always tells me that, and it seems to fit you, too. Have a great day!"

She really had needed to hear such happy news. Any news that had life and love involved in it was better than what she had been hearing lately. Her first interview was today, and John had promised to email or call her so she could ask him questions. She was looking forward to seeing if the church saw Gina the same way Gina's family had.

****

The church parking lot had several cars in it, and Jessie remembered there was a morning book club group meeting there today. She was happy to have others in the building. Melinda had come early to make coffee and set up.

"Wow, Jessie, you look nice today." Melinda walked up to her. "Fuchsia is your color."

"Thanks." She looked at Melinda's tamed hair, and polished pant suit. "You look pretty nice yourself."

Melinda preened a bit. "I don't look half bad, do I? I heard you're interviewing people about Gina and letting them talk. I want to talk to you, too."

"Sure, any time. I want to get it done before Pastor Rick gets back because I don't want to upset him with people coming and going in the office."

"He doesn't like anyone talking about her at all. He won't like it." She spoke matter-of-factly. "This is my book club, so I'd better get to the meeting." Melinda headed toward the room the club was meeting in.

Jessie walked down the hall to the office and unlocked the door. Each day she found herself getting more attached to the job and people. The longer she worked here, even with all the crazy things that had happened, the more she loved her job. Maybe it wasn't the secretary part as much as the thrill of a great story and the adrenaline rush she got from unraveling a mystery. She would know more when things settled down. She drank her coffee, enjoyed the cranberry scone, and got her small tape recorder ready for the interviews.

By lunch time, Jessie had talked to three or four people and all of them said, basically, the same thing. Pastor Gina was a wonderful pastor with a kind heart. She had a way of making each of them feel special and like an integral part of this church. They were heartbroken and felt like she had been stolen from them. They would have left, but they had been attending for a long time and they had good friends in the church. And the final area of agreement was that Pastor Rick didn't have the heart or the regard for them that Pastor John and Gina had had.

James Morris went as far as to say, "We are thinking about calling a committee meeting to boot him out."

She sent an email to Matt and told him the last part, which might impact the case. Then she ate her lunch. The chicken salad was great. All white meat, grapes, celery, walnuts, and apples tossed with mayonnaise served on raisin bread. It was yummy!

John's call had confirmed most of what Gina's parents had told her. Gina was indeed leaving for the West Coast and a new job, but the last statement he made was the one that seemed to torment him the most.

"I told Rick she was leaving after I promised not to tell anyone. It haunts me to this day. Especially since Rick is friends with Brad. At the time, I didn't think anything about it because I thought it was a chance for Rick to apply for her job. When Gina was murdered, I wondered if Rick or Brad might have had something to do with it. Could my son have such an evil heart?"

She wasn't sure how to answer him, but she couldn't stomach the torment she heard in his voice and wanted somehow to reassure him it wasn't his fault. She chose her words carefully, not wanting to give him false hope or premature conviction of Rick's guilt or innocence. "I'm not sure if Rick could do it, but some of the people he's working for might. From every indication I have, Brad loved his wife and was worried that someone would hurt her if she didn't stop the questions."

"Jessie, you do this old man's heart good. You're too kind to hurt me, but somewhere I must have failed as a father."

"Every parent fails sometime, Pastor John, but you didn't make the choices for him. He's a grown man and is responsible for his own life."

Jessie received the information she needed to finish Sunday's bulletin from the visiting pastor, attached with a promise to call her later. She spent the rest of the day at work on Gina's story, weaving interviews into it, bringing Gina to life as a warm and beautiful human being. She saved it on a file entitled Gina's Story, easy to find if someone snooped.

Pastor Mark called right before she left, wanting some information, and when she pulled out the papers from her drawer an unopened letter fell out onto her desk. This was what she had forgotten.

She answered Mark's questions turning the envelope over in her hand. It was probably instructions from Pastor Rick. She stuck the letter in her purse, locked up her office, and went to the local gym to work out.

****

She ran on the treadmill, which she didn't like as well as running outdoors, but she was still a little freaked about last night. She set a fast pace so she wouldn't have to work out as long, and her favorite tunes on her iPod kept her from being totally bored. When she was done, she made a quick stop at the desk to sign up for the spin cycle class two days a week. Until the case was solved, it would vary her routine a little.

She had just walked out the door of the gym when her phone rang.

"Hi Jessie, I'm at Angelo's with Dylan. Why don't you come have dinner with us?" Katie asked.

"I just walked out of the gym and believe it or not was thinking about ordering a pizza and taking it home. I'll be there in ten minutes."

"Okay, we just got here, and we'll get the table."

The thought of being with friends and not having to cook was just what the doctor ordered. When she got in the car, she put on some lip gloss and ran the brush through her hair.

Angelo's was hopping. Dylan and Katie were sitting at table by the front window. Jessie loved the aroma of this place. It made her realize just how hungry she was. She approached their table, smiled, and took the empty chair beside Katie.

"You look really great! That's definitely one of your colors," Katie exclaimed.

"It brightens up my complexion so I don't look like

I need sleep, which I do." She picked up a menu to check it out.

"Do you want to share a pizza? Matt will be along soon to share one with Dylan."

"Sure, what do you want on it?"

"What's this?" Katie gave her a look of mock shock. "You're not upset that Matt's coming? I don't know if you noticed, Dylan, that Jessie and Matt don't hit it off." Katie laughed.

"I've noticed all right." Dylan was grinning.

"Look, you two, you can just zip it." Jessie pretended to glare at her friend. "We do fine in a group, and we're making an effort to be civil."

"Why don't we do the Blue Cove Special in a medium size so we can take a couple of pieces home?" Katie paused. "Is that okay with you? The guys are doing Angelo's special, which has lots of meat and black olives."

"You know me so well. The only thing more perfect is to add a salad to the order." She turned up her nose. "Putting black olives on anything is just wrong."

"I'll be right back. I see one of the guests from the inn." Katie walked over to one of the other tables.

"How are you holding up? Matt told me about what's been going on. I'll be the one sitting outside your house tonight." Dylan handed her a card with his cell phone number on it.

"I'm doing all right." She reached for the card and slipped it in her purse. "I'll sleep better knowing someone is outside looking out for me."

"There's Matt." Dylan stood up and waved him over.

Matt took the empty chair beside Jessie. "Hi, Jess."

He laughed when she frowned.

Katie walked back to the table. "Hey, you took my chair." Katie glared at Matt.

"You don't expect me to sit by Dylan, do you?"

"Yes, I believe I do." She planted her fists in her hips. "Someone has to be a referee between you two." She pointed to the other chair. Matt went there, laughing.

The pizza was tasty, and the conversation lively. As the dinner progressed, Jessie felt anxious. She dreaded going home and walking into her dark house.

When they stood up to leave, Matt found a way to get her alone for a few minutes.

"You're too quiet. What's up?" He searched her face, his hand lifting her chin up.

"I'm still a little overwhelmed about last night."

"I'll have Dylan walk in with you so you don't have to go in alone. Okay?"

"Thanks." She didn't try to hide her relief.

"By the way, nice color, you look, uh, pretty good." His compliment seemed to take him by surprise as much as her.

"Don't choke on the words." She tossed her head and walked away.

As she started her car, she noticed Matt talking to Dylan. When she passed them, Matt lifted a hand to stop her. He opened her car door. "Wait for Dylan to follow you." He went back to speak to Dylan. She turned out of the parking lot and headed home with Dylan close behind her. There was comfort in knowing he would be out there, but she didn't like feeling dependent upon it. She needed a plan, and the sooner she could think this through, the better.

After Dylan checked the cottage, he went outside to walk the grounds, and she sat down at her computer. Jeremy had sent her a quick note saying he was getting close to figuring the source of the stream. The rest of the evening was uneventful: a little TV, a little reading, and lights out by ten o'clock.

Chapter Fifteen

The next morning Jessie was up early and decided to sneak in an early morning run just as the sun peeked out and began to rise in the sky, casting its beautiful glow on the water below. She followed a couple of guests from the inn and pushed herself hard, enjoying the brisk pace, running a little farther than the marina and feeling exhilarated by the time she returned to her house. All ready for interviews. What would this day hold?

When she arrived at work, she noticed the side door to the church was open. Her first thought was there was no way she was going in the building alone. She took her phone out of her purse and called Melinda.

"Hi, Melinda, this is Jessie, are you by chance in the church?" She waited, holding her breath.

"No." Melinda sounded puzzled. "Why?"

"The side door is standing wide open."

"Call the police, and for heaven sakes don't go in, just in case the intruder is back."

Jessie pulled Dylan's card out of her purse and called his phone. He didn't answer of course. He had watched her place last night and probably was sleeping. She hung up not wanting to wake him. Before she got the next call off her phone rang.

"What's up, Jessie?" Dylan asked.

"I just got to the church, and the side door is

standing open with no cars in the parking lot. I'm a little hesitant to go in."

"Don't go in. I'll send someone. Wait in your locked car until you see the police." He sounded urgent.

"Okay." She got into her car and locked the door.

In a few minutes, two police cars flew into the parking lot, and one of the officers approached her car. She told him she had called Dylan, and he told her to wait.

"It's always the right move in case someone is still in the building," the dark-haired young officer told her. "You remain here and lock your door. We'll clear the building before you go in."

She was just beginning to think she had overreacted when Matt came into the parking lot followed by Dylan. They also told her stay put and went inside. Melinda came next and close on her heels was James Morris.

Jessie got out of her car and told them the police were in the building. A couple more church people showed up including Reba Thomas. They all waited together, wondering aloud what was taking so long. Molly came from across the street.

"What's going on? I hate to say it, but watching all the police come this morning reminded me of the morning they found Gina."

"I found the side door standing open when I came to work and called the police." Jessie hugged herself, chilly in spite of the warm morning. "I was told to stay outside until they checked the building."

As they waited, two of the young officers came out and looked at the door. James went over and talked to them. He started back toward the ladies with a grim look on his face.

"They told me it was a forced entry and there is some damage inside, mostly in your office, Jessie, and some in the hall leading to your office."

"I thought someone was in your office that night," Melinda chimed in.

"I wonder what they're after and why your office? You're new to the church and the area," Reba added

Jessie's heart raced, and she once again was reminded this wasn't a game. These people were deadly serious about protecting themselves, and murder was an option they were willing to use.

The small town grapevine was working well, as more and more church people showed up. Molly went to the coffee shop and came back with coffee and fresh cinnamon rolls, and everyone waited, huddled together, most filled with memories of the last time they had waited to be told what had happened.

****

"I'll explain to the crowd what's going on. We'll play it up as a simple act of vandalism, maybe by some kids." Matt briefed Dylan on the way out the door. He walked over to the group huddled together. "Overnight you had some vandalism in the building. It's mostly some obscenities written on the walls and the secretary's office has been ransacked. It looks like the work of some kids, but we aren't sure at this point. Entry was the side door, which looks like it's been forced. After the police finish dusting for prints you can get in to clean up the mess." Matt spoke without showing any emotion.

"Why would someone target our secretary's office? She's new to town and the church."

"It may not be that at all. Maybe they were looking for money in the office and got angry when they didn't find any. It's hard to say." He looked over his shoulder at the police officer who called his name and held up ten fingers. "I was just told you can go in the building in ten minutes."

"Do you think I should call the insurance company?" James asked Matt.

"Yes, some equipment was destroyed along with some office furniture." He found Melinda in the group. "Melinda, you thought you saw an intruder the other night? I want you to talk with Dylan and fill him in about what you saw."

Melinda walked over to Dylan. After answering several questions, Matt found Jessie sitting on the front bumper of her car.

"I'm not going to pull any punches. You were definitely the target, and whoever did this is trying to scare you off." He folded his arms against his chest.

She didn't say anything, but handed him the note she had forgotten about until she had reached in her purse to give Molly some money.

Matt read the note, which was short and to the point.

Quit looking for things your eyes shouldn't see or like Gina you'll deal with me. Blue eyes will go the way of brown, only your body will never be found.

"Where did you get this?"

"It was on my desk, and I thought it was from Pastor Rick. It must have been pushed into some of my papers. It fell out yesterday when I was looking for information. I stuck into my purse to read later and forgot about it. I just remembered to read it."

"These guys must get off on scaring women." He frowned. "Are you ready to give up yet?"

"No, I'm angry." She looked at him and paused. "I'm concerned for this congregation though. They suffered a lot when Gina was murdered, now this. It's too much."

"At least this note makes more sense. It was taped to your broken computer." He handed it to her sealed in a plastic bag to read.

"*Strike one. You get three, after that there's only me.*"

"I guess that means you'd better hurry up and find him." She forced a smile. "I'm running out of strikes."

"Let's go in and look at the mess." He pulled her up, placing his arm around her waist to steady her.

****

After they were done, and he had gone back to the police station, Anderson called Matt into the office. "I heard about the church. Is Jessie okay?" Anderson had a concerned look on his face.

"She's fine. Her office was torn up, and a note was left." Matt sat down across from the chief.

"What did the note say?"

"It's in the evidence box and still on its way here." Matt was hesitant to give all the details.

"They must have been looking for her research. Does she keep it there?"

"Yes, she uses the computer there for her work." Matt lied, but he didn't know where the leak was coming from. He made an instant decision to play it safe, and let the chief know the truth later.

"Maybe she'll be left alone after this." He looked

hopeful.

"It could have been just kids messing around. Nothing seemed to be missing." Matt stood up to leave. "I'll get back to you later when I find out more information."

Chapter Sixteen

The next couple of days Jessie worked alongside church members to clean the church. Files had to be re-filed, walls painted, broken furniture replaced, and a new computer set up.

She had people around her all day, so she felt much more relaxed. Pastor Rick would be back in a few days, and she knew he was going to be confronted by the church committee. They were going to replace him. Matt had asked them to wait so as not to jeopardize his investigation. John had agreed, as long as the congregation wasn't in harm's way.

By Saturday night, the congregation was weary, but the church looked nice for the visiting pastor. Jessie locked up her office and told Gina to look after everything. A ghost whisperer, now. She smiled at the thought.

When she walked out the church door Matt, Dylan, and Katie were standing by her car waiting.

Katie walked toward her. "We stopped by to take you to dinner. You've been working so hard the last few days. How's that sound?"

"Good, but you might have to prop me up so I can eat. I'm so tired." She rubbed her neck.

"How about we get some take out Chinese and eat at your place?" Dylan asked. "Katie, you come with me, and Matt can drive Jessie home since she can hardly keep her eyes open. What do you opt for, Jessie?"

"Cashew Chicken sounds good to me."

"Can we trust you two not to fight?" Katie looked at them and smiled.

"She's too tired to put up a good argument. You don't have to worry about us."

Matt took the keys out of her hand and opened the passenger door, touching her elbow as she got in. He got behind the wheel and started her car. "I've been waiting for a chance to drive this sweet machine." She was still and quiet when he looked over at her.

"Don't worry I'm not asleep. I'm conserving energy," she murmured.

"Dylan knew I wanted to talk to you before were all together, again. We presented the information to Sheriff Taylor from the county sheriff's department and a state official, and it looks like we'll be getting some help. This is a big operation, Jessie. Thanks to you we've found out some key information. You've played an important role, but you've also become a target with huge bull's eye on it." His voice tone was serious. "We are going to do everything we can to keep you safe, but you're going to have to be careful and watch the people around you. Let us know your schedule and movement. Do you hear me?" He raised his voice, baiting her as his lips twitched.

"Of course, I can hear you. Those people in the car over there can hear you. The whole street will be able to hear you if you speak any louder." She yelled each word for emphasis and was ashamed of her reaction.

"Now there's my girl." He grinned. "I was beginning to worry that you'd lost your will to fight. I always bring out the best in you."

"Don't flatter yourself," she said sarcastically.

"The thing is, Jess, we will still be short of manpower, so there will be someone watching over you when you're tucked in for the night, but not all day, every day. We have too many people to watch in order to build this case. We won't get the extras eyes until Rick and the others return from India. In the meantime, the duty to look after you is split between Dylan and me." He gave her a serious look. "You're going to have to cut us some slack. Keep us in the loop in and try to be civil about it."

"Are you through with your lecture, professor?"

"Yes, but I do have one more request of you." His serious look softened as he reached over and touched her hand. "I'm trying to keep you alive, Jess. Could we possibly work as a team?"

"I get that, but don't treat me like a little kid always telling me what to do," she snapped. "Oh." She paused. "You asked, didn't you?"

"I'm sorry, Jess, for sounding harsh sometimes, but in the face of murder the niceties don't often apply."

Jessie wasn't sure why she always felt so surly with Matt. She was capable of reasoning, and he was trying to keep her safe. Yet every time he opened his mouth, she wanted to argue with him. She had never had a problem like this before, unless you counted Bobby Angel. Angel was not a good name for him. He was the fourth grade devil who had made that school year a living hell for her. For some reason, Bobby had picked her out to be his girlfriend, and he showed his affection by endless torment. She practically danced all the way home on the last day of school knowing she didn't have to see him for the whole summer. He was over her when fifth grade started. Lisa Marie Wilson had replaced her in his affection.

Once again, Jessie was determined not to let Matt get under her skin and to treat him the same way she did everyone else, with some amount of decorum. Maybe she should try being sweet for a change. "I understand. I'll give it my best shot. I haven't had to tell someone my schedule and whereabouts for a long time. It'll take some getting used to." She looked sideways at him, and her voice softened.

"A guy can't ask for more than that." A flicker of amusement lit up his eyes.

****

They turned onto Blue Iris Lane, driving past the inn to her house. As soon as the car stopped, she opened the car door and jumped out. He was step for step with her.

"Will you see Gina anymore?" His hand brushed hers.

"I have no idea. I don't know how this works." She moved over a little on the path.

"I guess we'll just have to wait and see." He grinned as he moved closer to her.

When they got to her back door, he took the house key out of her hand and unlocked the door, but blocked her way in. She backed up against the wall to get away from his close proximity. Matt stood in front of her putting his hands against the wall on each side of her head and looked directly into her eyes. "I want to have a serious chat with you, my sweet little adversary." Matt could see he had caught her by surprise. "I have no idea how long this will take, but just so you know, we belong together. Neither one of us may be able to grasp it right now, but it's still true. We are going to have to find a way to get on together." His eyes shifted to her lips. "I don't want you getting any ideas I'm going to let anyone else come along and take you away from me. I'm staking my claim here and now. It may not be today, we both may still need convincing, but we will be together." He was close enough to feel her breath.

Matt watched her surprised look turn to one of anger. She pushed her hands against his chest and slipped out from under his arms. "You can't just tell me you're staking your claim. I'm not a piece of property, for heaven's sake. You don't own me." Jessie sputtered, her hands on her hips.

"I meant every word. And I'm one boss that you're going to date."

"You don't even like me. You're always grumbling at me. Besides, we have to concentrate on this case. How can you possibly tell me we belong together?"

"I just did, so get used to it, sweetheart." His eyes challenged her. "I don't like it any better than you do. I didn't particularly want anyone in my life right now. You moved here, and I'm attracted to you, so live with it. I'm learning to."

She pointed her finger in his face. "I'm the only one who has any say in who can claim me."

"You will, but I've made up my mind. I'm going to chase you and wear you down until you say yes." He grinned. "If it works out the way I hope, it could be a win-win situation for the both of us."

He let her go inside. She gave him a dirty look as she passed by him. She was angry. He smiled. There would be a royal tug-of-war, and he was looking forward to it.

He was still smiling when Katie and Dylan arrived with dinner. "You look awful pleased with yourself, Mr. Parker, a little like the cat that just swallowed the canary."

"I just won round one in what could be a long drawn-out conflict." He grinned, Jessie was silent, and Katie looked puzzled.

****

The rest of the evening went off without a hitch. She actually had a good time once Katie and Dylan got back. They ate dinner, had a great political discussion, and watched an old movie with a big bowl of popcorn. She found another area where Matt and she where total opposites, and that was in politics, although Dylan's views were eye to eye with hers.

"What do you think about their stakeout on the property?" Katie asked Jessie when the two of them went into the kitchen to clean up.

"If there is someone suspicious in the area, then I'm glad they're out there." Jessie handed Katie the tea to put into the refrigerator.

"Me too! Next weekend do you want to have an old fashioned sleepover? I'll bring dinner from the inn, and we'll just hang out. It'll be like old times," Katie suggested delightfully.

"Sure, come prepared with memories, and be ready for our ritual pillow fight." Jessie burst into laughter.

"You got it, girl. You're going down."

"Now what are you two laughing about?" Dylan smiled as they giggled all the more.

Jessie handed Katie her cardigan. "I'm going to

church tomorrow. I told Pastor Rick I would be there to help the visiting pastor. Besides I want to make sure my friends are all doing okay. All the activities this week have brought back some pretty awful memories."

"Count me out. The last time was more than I wanted to handle in a lifetime," Katie confessed.

"Come on, Katie," Dylan called to her. "I'm walking you home to make sure you get there. I'll be back, Matt, to take you to your truck."

"See you both. Thanks for dinner," Jessie added.

"You have my number. I'll take a look around outside and make sure it's secure before Dylan takes me to get my truck. Dylan will be back for the night in about fifteen minutes. Okay?"

"Okay." She glanced at her watch. "I'm tired, so I'm sure I'll sleep fine."

"Dylan will call when he's back. Be sure to answer, or he might break down the door thinking something is wrong."

"Goodnight, Matt, and thanks for most of the evening." Her eyes twinkled with mischief.

"Sure." He sounded distracted. "Lock this door and bolt it now," he commanded as he stepped outside.

He was back to giving orders. Now this Matt she could handle.

****

Matt had heard a slight rustling sound coming from the side of Jessie's house, and with one fluid motion his gun was out of his side holster and the safety was off. Dylan walked back, near his car when he saw Matt's gun drawn, and he followed suit. Matt motioned him to one side, and he went the other way. Matt saw a huge figure take off running as he rounded the side of her house.

Matt yelled at him. "Stop. Police!" He held his gun up and fired a warning shot off. The guy kept running, crashing through the trees, and headed toward the cove. Matt lost sight of him after running for about ten minutes. He stopped to listen—nothing but silence.

There was no way he would leave her tonight. He wound his way back through the trees toward Jessie's. He couldn't imagine who this guy was. He was big. He didn't know if he could hold his own against him, and Jessie certainly couldn't.

Dylan saw Matt making his way back through the trees. "Did you hit him?"

"No. I wasn't trying to. He must have heard me coming and took off through the trees toward the cove. I lost him, damn it. I don't know how he got away, but it's too dark to find him now. I swear the guy was massive, and yet he seemed to blend into the shadows." Matt put his gun back in his holster. "There's no way in hell I'm leaving her alone for a minute."

"What do you want to do?" Dylan asked as he put the safety on his gun and put it back his holster."

"I'm going to stay inside with her. This guy is getting bold. He's a real bruiser, and Jessie wouldn't stand a chance if he got a hold of her."

He called and waited for her to pick up. "Hi, Dylan, I'm glad you're back. I think Matt heard something earlier. I'm sure I just heard a gunshot." Her voice was shaky.

"Jess." He cut her off. "This is Matt. I've been chasing a guy out here, but he got away. I fired my gun just as a warning. I don't want to leave you alone. Let me in, and I'll stay on the couch."

"I'll be right there."

He heard the deadbolt turn. When she opened the door, Dylan gave her a sympathetic look.

"Matt, I think we should both stay here. If the guy's as big as you say he is, it will take both of us to corral him," Dylan said. "That way both of us can take turns sleeping."

"Sounds good to me; the more the merrier." Jessie opened the door and let them in. "It must be the same guy that I've been seeing, and the one who messed up the church." She shivered.

"You aren't going to fall apart on us now, are you?" Matt stifled a smile as her temper kicked in.

"Could you give me a little credit? Have I ever done that to you, yet?" She glared at him.

"No, I'd say you've done pretty well." His eyes glinted with admiration. He gave her playful push, then shut and locked the door.

Out of the corner of his eye, Matt saw the pillow headed his way. He grabbed it and tossed it back so fast, Jessie had no reaction time. It smacked her in the head knocking her off balance. "Sorry, it comes from living with brothers." He went to steady her. Instead, he watched her dissolve into a fit of giggles holding her side.

"Goodnight." He grinned at her.

He didn't say anything else until he heard her close the door.

"This guy is serious, but I have a feeling he's only here to scare her off," he told Dylan. Someone else is giving the orders. I believe this could be the same guy who followed Gina, but I'd be surprised if he was the one who killed her."

"What makes you think that?" Dylan stretched out on the couch.

"I don't believe this bruiser has the touch." Matt sat back in the chair and stretched his legs. "There's no way he could have removed Gina's eyes that way, so precisely and neatly. Nor do I believe he could have made the small incisions we saw on her body. His hands would be too big and clumsy. He was built like a boxer. He could have definitely scared her, beat her, and even dumped her body, but I don't believe he has the finesse to do what was done to Gina's body."

"What are we talking about then?"

"He is just the tip of the iceberg, and that scares the hell out me."

Matt turned on the TV while Dylan caught a little shut eye, and then around two-thirty it was Matt's turn. By the time Jessie's alarm went off at seven-thirty, both of the guys were gone.

****

Jessie wondered, as she dressed for church, if she would ever feel safe again. Even with the two guys here last night, she had awakened several times through the night. She didn't like this cat and mouse game. Closure would only come from knowing who'd killed Gina and why. Matt wasn't helping, either. This new Matt was hard to handle. One minute he was lecturing her, and the next he looked like he wanted to kiss her.

The church service was pleasant, the people were all sympathetic to each other, and Pastor Mark did a great job. He actually sounded the way a pastor should. After the service, Jessie said hello to Andria and told her she had given Gina's letter to the police. Reba was the next to get a hold of her.

"Jessie, dear, are you doing okay?"

"Yes." She nodded.

"I had the strangest dream last night. It was about a large man, crashing through trees. He kept yelling strike one, which hardly makes sense." She patted Jessie's hand. "Unlike his prediction, I don't believe for a minute strike three will be the end for you. Maybe for him, but not you. He's only the distraction."

How did she know these things, Jessie wondered. When everything was over, she would have to sit down with Reba and let her know how much she had gotten right.

She walked out the church doors into a glorious day. A nice breeze from the ocean kept it from being too hot. Just once, she would like to enjoy the beauty of her surroundings without worrying about what was waiting around the next corner.

Chapter Seventeen

Jessie picked up another of the great chicken salad sandwiches from Java Joe's and headed home. She changed into shorts, a T-shirt and sandals. She left a message for Pam Bradley to let her know she was sending a copy of part one of Gina's story to them.

"Please feel free to make any changes, deletions, or let me know any additional items that you would like to see included in the story."

She got some iced tea from the kitchen and sat down at her computer to read her emails and eat lunch. She really did like Joe's chicken salad.

I can't believe I'm thinking about chicken salad. She laughed at herself. Shouldn't she be considering deeper things with everything else going on in her life? It showed how crazy she was or how resilient. Life still goes on even in the face of fear, she thought.

She noticed an email from Jeremy saying he would call her after five and maybe she should have someone from the police department there.

Jessie finished lunch and decided to go outside and sit in the sun. She would call Matt in a little while, but for now, in this moment, she wanted a little peace and quiet. She didn't want to read her book, which was a murder mystery. Why read it when she was living it? The warm sunshine made her drowsy. She closed her eyes, and her last thought was that she needed to get Matt to come at five if he could make it.

****

Jessie jumped as Matt touched her shoulder. "Jess, what in the hell are you doing? I've been calling you for the last hour and a half." He glared down at her. "I didn't know what to think. Your doors are unlocked and you're sleeping outside; could you give this guy a bigger invitation?"

"I came out here to enjoy the warmth. It was so peaceful, and I must have fallen asleep." She stammered the words out, still groggy.

"Why isn't your phone with you?" The muscle in his jaw flexed. "In case you haven't noticed, the sky is dark. There's a storm building."

As if on cue, a clap of thunder rumbled in the distance. "I'm sorry I worried you." She returned his glare, wide awake now. "I didn't know when I sat down that I would fall asleep. I was going to get my phone and call you to see if you would come earlier. Jeremy is going to call at five and said I should have someone from the police department here. I guess the warm sunshine and peace was a sleep inducer."

Matt wasn't finished yet. "What if the guy that was outside your house last night had come back today and found you like I just did? Geez, Jess, I can't imagine what he's capable of." He scanned her face. "We're going to talk about this again." He kept his voice even. "Keep me in the loop, keep your phone with you at all times, and need I add, no sleeping outside, leaving doors unlocked, or giving an open invitation to a criminal."

She straightened in her chair. "If you think…"

162

He put his fingers to her mouth to silence her. "The thing is, you *weren't* thinking or you wouldn't be out here like this. You know I'm right, Jess."

"Point taken." She raised her hand in a conciliatory gesture.

He was right, she hadn't been thinking. She was overwhelmed by too many events to manage. There must be a way to process this sanely. Fear started to grip her. How could she possibly control the whole mess? She was dealing with some kind of white collar crime syndicate, a ghost, an intruder, and threats on her life. All she wanted to do is sleep and forget about it.

His voice eased her budding panic. "It'll be okay. We'll manage this together with the help of a whole lot of people. But, and this is important, Jess, you can't do things this stupid. You're strong, but you're not invincible."

"I know," she said quietly.

"I'll try not to lecture you if you try to use the astuteness that I know you are capable of. Truce..." He extended his hand to shake hers.

"Truce..." She took his extended hand.

He held on to it, liking the feel of it in his. "What were you saying about Jeremy?"

"He's calling at five and told me to have someone from the police here. Put simply, he's found something too important to put in an email."

"Do you have something we can make for dinner? I might as well hang out here until he calls. It's my night to see you tucked in and shut up tight."

"I have plenty of food. We could barbeque some chicken if the rain holds off, or I can bake it in the oven," Jessie answered. She slipped her hand out of his and walked inside.

Matt turned on the TV to watch the Yankees play, and Jessie answered emails, talked to her parents, and her grandma Sadie. Then she went into the kitchen, put the chicken into the oven, along with two potatoes. She put together a fresh salad with raisins, sunflower seeds, green onions, tomatoes, cucumbers, and avocado and put it in the fridge to chill.

To an outsider it might look like a very domestic Sunday afternoon scene. But to one dark figure, it meant he had to wait another day.

****

He had been just a little too late getting there. If he hadn't stopped for the hamburgers...oh well, he was a patient man. He would officially give the second strike before his boss returned.

He had gotten there just in time to see her sleeping so peacefully, unaware that he was less than a hundred feet away crouched behind the tree. She was pretty. He almost hated to mess up her face. Almost. He grinned. He would do it and relish the job. It would have been done now, but the cop had come around the corner. He was hanging out at her place a lot lately. He wondered if she was the cop's woman. It would make it even better, because his boss wanted him gone, too.

The dark clouds started producing a gentle rain. The droplets trickled through the leaves on the tree, splashing his face. Maybe there would be more money in it for him, a bonus of sorts for wounding two with one punch so to say. He smiled with smug satisfaction at his own pun and watched the two of them for a few more moments, not minding the rain, before he slunk back the way he had come.

Chapter Eighteen

Jeremy's call came promptly at five, and Jessie put it on speaker as soon as she told him Matt Parker was there, and he was the officer in charge of the investigation.

"First, I have to say this is a pretty big operation with some fairly well-known individuals. They have an elaborate technical monitoring device protecting their information, and they're good, but I'm even better." Jeremy's voice came through the speaker clearly. "And as you know, I taught you all I know about inscription bypass," he added. "Someone who isn't familiar with firewalls could inadvertently trip their warning devices and be known instantly to have been an unwelcome visitor in their information."

"Maybe that's what happened to Gina." Jessie winced.

"I'm glad you called me and didn't attempt this yourself. Anyway, I found two streams of money that went to all the accounts. Most of the ones you named seem to be the small fish. They're the buyers in the organization."

"What is their primary function in the organization?" Matt's hand curled into a fist.

"They visit the countries and arrange to buy organs through brokers from the sellers in that country."

"Who are the sellers?" Jessie wrote down notes as

Jeremy talked.

"The sellers may be people selling their own organs or a person selling kidneys taken from someone without their permission."

"So basically, they could buy anyone's kidneys." Matt was angry.

"Yeah…It used to be that a kidney had to come from a close relative, but now because of anti-rejection drugs, that is no longer necessary. Buyers can get a kidney from anyone, anywhere. Unscrupulous as that sounds, what's worse in the black market buyers mart, a kidney taken from a living donor will keep a person alive twice as long as one taken from a cadaver, so it's worth more money."

Jessie frowned. "Now that's just sick."

"That's probably what this trip to India is all about." Jessie saw Matt's jaw flex and knew he was angry.

"Yes, and I'm sure there are a few brokers intermingled in the group to watch over their clients' interests. There are a lot of people living in the slums willing to sell their own or someone else's organs. And, believe me, there is always someone here trying to buy one for a family member, and they are willing to pay." Jeremy paused.

"Whether by accident or design, some top surgeons in three hospitals that I tracked have been transplanting black market kidneys from residents of some of the world's most impoverished slums into some of the world's wealthiest failing bodies of dialysis patients."

"How do you figure that?" Matt asked.

"The story is all in the money. For about $100,000 to $150,000, a broker will connect buyers and sellers and guide them to broker-friendly hospitals. I traced the flow here to three hospitals and transplant teams."

"This is unbelievable." Jessie shook her head.

"Here's the kicker—you mentioned clergy and a rabbi. Brokers often pose as clergy to accompany their clients to the hospital to ensure the process goes well. It makes it all appear above board. It seems to me these men are going to broker and buy organs to bring back and sell to their clients. Some goodwill tour, huh?"

"So where is the money coming from?" Matt frowned.

"The brokers and buyers are getting paid from the hospitals. Clients and some other sources are giving the brokers money to buy the organs. I would say, and this is my opinion only, Brad is a buyer, along with your mayor and city councilman. The pastor, rabbi, and most of the clergy are brokers. They get paid larger pay-outs for a single transaction. Although, Brad got a hundred thousand, I notice a couple of dates for that. Still $30,000 to $50,000 is nothing to sneeze at."

"Who is the other source?" Jessie asked

"The other source is one of the pharmaceutical companies that market the anti-rejection drugs. With the long wait lists for transplants and the very rich who get promoted to the head of the lists, it's easy to understand how about one-fifth of the seventy thousand kidney transplants world-wide every year come from the black market, and then the drugs are needed for the rest of that individual's life. It makes for big money all around."

"Is there any way we can prove any of this or get any convictions?" Matt asked.

"In my opinion, the hospitals are safe and so is the

pharmaceutical company. They'll be able to say the money was given to promote research, and because the hospital is helping patients, they'll claim they thought the donors were legitimate. However, you'll be able to get the brokers and the buyers and stop this black market ring. I'm sure there will always be more willing to take their places. One of these guys is the head of this ring. I'm not sure yet who." He paused to take a deep breath and then added, "The money is a major draw. Hopefully in the process of rounding up this group, you'll find the murderer you're looking for. Oh and by the way, Jessie, the letters HC are the initials in the name of their group. They call themselves the Harvest Club."

"It's a fitting name," Matt said sarcastically.

"Jeremy, how can I ever thank you?" Jessie asked.

"You can come to New York or, better yet, you can ask me to your place and feed me dinner. I'll keep looking. I know the head guy will surface. Talk to you later, Jessie, and be safe."

"You have an open invitation. See you soon." She let out a deep breath.

"From the moment I saw Gina's body, my gut told me it had to do with organ trafficking." Matt started pacing. "You helped push the case along when you got the information from their bank accounts, and bringing Jeremy into this was brilliant."

"So what happens next? Will you arrest them when they get back?"

"No, the long process of building a case against these guys begins." He paused to look at her, and then resumed his pacing. "It must be meticulous, thorough, and well documented."

"Sounds like what Neil demanded of me."

He nodded and grinned. "What's needed is admissible evidence that won't be thrown out because we didn't do our job right. We could bring some of them in for questioning, hoping someone will crack, but these guys have been pretty good about covering their tracks up to now. Murdering Gina may have been their one real mistake."

Jessie went to the kitchen to check on dinner. Everything was ready so she set the table. Lightning lit up the room, and the thunder boomed close on its heels. The gentle rain turned to a real gully washer in a matter of a few minutes. She was glad she had opted to bake the chicken.

Matt asked what he could do to help, so she let him get the salad and dressing out of the fridge and fill the glasses with tea. They ate quietly, lost in their own thoughts. Jessie was wondering how long it would be before Gina could rest in peace.

"Jess, I have a major concern I need to talk to you about. The big guy who has been around may be the decoy. He can and will try to hurt you and scare you off, but he's not the one who might really hurt you. You're going to have to keep your eyes open for someone else. They may be following you or hanging around some of the places where you go."

"What do you mean?"

"The person responsible for Gina's murder, the one who harvested her organs, had to have had medical knowledge. The incisions were barely noticeable and had been done with precision. The bruiser's hands don't fit the criteria. Someone else may be your biggest threat. Keep your eyes open."

"As if I don't already have enough on my plate, now you tell me there may be someone even more dangerous. You must be kidding or trying to kill me with fear yourself!" She gave an exasperated laugh.

"I want you to be aware of your surroundings. Watch for someone who shows up at the same places you are often enough that it no longer seems like a coincidence. He might be someone nondescript who can fade into the background, or a real lady killer."

"Okay, I'll keep my eyes open."

"Enough of the serious talk." Matt rose to take his plate into the kitchen. "You need to chill for a while."

"Duh, you think?" she replied smartly. "If I don't, you'll have a raging or perhaps a weeping woman on your hands. I think the latter would bother you most."

"Lady, you've got that right."

The rest of the evening was a relaxing one. They presented the idyllic picture of two friends enjoying their favorite programs, shoes off, one pair of feet with a hole in the socks propped on the coffee table, the other pair tucked neatly under her. A shared bowl of buttered popcorn, his choice, cherry coke, hers, both of them picking arguments over everything from who done it to who would win the Sunday evening baseball game.

When the news came on, Jessie got up and got a sheet and pillow for Matt. Setting them next to him, she smiled at him. "Thanks for the evening. It helped to forget for a few hours. I'll keep my eyes open and you…" She smiled at him. "Be careful too." She heard thunder. "It's still raining pretty hard, so I imagine he won't be around tonight. Goodnight." She turned to walk out of the room.

"Goodnight." He paused and then added "Jess…"

She smiled. Right now in this moment, she felt safe, and she would go with it. Who knew what tomorrow would bring. Once her head hit the pillow, she was out.

****

Matt was wide awake listening to the sounds of the night, sleep eluding him. She was sleeping in the next room, and he was painfully aware of it. He didn't know how much more of the close quarters he could take. Moving on. He had to focus on keeping her safe.

He played back the conversation with Jeremy and events of the past several days. He was more convinced than ever that someone with medical know-how had killed Gina, probably someone reputable in the community with a wife and children. Maybe he had lost someone close to him because of a shortage of available donor organs, so he set out to make sure it wouldn't happen to anyone else. In some twisted way, he supposed they all could justify that what they were doing was helping people. Somewhere along the line, it had gone from a noble cause to greed, and finally, to murder to cover their greed.

Jessie was starting to get to his heart. She had moved to the small town to be near her friend and had been welcomed into a living hell. Was Gina trying to reach from beyond to find her killer? How had Jessie become the target? Had Rick played a part in drawing her in? He knew she was a journalist when he hired her. Was he hoping she would snoop?

He couldn't shut his mind off. He went over the plan again that would be in place when the men returned from their trip. There were officers who would watch them from their arrival at La Guardia, to their return home, and anywhere else they might stop in between.

This case was big and complex. The group could be as large as thirty people or more. Somewhere hidden in their midst was a murderer. If Brad hadn't ordered Gina's death, he sure as hell knew who did. He hadn't been the same since Gina died.

Tomorrow was his D-day in Blue Cove. He was ready. Assignments had been made, the extras were coming in, and the command post would be set up here in the spare room right on schedule. He was prepared to put the greedy bastards out of commission. It was the waiting that bothered him most. Their crimes might still be undetected had Gina not been murdered and somehow involved Jessie. It was a hell of a case.

Chapter Nineteen

Matt was gone when Jessie got up. She noticed the neatly folded sheet and pillow on the couch. Pastor Rick would be back in the office Wednesday, so she had only today and tomorrow to formulate her plan.

By 8:15 she was ready and out the door for work. Jessie wanted to get a few things out of the way. Rick would be surprised by the new office furniture and computer or maybe not. Nothing was as it seemed.

"Thank you, oh, thank you," Jessie whispered when she saw all the cars in the parking lot. She wouldn't be in the building alone today. She had forgotten this was the day the District Conference was scheduled to meet with the nominating committee.

"Hey, there, Blondie. You're here early this morning." Melinda rushed toward Jessie. "This is my youngest daughter, Megan."

"Hi, Megan." Jessie smiled at the little girl. "I wanted to get a few things done before the pastor gets back."

"There's some kind of big meeting here this morning with all the uppity ups and the biggies." Melinda gestured wildly with her hands. "Reba will stop by afterwards to talk to you. She had a run in with you know who this morning."

"Thanks for the information, Red." She turned and walked down the hall.

When Jessie put the key in her office door, a cold chill went down her back. She turned expecting to see Gina, but she wasn't there. Yet, the apprehension she felt was so strong she didn't want to open the door.

Slowly she opened it, peering inside, then she flipped on the light switch, and her eyes saw him. The next thing she became aware of was her own voice screaming, which brought several people running from everywhere in the building.

Hanging from a noose over the beam was a man, an obviously dead man with a note attached to his shirt.

"Don't touch anything. This here is a crime scene," James told the crowd as he took charge. "Reba, you get Jessie out in the hall, and, Melinda, you call the police."

Within the space of ten minutes, several police cars roared into the church parking lot for the second time in less than a week. Molly stared out the window as the police moved quickly into the building. "What in heaven's name is happening at that poor church?" she asked loudly.

****

Matt and two other officers walked down the hall with Melinda leading the way. Jessie followed them into her office and stood in the doorway listening, but trying not to look. "Geez, you were the one to find him?" She nodded. Matt read the note. It was tagged and put in a plastic bag.

"*Jessie, my blue eyed girl, can you come out and play? You'll run and I'll chase you. You'd better not let me catch you or strike three you're out. Kind of like Matt's friend and your new office companion.*"

"It's Mr. Yamamoto," she said softly. "I've talked with him a few times. He worked in the gardens at the inn." Matt nodded at her.

"Let's get the body down." He looked at Jessie studying her pale face. "I had a call this morning from Blue Cove Funeral Home about a missing body. Mr. Yamamoto needs to get back to the funeral home for his funeral tomorrow. He died of a heart attack a few days ago."

"Geez, a man can't be left alone even after he's dead." The officer shook his head.

Matt called the funeral home to let them know Mr. Yamamoto's body had been found, and they could pick him up at the church.

Matt walked over to her and draped his arm over her shoulder. "How are you holding up?"

"Why would they steal his body and hang him like that?" She shivered. "Was it just so they could scare me?"

"Probably. I hate to do this to you, Jess, but you need to read this note." He handed the plastic bag containing the note to her.

She read it once, twice, and then over again.

For Matt this was a moment wrought with uneasiness. He wanted to comfort her, but he didn't know the right words. He felt awkward and not up to the task. He stood beside her patting her on the back a little too hard, not sure what he should say or if he made sense at all.

"Matt, I'm all right, really I am." She smiled at him. "I've come to understand you're not a man that is good in this kind of moment." She lifted his hand away from her shoulder.

"You're getting to know me pretty well." He gave her a lopsided smile. "The suspect has connected us in his mind, which means he's been watching your house. He believes in hurting you he's hurting me and vice versa, which empowers him." He paused hoping she would respond.

"I don't know about you, but I'm mad. When I went to open my office door this morning, I think Gina was trying to warn me something was wrong." She straightened in the chair. "I'm getting used to her hanging around." She creased her brows. "I don't believe I'll ever be able to walk into the office again and not see poor Mr. Yamamoto swinging like that."

He took her hand in his, lacing his fingers with hers. "Will you be okay?"

"Yes."

"Are you going to work today?" He tightened his hold on her hand watching her face. He could look at her all day. He practically did anyway. She was in his head even when he couldn't see her. Staying away was no help at all.

"Yes, I'll use the Sunday school office to answer the phones. I don't want to be in my office today. I have to stay until 8:00 tonight because the town book club meets here, and I have to lock up when they leave. I usually go eat about 6:00 and then come back to lock the church."

"Call me when you're ready to go, and I'll stop by and follow you home." He gazed at her thoughtfully. "I'll see you later."

He handed them the note to put into evidence and walked out heading toward the exit. He passed the guys from the funeral home coming in with a stretcher to pick up the body. He told James he could have the office back to clean up for the second time in a matter of days. He held up ten and told him they were wrapping it up now.

Matt made it to his car before he allowed himself to think about what had just happened. He was angry. He didn't like bullies, especially ones who picked on people he loved.

He admired Jessie and the way she was bearing up under everything. He had to admit she wasn't the selfish, witless, shallow person he had originally thought she was. She had been an asset, a pretty one at that, and he was feeling pretty damn protective of her.

He knew that Gina's murder was connected to the Harvest Club. The HC had been very active for the past five years, and it was time for them to be shut down. Gina's murder may have been their first major mistake, but today was their second. He was mad as hell and felt like putting his fist into someone's face. He drove back to the station.

****

Phase one was to tail the members and apply pressure. Hoping to get them to turn on each other and sing like little choir boys. He was prepared for the long haul, either way.

"So what's the plan for tonight and tomorrow?" Dylan popped his head in the office door to ask him.

"I emailed everyone their assignments. You and I will be tailing Pastor Rick and taking care of tucking Jessie in at night. She seems to trust us, and as much as she's been through, I hate for her to have to get used to someone else. I'll follow her home after work, and you can come by after dinner. I already have Joe and a couple other guys on call during the day if she needs them. I think we'll both stay there tonight because everyone is coming back tomorrow and if that guy is supposed to do something to Jessie, time is running out. He may throw caution to the wind."

"In other words, she needs both of us to be there to protect her." Dylan nodded.

"My gut tells me we need to stay close to her right now. The information we gained because of her puts her at greater risk."

"I'll eat dinner and come over about 7:00, if that's okay?"

"She's working late tonight and won't be home until about 8:30. You won't need to come until then."

****

Matt worked on the HC case for a while when he noticed a typical summer afternoon storm was building. He tapped his fingers on his desk, reaching for his phone. He put it down only to pick it up again.

"First Community Church. May I help you."

"You sure can. I need to eat dinner before I tuck you in and would rather not eat alone. Meet me at Patterson's after work, say about 6:00. See you there. Oh, you might need an umbrella. It looks like rain." Matt hung up before she could respond.

He made it to Patterson's by 5:45 and got a table by the front window, so he could watch her come out of the church and cross the street. He ordered a Guinness and set back to wait.

She was prompt, and he didn't have to wait for long. He watched her cross the street. Her long legs looked amazing. The dress she was wearing showed them to perfection. With her hair blowing slightly in the wind and a smile on her face, she looked like a model at a photo shoot.

Jeez, Matt, he thought, fate sends you a beautiful woman and practically hands her into your care. You need to stop lecturing her and thank your lucky stars.

He watched her come in the door. Patterson himself went over to talk to her. She smiled at him and said something that made him laugh. Patterson's whole demeanor changed after a few moments with her. She had a way with people. The people at the church loved her. Hell, Patterson never smiled, and she'd won him over. What did she think about him, he wondered? Or did she ever think about him? She was always in his thoughts. He frowned.

"Hi." She smiled and sat down in the chair across from him.

"You're late." He knew it to be a lie the minute he said it.

"No, I'm not." Her chin came up. "Did you ask me to dinner just to fight? If so, I'm leaving." She gathered her purse and the umbrella she had just set on the chair beside her.

"I'm sorry. I'm just having a bad day. Please stay." His excuse sounded lame even to him.

"Of course you're having a bad day. I should have been more sensitive. It's this case." She placed her stuff back on the chair and smiled at him again. As if without thinking, she grabbed his hands. "Let's eat, I'm starving," she said, watching the storm clouds start to build.

Chapter Twenty

The storm brewed out at sea, blowing huge threatening thunderheads toward Blue Cove. Lightning lit up the sky, casting eerie shadows on the buildings. Thunder rumbled in the distance and waves crashed ashore. The air was muggy. A perfect backdrop for his plans. He crouched in the darkness behind the Dumpster, watching the door as he waited for her to come out. He rehearsed in his mind how he would take her by surprise and grab her before she could get in her car. He knew her daily movements as if they were written on the back of his hand. His boss, the meanest S.O.B. to walk the earth, had told him to rough her up and scare her. Something he was real good at. His notes and the hanging gardener in her office had been a nice touch. A little extra. Dressed in black from head to toe, he enjoyed looking the ugly brute part. It was an advantage in his line of work. She was one sweet looking job. Gina hadn't been bad ,either. He was really going to enjoy this. Fact was he was getting high just thinking of it.

"What's this?" he whispered. She emerged from Patterson's with that cop fella, and people were coming out of the church. He retreated farther into the shadows. "She's messing with my head. Be patient, it's only a matter of time." He watched them cross to the church and go in. He heard the cop tell her to wait in the lobby he would lock all the other doors.

Her car was the only one left as he crept around to the front of the church. She was at the door standing alone when he heard her call to him.

"I'll lock the front door and meet you at my car." She stepped out of the door.

He was in luck, she hadn't noticed him moving out of the shadows. Lightning lit up the sky followed by a big boom.

****

The crack of thunder startled Jessie. The scream stuck in her throat, and then she saw him, his sinister face, lusting eyes, and sheer size. She screamed, dropped her keys and ran, realizing too late she was running toward the graveyard and wooded area just beyond. Stupid. Too late to run to Matt now. She gasped for breath, heart pounding in her ears.

Making it through the graveyard to the trees, Jessie ran along them, hoping she was headed back toward the church and the lighted parking lot. He was closing in fast. Tripping over a tree root, she pitched forward into the darkness, sliding sideways down a steep embankment, grabbing at the muddy grass. She choked off a cry as she fell several feet to a ledge below hitting her head on something hard.

She lay winded on her back, struggling for breath, looking up in the mesmerizing light show as a fork of lightning unfolded across the sky. On any other night it would have fascinated her, but now it was like a scene from a creepy movie. As she breathed deeply in and out, her racing heart started to slow down.

"Jessie, sweet Jessie…" The man's mocking voice floated down to her. "I'll be back to play another day."

His words rang like a song refrain in her head as she crouched in the darkness. Then the heavens opened up, and it rained. She listened and waited for what seemed an eternity. Finally, wet, bruised, muddy, and tired, she inched slowly up the way she had slid down. There waiting quietly at the top was Matt with a look that said he was going to give her hell.

Neither of them spoke a word as he took her hand, winding them through the trees back through the cemetery to the front of the church. He pulled. She tripped and limped, never complaining. But if looks could kill, she would be dead. Once in the light he could see her and swore under his breath. Lifting her up into his arms, he pushed her face against his chest.

"What did you say?" she asked.

"Nothing for your ears to hear." He paused. "We need to get you home, cleaned up, and into some dry clothes. Your dress is ruined. You're soaked."

"I think I lost my keys." She sounded defeated.

"I have them, and I'll drive." He opened her door, setting her down. He took a deep breath, obviously struggling for calm before he got in the car.

The silence between them was deafening. When they got to her house, Katie was there with a blanket to wrap her in. Dylan had the door open and lights on in her place.

"Let's get you inside," Matt said. He picked her up and carried her in.

"I'm okay, you don't have to carry me." She felt her face heating.

"I want to and besides we're in now." He set her down on the chair.

"Why didn't you just throw me? It would have

been faster." She reacted to his tenderness.

"Jessica Lynn Reynolds!" Katie imitated Jessie's mom. "Your pride may be wounded, but it didn't hurt your tongue."

Matt ignored Jessie's remark. "Katie, would you help her get cleaned up so we can see how bad her injuries are?"

"Sure, hopefully it's not as bad as it looks. But no matter what, she's going to be awful sore," Katie remarked.

"Help her get dressed too, and we'll take her over to the emergency room." Matt's jaw flexed, and his hand tightened into a fist.

"I'm going too. She may need me." Katie put a hand on Jessie's shoulder. "Besides, you guys aren't good in the comfort department."

About twenty minutes later, they were ready to go. Jessie limped. Her ankle was purple and swollen. Her big toe, which had hit the tree root in an open-toed sandal, was huge. The pounding in her head was making her irritable and Matt wasn't helping, either. The lump on the back of her head, the scratches, and the pain every time she moved completed her misery.

Matt carried Jessie into the emergency room and carried her out. Her ankle was wrapped, her big toe taped, and Katie carried the crutches. She was told to walk only with the crutches for the next few days and stay off her foot as much as possible. A few pain pills and a good night's sleep was part of the prescription.

"You guys were watching Jessie all along, weren't you? She was your stake out. Why didn't you tell me? I could have stayed with her, making sure she wasn't ever alone. I'm mad at both of you." Katie glared at their backs. "You could have told me, Jessie. After all I'm your best friend." She looked accusingly at Jessie.

"What, and put your life in jeopardy?" Jessie frowned at Katie. "I was asked not to tell anyone because the case was sensitive and still is. I wouldn't even be involved had it not been for Gina's ghost."

"What's this about Gina's ghost?" Dylan inquired.

"Let's get her in the house, make her comfortable, and then she can tell you about how she got involved. Jessie, you aren't going to work tomorrow." He said this definitively.

Jessie stuck out her tongue at him. Matt caught the gesture in his rearview mirror and smiled.

Katie helped Jessie into her night clothes, and she stretched out on the couch with a pillow under her foot. She recounted the story all over again about Gina.

Katie stood up and fluffed her pillow. She went into the kitchen and brought Jessie a glass of water. "I want to see you take these pills. They'll help you sleep." She waited for Jessie to swallow them. "Can I get you anything before I leave? I need to go make sure my guests are settled for the night. Do you want me to come back and to stay with you tonight?" Katie asked her.

"No, I'm really tired, and besides, you're supposed to stay this weekend when I'm hopefully feeling better."

"Sweet sleep, friend, and I'll check on you tomorrow." She spoke over her shoulder as she headed for the door.

Dylan walked with Katie back to the inn leaving only Matt, Jessie, and the silence as thick as the muggy air outside, between them.

"I know you've been itching to yell at me all night, but before you do, let me speak in my defense. I was standing at the door waiting like you told me to, and I hadn't gone to my car to meet you. I stepped out to lock the door, and there he was."

"You should have never stepped out the door without me. I don't blame you entirely. I never should have left you alone."

"Look, Matt, there is no way you can be with me every minute. Strike three wasn't out for me just like Reba said. Maybe it will mean he's out."

She rambled. "The guy was enormous. His fist could have leveled you. I'm glad you weren't there to protect me." She paused and then added, "He might have hurt you."

"He did hurt you," Matt reminded her.

"Not really. I hurt myself when I decided to take up flying off that embankment."

"You were lucky. I still shudder to think what would have happened if he caught you."

"Matt, the one thing I'm good at is running. I can be fast if I need to be. I ran the wrong way is all. I got spooked and what bothers me is I forgot all my training and ran toward the darkness instead of Patterson's or someplace where there were people. I paid the price for it, but in some regards I would have rather slid down that slope than have had him get a hold of me." She added with emphasis, "I did see him clearly though, so if he has a mug shot I could pick him out. I could also describe him to a sketch artist."

"When I came out the door, I saw your keys on the ground and then saw him chasing after you. My heart almost stopped. I realized where you were running and

I thought you were as good as dead." He shook his head.

"You can yell at me if it makes you feel better, and I certainly don't blame you." She closed her eyes. The pain meds were kicking in.

****

He let her sleep on the couch, not wanting to disturb her. He pulled the light blanket up over her, softly stroked her cheek, and smiled at her. "Finally, I've tucked you in for the night."

When Dylan came in, he told him he would take the first watch and for him to sleep in her guest room. Dylan opted to stay up for a while and watch the baseball scores on ESPN.

"She's sure out," Dylan said looking at Jessie.

Matt ran his hand through his hair. "This has been one hell of a night. She could have been killed." He heard Jessie's phone ring.

"But she wasn't." Dylan knew what he was thinking. "You aren't to blame for this."

"No? Then tell me who the hell is? If it wasn't for the fact she's one damn good runner and stronger than any woman I know, this night would have had a far worse outcome." He stood up and paced back and forth.

"Look, Matt, you were with her and stepped away for a moment. This guy wanted to get her and would have, whether you were there or not."

Matt scowled. "I need to call James Morris and let him know Jess won't be there tomorrow. I want to keep her with us and have her take a look at mug shots."

He pulled out his phone. "James, this is Matt Parker. I know it's late, but I needed to tell you Jessie was in an accident and won't be able to work for a few days. She's on crutches and will need a few days to recover."

"That poor girl has had a rough few days. I'll get someone to cover for her, and you tell her not to come in until Monday."

"Will that be okay with Pastor Rick?" Matt heard Jessie's phone ring again.

"He won't have much say in the matter. I'll let my wife know, and she'll get some of the ladies to bring in some meals in the evening."

"Sounds great, James, I know Jessie will appreciate it."

"Is everything settled?" Dylan asked.

"Sure is. At least we won't have to worry about her being around Rick at work for a few days. The church board is going to give him the boot. I asked them to wait a few days, and they gave me until Friday. Jessie won't be there when they tell him."

"Good." Dylan nodded and went back to his baseball scores.

When Jessie's phone went off for the third time in the past several minutes, Matt decided he should check to see who was calling. Two of the missed calls were from Sadie and one from Jeremy. While he was holding the phone, it rang again.

"Hello. This is Matt."

"Young man, what are you doing answering my granddaughter's phone? Is she all right? I've been worried about her all day, and I know when something is up."

"The answer to your first question is that your granddaughter is sleeping, and I'm the on-duty police protection assigned to her. Second, she is all right but a little beat up from hard run and tumble she took. You were right to be concerned for her."

"She didn't just run and fall down, did she? I'm not naïve." Sadie's voice was firm. "Someone was chasing her."

"You're right, ma'am."

"Did you catch the guy?"

"Nope, he got away, but she got a great look at him and she can ID him."

"What're the extent of her injuries? You did have her checked out, didn't you?"

"Yes, ma'am, I did. She has a broken big toe and a sprained ankle. Add to that, some scratches, bruises, and the bump on the back of her head, and I think you're getting the picture. She's sore."

"But thank God, she'll live. Young man, are you the one that she's always fighting with?"

"That would be affirmative."

"Let me tell you a secret about my granddaughter. She's just like me you know."

"I wouldn't doubt it." He was glad she couldn't see his grin.

"The minute you tell her not to do something, she'll do exactly what you told her not to do. Her dad has tried to run her life, and she wouldn't have grown into the woman she's become without defying him and standing on her own two feet. She was an only child, and he never wanted to let her out of his sight." She paused. "Don't lecture her or tell her, young man, ask her. She'll think it through and do what she thinks is right. She really is a remarkable young woman."

"Yes, I've noticed." Matt's grin broadened.

"Young man, have her call me when she's up to it.

Watch over her and try to appreciate the gifts she brings you. You just might find fate has handed you a treasure. If not, the worst you can do is have a loyal friend, which given the chance, she will become. It isn't really a test of the strongest will, but how to take two strong people and combine them as a team. I think I like you, Mr. Parker."

"Thanks, I take that as a compliment coming from you."

"You should. Stay safe and keep her safe."

When Matt ended the call, he couldn't stop smiling. Sadie must have given the boys a run for their money when she was young. Actually, she still probably could. He liked her.

Keep her safe echoed in his mind. With Jessie's cooperation, he would!

Chapter Twenty-One

"Did you get the job done?" Buddy wasn't dumb. He answered on the speaker and turned on the tape recorder. This was his protection against his boss ratting him out.

"Yes, sir, it's done. I mailed a copy of her article about Gina to your office. It should be there by the time you arrive back in town."

"Lie low for a while. She might be able to ID you." He sounded irritated. "This would be a good time for you to leave for a nice warm vacation spot. You know what to do, just get out of the area for a few weeks. We'll let them think everything is done, and then who knows what might happen? It all depends on where she decides to stick her pretty little nose next."

"The police in all of these small towns are no match for us. Hell, we've been operating right under their noses for close to five years. They'll never catch us."

"Before you gloat too much, remember I told you to get the hell out of there. If you get caught, you may end up like one of your victims."

"Don't worry. I'll disappear until you want me back. Call me when you need me."

"That's more like it. You know how important this is to so many people who are counting on us. The money is secondary." He chuckled. "Hell, who am I kidding. It's the only reason for sticking our freaking necks out. Rick was a damn idiot for bringing her here."

"You have to admit she's a looker."

"So was Gina. Pretty women are a dime a dozen. You can find another one just around the corner. I didn't spare Gina, and I won't spare Jessie if she gets too close to the truth." His tone hardened. "You do what you're told, and you can retire a very rich man. Let me down, and you'll retire a dead man minus a few parts." He snickered.

"You don't have to worry about me, boss. I'm out of here." He cursed the man under his breath.

"Go, but be ready. I may need you back here at a moment's notice to deal with her or him. Maybe both, it's my choice." He chuckled. "I'm not who people think I am, that upstanding elected official or better yet a nondescript little nobody. Even my wife, God rest her soul, used to ridicule my lack of stature, but who's laughing now?" He snickered. "I made her disappear. The good and moral citizens believed me, the model of propriety, when I told them she had died of a heart attack. They never thought to check and see if there was more to it. There are so many drugs. You can add a little here and a little there, and over time, goodbye, nagging bitch. But you know, Buddy, what I'm capable of."

"Yes, sir, I sure as hell do."

"When I say jump, you jump, no questions asked. If I say kill, you do it, and if I want you gone, you go." He laughed as he hung up the phone.

He was one crazy bastard, and Buddy knew he would be stupid not to fear him. He took the tape and slipped into his pocket. It was going with him.

****

Jessie awoke to find Matt and Dylan still there, the pleasant smell of bacon and eggs filling the air. Her stomach grumbled, reminding her she hadn't eaten for a while. She tried getting up, groaned, and lay back down. Every part of her body hurt, even her eyelids. Her head felt like a hatchet was buried in the back of it. But the aroma of coffee kept her struggling toward a sitting position.

"Good morning, sleeping beauty." Dylan smiled at her. "How are you feeling?"

"Wrong analogy, I feel more like the wicked witch of the west this morning."

"That good, huh?" Matt smiled at her quip.

"I need to get up." She reached for the crutches. "I'm surprised you're still here." She swayed for a moment, trying to get the hang of the crutches.

"Everyone has their assignments, and we were waiting for you to get up. You have to come with us." Matt paused and reached across to turn off the stove. "By the way, you're not expected back at work until Monday. James said he would take care of a temporary replacement. His wife is arranging to have meals brought in, and your grandmother called. I had a nice talk with her."

"I just bet you did." She frowned. "You didn't worry her, did you?"

"She called because she felt something was wrong. She was right, wasn't she? I was careful what I said. You and she are two peas in pod." He laughed. "There's been a change of plans, by the way. You will be our shadow for a few days. I'm afraid you'll have to tag along with us."

"Something smells good. I'll be back in a few." She spoke over her shoulder.

When she came out of her room, she had managed to get dressed. She had on a simple sundress, thongs, the only shoes she could wear with her toe, and she had pulled her hair into a ponytail.

She noticed both of them looking at her. "What, isn't this okay?"

"Actually, I was thinking how pretty you look," Dylan stated.

"Thank you." She ate and listened to them going over plans as they talked on the phone with their field operatives who were at various locations. The plane from India was due in at three.

"As soon as you're through here, I want to get you over to the station to look at mug shots. I would like to believe we'll have him behind bars this afternoon, but I bet he is already underground," Matt told her pointedly.

Dylan got the dishes loaded in the dishwasher, the kitchen cleaned up, and handed her the meds from the doctor. "You should put these in your purse. You may need them to take the edge off the pain. It's going to be a long day for you."

"True. Before the day is over, you'll be wishing you were back here on this couch. I don't know how else to watch over you except by keeping you with us. With all the help, we're still shorthanded." Matt handed her the crutches, his tone all business.

"I'll bring a good book, and I'll be fine." She grabbed her book from the table and shoved it in her purse. Matt apparently didn't have the time or patience for her to hobble to the car. Before she could say no, he picked her up and carried to the car. She fought him all the way, trying to keep her dress from riding up. A struggle ensued getting in the back seat.

Dylan had a pillow for her head and one for her foot. He tried to make her as comfortable as possible. Matt was already behind the wheel, fidgeting. "Dylan, get a move on it."

While Matt drove to the station, Jessie checked the messages on her phone and noticed she had missed several calls. She started returning calls and texts. The last two she had to take care of were from Katie and Mrs. Morris. "What time should I tell Mrs. Morris to bring dinner?" Jessie threw out the question.

"I think 6:30 would be a safe bet," Matt responded.

"Dylan is going to be on stakeout tonight, and I'll be with you. Your house will be my command center for a little while. So they'll be setting up some equipment in there today, if that's okay." He looked at her in his mirror.

"Fine by me." She smiled in agreement.

"I'll need to give them a key." He glanced back at her.

"Okay, I have an extra one."

Matt and Dylan started talking so she used the moment to call Katie.

"Hey, it's me."

"Where are you? I just saw Matt's car go by."

"I'm in the backseat of the car on my way to the station to look at mug shots."

"Did you take the pain meds the doc gave you so you don't hurt all day?"

"No, I need to be clear headed. I'll take it when I'm done."

"Don't let it get too bad, or it will be hard to get it

under control. I'm still upset with you for not telling me about all the things that have happened to you. I just heard about the bizarre notes and Mr. Yamamoto."

"Sorry, not telling you is one of the hardest things I ever had to do." She smiled. "You know me and secrets, Katie. I can't and never could keep one. I had to tell someone, and it always seemed to be you."

"You've had an awful week, friend." Katie's voice cracked.

"Mr. Yamamoto was by far the worst. You never told me he died. I don't believe I'll ever be able to go into my office again without seeing him in my mind, hanging there." Jessie paused. "It was awful."

"I can't imagine. Add to that, being chased by some big oaf. It's amazing you want anything to do with this town."

"If it doesn't kill me first, I think I might actually grow to enjoy living here. Oh, I needed to let you know in case you see someone going into my house that the police will be bringing in some equipment today, and Mrs. Morris will be there at 6:30 with dinner from the ladies at church."

"Be careful, Jessie, I'm afraid for you."

"They'll watch over me, and I'll be fine." She paused. "Katie, I hope you know I'll tell you what I can, whenever I can. You are the one person who always gives me perspective."

"I know. I'm just bent out of shape. I could have lost you, and that's not an option for me. You have to be the maid of honor at my wedding."

Jessie started grinning. "Are we talking about the near future here?"

"It's wishful thinking for now, but I did meet

someone who causes my little heart to flutter."

"Now, who is the one holding out? Is it who I think it is?"

"Not Dylan, although I like him, too, but he doesn't seem too interested. Bruce was a guest at the inn, and we have been emailing back and forth. He'll be here at the end of July for a visit."

"We're at the station so I need to go. Walking on these crutches is harder than it looks. It takes me forever to get anywhere." Jessie laughed. "You'll have to tell me all about him this weekend. By the way, the best way to jump-start something is let someone see there's some competition."

"And people think you're just a dumb blonde. Talk to you later."

As good as her word, Jessie struggled, but kept trying to use the crutches to get to the door from the parking lot. She could tell Matt's patience was wearing thin. He was about to pick her up and carry her, yet again.

"Don't even think about it!" she snapped at him. "I need to learn to use these things, and I will even if it kills me." She worked at it, and by the time she got to the door, she was starting to get the hang of it. Once inside she was also ready to plop down in the nearest chair and hope she didn't have to move again for a long while. Every drop of spare energy she had in reserve had been used up getting her in the door.

She propped herself up with the crutches leaning against the wall, hoping she didn't look as depleted as she felt. If she had to get away from anyone today, she was in deep trouble.

"Joe, escort Jessie into the conference area, and

bring her the book of mug shots to look at. It'll take her a while to get there." He looked at her. "I'll be back to check on you, later."

"Go. I'll be fine. Joe, pay no attention to him." She grinned. "I'm making good progress for being a new student in the fine art of using crutches and hobbling."

Jessie was so happy to reach the conference room and to sit down. She thought she would be content to look at the faces of criminals all day if she didn't have move again. She spent about thirty minutes looking at every kind of face imaginable, but she knew him the minute she saw the photo of him. His name was Buddy Maxwell, and as she stared at the black and white photo, the saying "a face only a mother could love" came to mind. Buddy's face looked like it had been worked over several times by a boxer. He was a huge, homely man, all six feet eight inches of him.

No wonder she'd lost all common sense when she saw his face with the lightning as a background. She shuddered to think of it, now.

Dylan popped his head in the door. "How's it going?"

"I found him." She pointed at the photo. "I need the ladies' room, and I really hope it's not too far away."

"It's right across the hall. I'll get Matt and meet you back here."

She kept them waiting for more than ten minutes. When she finally came in the room, she felt pale and clammy. Her head was pounding. Several guys were standing around looking impatient, but when they got a look at her face, their demeanor changed. She was helped to a chair, a glass of water was brought in, and

Dylan grabbed her pain pills out of her purse.

"Sorry, Jess, we keep forgetting your injuries are only a few hours old. Can you show us the photo?" Matt was all business as she pointed.

"It's Buddy Maxwell." She tried to find a comfortable position, shifting in the chair.

Matt was on the phone instantly barking out orders, and the room was suddenly empty as officers scrambled to the address given for Buddy. It was at least an hour's drive from where they now were, but the details of the various agencies cooperating had been worked out in advance because the Harvest Club members involved so many jurisdictions.

Matt had forgotten she was there, and no one was left in the room but her. She took the pain pill, called her grandma Sadie, and hoped she would remain upright in the chair. She tended to get loopy or fall asleep when she used pain pills. Her last coherent thought was that she hoped Buddy was underground because it would take every one of them and maybe more to take him down.

Chapter Twenty-Two

Buddy lived in small house on the outskirts of Rocky Pointe. Matt had called ahead to Rocky Pointe, and in the time it took his officers to drive there, a judge had issued an arrest and search warrant on probable cause and a witness's testimony. Officers from Rocky Pointe, the county sheriff's, and Blue Cove converged on his house. With guns drawn and a sharp shooter on the roof of the house across the street, they entered Buddy's house.

Once the house had been cleared, Matt told the officers, "We need to do this search by the book. That means gloves on, tag it, and bag it. We don't want this guy let out on a technicality. Get it right the first time."

Room by room, they systematically made their way through his empty house looking for any potential evidence and anything that might incriminate Buddy. They meticulously documented and photographed the premises, creating their visual record. Dylan helped tag, log, and package evidence, trying to keep it uncompromised and intact.

Mr. Murphy, Buddy's neighbor, approached Matt. "I saw him leave with a bag about an hour before you got here. He told me he was taking a trip."

"Has he ever caused any trouble?" Matt asked him.

"To tell you the truth, I hardly ever seen him. He's a giant of a guy and a little on the menacing side, always dresses in all black. He basically kept to himself. What did he do?"

"I can't talk about the particulars of the case, but thanks for your information. Give your name to Bob standing over there, and tell him what you told me. If you see him come back around, please give us a call." Matt handed him his card, shook his hand, and walked into the house.

Mr. Murphy gave his name to the officer and then walked back toward his house, sat down on a chair to watch all the comings and goings.

The evidence was gathered, including pictures of Gina and Jessie, which Buddy had lining a wall in his office. He must have been watching and photographing them for a while. He also had pictures of the church office and Mr. Yamamoto swinging from the rafter. Buddy's computer was confiscated, along with several other items. Maybe they would gather some information from his files. Matt could only hope this guy wasn't as savvy as the rest of the Harvest Club. All his photos were evidence that either he wasn't too smart or maybe overconfident that he wouldn't get caught.

"Man, this place is a dump." Matt looked around him noticing the trash, dishes in the sink, and clothes lying everywhere.

"He had a hell of fascination with these two women," a deputy said.

"At least he has good taste."

"He is one ugly son of a bitch. It's probably the only way he'd get a woman like this, in a fantasy."

By the time Matt returned to Blue Cove, a few hours had elapsed. He found Jessie sound asleep, her head resting on her folded arms on the table. She had to be uncomfortable, but she didn't stir when he walked into the room and sat next to her.

He touched her shoulder lightly. "Jess, I can take you home now."

She startled, flailing, as she tried to awaken from the drug-induced fog she was in.

"Easy, it's okay, Jess." He tried to calm her as he put his arm around her.

He noticed her face was wrinkled from where her hand had pressed into it. She was safe, but she really needed to be home where she could get comfortable. Her eyelids opened, and her blue eyes tried to focus on his face.

"Hi." He gave her a lopsided grin. "Having trouble waking up, are we?"

She nodded, swallowing convulsively, her cheek wet from drool, not yet able to put together a coherent thought.

"Is she okay?" Dylan asked when he walked in the room.

"She's loopy from the meds and sleep." Matt chuckled.

"Watch who you call loopy, bud, that's all I have to say." Her voice was slurred.

"It didn't hurt her tongue any. It's still sharp even when she's half lucid." Matt grimaced when she hit him. "You can go home now. Any work I have to do can be done from your house. Do you think you can stand, or do want me to carry you?"

"Oh please...I can manage myself." She glared at him.

"You two are something else." Dylan laughed. "Together you're a lethal combination like fire and gasoline. Kaboom!"

As soon as they got back to her house and were inside, Jessie sat down on the couch and was out in just a few minutes.

Matt took the time to have Gary Madison show him all the equipment so each of the teams could be reached and call in. He hoped she didn't mind that it was all set up in the spare bedroom.

"How is it possible for anyone to fall asleep so fast?" Gary asked. "She sat down, said hello, and was out."

"I think it's the pain meds she's on." Matt laid her down, covering her legs, and putting a pillow under her foot. He accidently banged her toe, and she moaned, mumbling something, but slept on. She even gave him hell in her sleep.

"If I have to be stuck here for the next several days, at least I can enjoy the view." Gary pointed at her.

Matt frowned and was about to say something when the first calls starting coming in and everything else was forgotten.

Dylan was outside of Rick's house. Team A was following him from the airport. Cars were in place at Ed's and Jason's, and team B was following them from the airport. They had some addresses and names of the other Harvest Club members, but not all of them. So they followed those they could. There were about ten teams in the field now and ten ready to take over for the night shift.

Matt heard Jessie's phone and answered it when he saw that it was Jeremy.

"Hey, Jessie, I've been trying to reach you. I'm on to something."

"Jeremy, this is Matt. Jessie had a run in with one of the suspects yesterday, and she's sleeping with the help of some meds."

"Is she going to be okay?"

"She'll be uncomfortable for a few days, but will be fine. What did you find?"

"I found a recruiting web site for the Harvest Club. I sent the link to Jessie's email. It reads like a who's who in America. There are thirty members in this particular group, but there seems to be an indication of other groups in Pennsylvania and on the West Coast. It seems there is one main guy controlling all of them."

"Does this guy have a name?" Matt asked.

"I haven't got it yet, but I'm working on it. I know this much, he might be a politician. In time, I'll find out his identity. This site refers to the founder of the Harvest Club, but never gives his name. Most of the members are politicians, religious leaders, or lawyers. I've checked into the backgrounds of the men listed on the site. They are all model citizens, clean records, no trouble with the law, and are civic and community minded."

"Great, we're dealing with freaking saints with criminal minds. These guys pose a danger, if not in this country, then to the poor of other nations who sell their own organs or worse yet, have them taken without their consent. It's a real comfort to know these guys are the leaders and pastors in some of our towns."

"Weird, if you ask me."

"You haven't found anyone with some background in medicine, have you?" Matt asked.

"No, not yet, why?"

"We've kept it under wraps, but when Gina was

murdered her eyes and kidneys had been removed with precision. It would take a surgeon and someone skilled to have done the job."

"I'll keep searching. Something more damning is bound to turn up. In fact, you gave me an idea. They obviously have had to check out the candidates who apply on line. I think I can do a trace. I'll get back to you as soon as I find something."

"Thanks, Jeremy, stay in touch.

Matt thought it might be time to pay a friendly visit to his old high school friend, Jason Cummings. All he needed was an angle. He didn't want him getting jumpy or thinking he was on to him.

Chapter Twenty-Three

She was fully awake without the fog. Jessie could feel some pain, but decided no more pain pills in the near future. It wasn't worth the effect. She would have to get by with the over-the-counter pain reliever from now on. She could hear Matt and Gary, whom she vaguely remembered having met, talking in the other room.

It was time to get moving. She grabbed her crutches and, standing up, hobbled to where their voices were.

"I'm glad you chose this room, so when people stop by they won't see the equipment." She leaned her hip against the door.

"Mrs. Morris should be here any time now. You also probably have several messages on your phone. It's been going crazy the past several hours." Matt couldn't resist adding, "You were dead to the world."

"No more of that," she said briskly. "Those pills knocked me out, so it's over-the-counter stuff for me now."

"I think that's the whole idea. Sleep so your body has time to heal. Hell, I would like a little time to sleep." Gary smiled at her.

"It doesn't matter. I kept thinking if I needed to get away there was no way I could run, but even worse, I couldn't wake myself up. I don't like the feeling of having no control."

She turned and hobbled into her room and then back out to the living room. Jessie listened to her messages, answered texts, and checked her emails.

Several ladies from the church arrived right at 6:30, bringing dinner, a beautiful bouquet of flowers, and a card signed by the church members. Andria sat down beside her while the other ladies were talking in the kitchen.

"You didn't just have an accident jogging, did you?" She looked around the room making sure no one was listening.

"No, I was being chased by someone and fell down an embankment," Jessie whispered. "But don't worry, I was able to identify him, and they might already have him in custody. I wasn't able to talk to Matt yet. I slept the afternoon away in a pain pill fog." Jessie watched the ladies working and chatting away. "What is Mrs. Morris' name?"

"Her name is Beth."

"Beth," Jessie called out to her. "Thank you for arranging all of this. I really appreciate it. Everything smells wonderful, and the flowers are exquisite."

"You are so welcome, Jessie. The wonderful chocolate cake is from Reba, and she wanted you to know she'll be by in the next few days, but she'll call first. We're all taking turns in the office, and I'm doing the bulletin for Sunday. Of course, Pastor will be back in the office tomorrow, for how long no one really knows, but that's neither here nor there. Let's go, ladies." Beth walked over with a beautifully appointed tray for her. The meal smelled delicious and included all of her comfort food favorites, pot roast, potatoes and gravy, a salad, broccoli, homemade dinner rolls, and chocolate cake for dessert.

Get well wishes and goodbyes were said with another promise of a meal tomorrow. When the ladies left, it seemed to Jessie all the positive energy was sucked out of the room with them.

Matt was summoned by the smell of the food. Filling his plate, he hurried passed her, barely acknowledging her as he went back into the guest room, and he was followed by Gary. Gary was filling his plate when Katie came through the door.

Jessie watched Katie stop, her eyes lighting up with interest when she saw Gary. Katie was really in a serious search for her soul mate.

"Katie, this is Gary. He is the tech guy who's been working with Matt."

"Hi." Katie gave him her killer smile.

Gary nodded and went on his way back to help Matt monitor the incoming calls.

"Jeez, I just gave him my best smile, and he hardly acknowledged it." Katie nudged her.

"Seems to me there are two major things working against you. First is the call of food, and second is the technical equipment, which calls to the male mind as strongly as a pretty woman. Depending of course, on what he has need of most. Right now, Gary is hungry and monitoring incoming calls. When he's full and bored, he'll be back. You can say something witty then."

"Jessie, doesn't all this testosterone and these good-looking men get to you?"

"So far I've managed okay." Jessie rolled her eyes. "I've been running from them, fighting with one, or sleeping through them. The nicest guy, my best friend is interested in, so he's off limits. I would say my singleness is intact. Maybe when this is all over I can think of them as just guys again. Right now their presence reminds me I can't be left alone, I'm in the middle of a nightmare, and I'm just trying to survive it."

"You're right, I keep forgetting. I came over real quick to see how you're doing. I had a few minutes down time. I was distracted by Gary. Is he married or do you know?"

"I don't, but I'll try to find out. Feel free to stop by and see him anytime." Jessie winked and forked up more pot roast.

"I'll let you finish your meal. Believe me, I'll be stopping by again." She popped up and headed for the door.

"What about Bruce?"

"What about him? I'm an equal opportunity employer. I want the best candidate for the job as my husband," Katie said over her shoulder as she closed the door.

Jessie was still smiling when Matt and Gary came in to fill their plates again.

"Where's your friend?" Gary looked around the room.

"She blew in and blew out again." Jessie smiled at his interest. He must be getting full and bored.

Matt walked passed her into the other room. "Gary, it must be hard to be away from your family when you do these kinds of jobs."

"I'm not married. It actually keeps me busy. I don't get a meal like this very often." He carried his full plate past her.

Jessie smiled at him. "Even so, I'm sure your girlfriend will miss spending time with you."

"I don't have one of those right now."

"One of what?" Matt asked as he came into the room to get his glass of iced tea.

"A girlfriend."

"Who'd want you?"

The male bantering began, and she could hear them going at it for the next few minutes and tried hard not to laugh. She had gotten the information Katie needed rather nicely.

Jessie finished her dinner and set the tray on the table. She went into her room and changed into some comfortable clothes. She was getting tired again, her body was aching, and she wanted to watch TV.

She took two Advil and headed for the couch. She hopped, not wanting to use her crutches.

Matt was standing there with her crutches in hand. "What are you doing without these?" His arrogance firmly in place, he glared at her.

"It takes so much effort to use them, and I wasn't going that far. I'm back in one piece as you can see."

"Use them." He walked out of the room.

She stuck her tongue out at him. "You're not my father," she whispered.

"I heard that." He laughed.

"Since your ears are so good, what happened today?"

"He was gone when we got there. We found pictures of you and Gina on his office wall along with some other photos. His computer was confiscated, and Gary is going through it now. I'm not sure if we'll find

209

very much though." He ran his fingers through his hair. "Waiting is always the hard part. It's easy to let down your guard when nothing happens for a few days. They're banking on you getting careless so they can go in for the kill."

"I understand, so you can stop the lecture." She pointed at him. "I have a message from Pastor Rick. He wants to stop by and see me. What should I tell him?"

"Tell him yes. I'll hide my car, and Gary and I'll stay put in the other room. You've got a nose for news, read between the lines."

Jessie sent Rick a message telling him he was free to come over. He responded he would be there by 8:00.

True to his word, Rick was there at eight with a bouquet of red roses, which he put into one of her vases, a card, and a journal that he asked her to open after he left.

"How are you?" His eyebrows furrowed as he looked at her. He sat down in the chair across from her.

"Tired, sore, and unable to summon the energy to do anything, but other than that, I'm fine." She smiled adjusting the blanket around her.

"Can you tell me what happened?"

She had a moment to decide whether to tell him a story or part of the truth. Her instinct told her to tell him what happened. She told him about people talking to her about Gina, meeting with her parents, and writing a human interest story about her. Jessie recounted the story of Buddy chasing her, leaving out the details of his name and her being able to ID him.

Rick was sweating, and his complexion took on an almost gray cast. His eyes darted around the room, and his foot tapped nervously.

"Do you have some place where you can go to be safe until everything blows over?" he asked.

"Until what blows over?" she asked innocently.

"There were people who were angry at Gina. That's why I didn't want anyone talking about her. But now I can see it wasn't a smart choice. I can't stop these people. I don't believe anyone can. Just by talking about Gina you've become guilty by association." He stood up and paced. "I don't want anything to happen to you. I'm sorry for ever bringing you here."

"I don't understand." She questioned him with her eyes. "What people are we talking about?"

"I've already said too much. You need to get out of here. It's too late for me." He bent his head to a few inches from her face. "I would have loved getting to know you. You're funny, sweet, and kind. I've messed my life up, but I don't want to add the guilt of destroying yours. Leave while you can."

"Why don't you tell the police what you told me? You could be put in protective custody."

"You don't get it. I'm in too deep. Death is the only way out for me. I've gone against everything I've ever known, and I'm an embarrassment to my father. My only defense is that I was told in the beginning I was helping people." He rubbed his temples and wiped the sweat from his forehead. "If only you'd come into my life sooner. I have to go." Agitated, he bolted out of her house.

She yelled for Matt, and he came running out of the room. "You have to stop him." She pointed at the door. Before Matt got the door opened, she heard the gunshot and knew what Rick had done.

Matt and Gary ran outside and found Rick slumped

over on a bench with a self-inflicted shot to the head. Jessie had managed to get as far as the door and heard Matt call for an ambulance.

The rest of the evening was a blur for Jessie. Rick had been remorseful, and she knew John would need to know that. That poor church was going to go through yet another tragedy.

She opened the card first and read his note to her.

Jessie,

I'm sorry for bringing you into this mess. The church loves you, and I must admit you've been the one bright spot to come into my life in a long time. Seeing you at work the last few weeks inspired me to try and be a better man.

The church is going to fire me and rightly so. I was never a pastor. I've been using it as a cover for some illegal activities. You are reading this because I finally made the right decision to end all the pretending. You're free to give this to the police. Please let my dad know how sorry I am for everything.

Sincerely,

Rick Robertson

When Matt came back in, she handed him the card. His glanced at it. "I guess he couldn't live with the guilt any longer. What he saw in India had to change everything for him."

She held up Rick's journal. "There is some pretty crazy stuff in here about a Harvest Master and Grimm Reaper." With a shaky voice, she read a passage to Matt.

"Today for the first time since I joined the Harvest Club, I'm scared, really scared. I

think I'm going to be physically sick. I've never been in the field before—now I'm in India. The long flight, customs, and the crowded airport—I'm on sensory overload. Gulping for air, I want to escape the pungent aromas of food, exotic spices, and body odors that are making my stomach turn. The visual chaos, bright colors, and noises are battering my senses. I wish I could make it all go away.

I've seen the cost of my choices in human terms, and I can't live with myself. God, I wish for freedom from this awful guilt ripping my insides."

Jessie stopped reading, handed the journal to Matt. There were no words she could add. She pulled the blanket up around her. She was weary and closed her eyes.

Chapter Twenty-Four

It was a long night for Matt. The next of kin had to be notified, the horrific scene processed and cleaned. Rick's house was searched, his computer confiscated, his suicide note found. His journal was filled with details of his illicit activities and his part in leading Gina to her death, but no information was found about any other Harvest Club members unless it was on his computer. One could only hope. Even death couldn't free them from the monster running the group. Who was he and why were all of them so afraid? Grown men afraid of what? Sure, they would go to jail for operating in the black market, but what did he have on them to control them?

He remembered the look on Jessie's face. She knew what Rick was going to do and afterwards she had looked devastated. How much could one person take? She had very little opportunity to adjust from one terrifying event to the next. Brad's wife was murdered because of his participation in the group, and now Rick had killed himself.

Rick was obviously feeling guilty about Gina's murder and the attack on Jessie. Without Gina's death, no one would've been any wiser, and the Harvest Club would still be an unknown.

Sitting in the chair across from Jessie with Gary asleep in the other room, Matt watched her face. He

214

could see she was having a troubled sleep. He continued to read Rick's journal. A plan formulated in his head. She would have to be strong and ready. He knew she was capable of it and much more. Even though at this moment, she was physically and emotionally weary. He wanted to enlist her because he believed it would flush the head guy out once and for all. He also wanted to get her certified to use a gun. She needed to be able to protect herself.

He closed his eyes, but jumped any time she murmured or whimpered in her sleep. When he opened them again, she was sitting there watching him. Dressed in a floral skirt and a yellow blouse, she looked great. He was intrigued by how quickly she seemed to recover herself.

"How did you sleep?" He stretched trying to relax his stiff muscles.

"All right. The question is did you get any sleep? You look weary." She flipped her hair over her shoulder in what he thought was a feminine gesture, pushing a few strands out of her face. "You look like you have something on your mind. What is it?"

"I have a couple of ideas that I've been thinking about all night. I would like to give you a few days to recover, and then I want to teach you how to use a gun and get you certified. "He watched her shake her head no. "Yes. I also want to work on a plan to flush these guys out. Are you game?" He stood up and stretched and walked toward the other room before she could answer.

She heard the shower, and when Matt came back his hair was wet, he had changed his clothes, and he looked a little more awake.

"Why do I need to use a gun? I'm a writer, not policewoman."

"You need to be able to protect yourself if you work on more cases with me. If nothing else, it will give me peace of mind."

"I don't know if I can get over my fear of the stupid things."

"Sure you can." He nodded. "I've got it set up with the chief, and he thinks it's a good idea. I'll work with you until you qualify. You won't be afraid of using a gun when I'm done with you, and you'll handle it safely. You have my personal guarantee, okay?"

"Okay." She looked skeptical.

"What was your self-defense class like?" He changed the subject.

"You know, the basic stuff to do to keep safe—awareness of your surroundings, pepper spray, something to make noise, doing everything possible not to be taken in a car against your will, and the big one, never run toward an open field or away from people, but toward them."

"You might need to relearn that last one." He chuckled.

"Ha-ha. What else are you thinking about doing?"

"I think you need the rest of the week and weekend to get back on your feet. On Monday, you have to go back to work. The church will be dealing with a lot, and I know you'll be needed there." He paused. "I thought you could write an article for the town paper about organ trafficking. I also thought you and I could pay a visit to the mayor of Blue Cove, the not so honorable Jason Cummings, and drop the hint that you have learned about the Harvest Club. I'll set up an appointment."

"Okay." She studied his face as she asked her question. "I want to help in any way I can. Is it possible for Dylan, Gary, or you to take me to the church today and maybe to see John? I need to tell him what his son told me."

"Are you up to it?"

She nodded. "I need to do it. Is it okay if I let him read Rick's card to me?"

Matt nodded. "Gary is monitoring the incoming calls, and Dylan is watching Brad. We're not sure how he will take the news of Rick's death. I'd be happy to take you. I just don't want to put you in harm's way until you're a little stronger."

"Java Joe's?"

He nodded on the way out and they stopped for coffee. Matt wanted a breakfast burrito.

"Hi, Jessie." Molly eyed her crutches. "Everyone is talking about what happened to you. And now, Pastor Rick's suicide. What's happening to our town?" She winced as she asked it.

"I know it's crazy." Jessie frowned. "I hope people don't associate all this trouble with my coming to town."

"No, it started with Gina. You just walked into it." She looked at Matt. "I didn't mean to ignore you. What can I get you both?"

"I would like a coffee and a breakfast burrito, the number three." He nudged Jessie. "How about you?"

"I'll have a decaf coffee with a ham, cheese, and egg croissant."

"Decaf? What's the use of drinking coffee at all?"

"I like the taste without the shakes." She smiled.

Molly handed Matt their coffees while Jessie sat down.

"I suppose you want cream and sugar, too?" His voice was tinged with sarcasm.

"Cream, no sugar." He sat down beside her and they talked until Molly brought their order. They ate while Molly served a couple of other customers.

She walked back to their table. "Did Kenny ask you to be in our wedding?"

"He sure did. I'd be honored to stand up with him." He smiled at her. "He also asked about coming to work at the station and what it would take."

"Jessie and Katie are also going to be in it, too." She lowered her voice so only they could hear. "It doesn't seem right to be so happy when so many folks are hurting right now."

"Of course, you should be happy. This is a special time for the both of you. Enjoy it guilt free. Hard times come and go in everyone's life. I say enjoy the special moments extra." Jessie's smile lit up her face.

They finished and filled their cups one more time to take with them. Molly was serving other customers, and so Jessie waved goodbye and headed for door, where she stopped.

"Wait a minute, you two." Molly picked up a bag and hurried after them. "Here's something for later. It's one of Jessie's favorites, fresh lemon blueberry scones." She smiled at Jessie. "Have a good day."

"Thanks, Molly." Matt took the bag, opened the door for Jessie, and closed it behind them.

****

Matt pulled the car into the church parking lot, which was already filled with cars. Jessie and Matt made their way slowly up the stairs at the front of the church. The minute Reba saw Jessie, she opened the doors.

"My dear girl, it's all too much for you and for everyone. Please tell me you didn't come here to quit today." Reba looked at her, eyes glistening with moisture.

"I'm not quitting. I came to see if you're all doing okay. I also want to talk to John. Rick talked to me before it all happened. I think John needs to know what his son had to say." Jessie sat down in the nearest chair.

"You shouldn't be out yet. You're still recovering, yourself." Reba watched Jessie with a concerned look on her face.

"I'm doing okay. I needed to know all of you are too."

"We all sort of migrated here today. It was spontaneous, and we needed to be together. Since Gina's murder, there have been too many sad things." She sat next to Jessie patting her hand. "I know we were going to let Rick go tomorrow, but we never could have imagined this. Why? Was it because of his job?"

Silence fell as Pastor John walked into the church with James. His eyes lighted upon Jessie, and he sat down in the chair beside her.

"How are doing, young lady?" His eyes searched her face.

"I'm improving every day." She noticed he looked tired and frail.

"I'm so sorry my son drew you into this mess, and then to kill himself at your house on top of it all." Tears filled his eyes. "He was never any trouble until a few years ago."

"Your son had come by to apologize to me. He was so remorseful. I think he felt there was no other way out for him." She handed him the card to read.

"Thank you for letting me read this, Jessie. I felt he had made a decision before he left for India. He was nicer to me than he had been for a while. It was as if he had settled something, and he wasn't as stressed. He told me we needed to talk when he got back. We never had the conversation. When he arrived on Tuesday, yesterday, it seems so long ago. I told him what had happened to you, and he became agitated and said he needed to make sure you were okay." His voice quivered. "That's the last time we talked. Although, he told me when he walked out the door, 'love you, Dad'. I hadn't heard it from him in years."

"I'll be to work on Monday, and I'd be happy to help you any way that I can." She leaned forward in her chair.

"The service is on Wednesday, July 3rd, so that family can get here and take a few days going home with the long weekend. It's still hard for me to wrap my head around this." He rubbed the back of his neck.

They continued to talk for a few more minutes. A couple from the church wanted to talk to John and stood by his chair. Jessie said her goodbyes and got ready to leave. It was still a major and time-consuming ordeal for her to move anywhere.

Standing, she grabbed her crutches and leaned on them. "John, feel free to call me any time you need to talk. I can't imagine how hard this is for you."

Jessie looked up to see Matt talking on the phone. His facial expression told her something was up. She made her way toward him talking to people along the way. Her phone signaled an incoming message. It was from Pam Bradley asking her to call as soon as possible.

Her purse kept slipping off her shoulder as she hobbled over to join Matt, banging against her crutches. Every few steps she had to stop and push the strap back up, only to have it slide down again, a few feet later.

He walked toward her. "Here, let me take this stupid contraption before you hurt yourself."

"It's called a purse, Matt, and aren't you just a little worried it'll hurt your manhood carrying it and being seen as semi-chivalrous?" Her eyes sparkled with amusement.

"Nope, I haven't got all day to watch you trying to get here. All our suspects are on the move and seem to be headed somewhere for a rendezvous. Dylan and those watching in this area are waiting to see if their guys go." He took her purse and motioned her toward the doors. "How's John doing?"

"As good as anyone can under the circumstances. He's getting a lot of support from people here." She walked by Beth and said hello.

"Your meal will be there at 6:30 and you need to go home and put that ankle up," she scolded. "Your toes are a little purple. Matt, you help her get that foot elevated. You hear me?"

"Yes, ma'am, consider it done." He picked Jessie up in front of everyone, handed the crutches to Melinda, and carried her through the doors. She smacked him on the shoulder, which he ignored, and those around them laughed. After getting her situated, he put the crutches in the backseat on the floor next to her and thanked Melinda.

"Take care, Blondie. I'll see you on Monday."

"Okay, Red."

As soon as the door closed, Matt began a new lecture. "Damn it, Jessie, you've got to tell me when you're tired or hurting. I won't know it by just looking at you. I'm going to take you home and let Gary watch over you. You need to keep your foot elevated all day."

"Yes, Dad," she said sarcastically.

No more vinegar, she reminded herself, try using a little honey. She smiled. "That isn't necessary. Some of the purple is from when I hit my foot on the tree root. I actually feel fairly good, not nearly as sore as yesterday." She looked at him in the mirror. "I forgot to tell you the funeral is on Wednesday, which gives the family time to get here and the holiday gives them a little more time going home. I was thinking we need to wait to drop our hint until after the funeral and have the benign article show up after the Fourth celebration. I have a feeling that, as egotistical as some of these guys are, they will come to the funeral."

"Good idea, I think you're right about that, but I'm still going to take you home. Katie has been trying to get hold of you, and I'm sure you have better things to do then sit in the back seat. You are not putting that foot down or hobbling on those crutches unless it's to take care of business. Besides you need to get busy writing that article."

Jessie called Pam back, and they'd loved the first draft of Gina's story. They didn't see the need to change a thing. When the call was finished, Jessie felt a certain pride in the praise Pam had given her about Gina's Story.

She looked at Matt. "I think we should do Gina's

story first, followed by the black market organs story." She was excited to have others read it.

"Okay. I already talked to Max at the local paper, and he said he would print anything we send him. I'll write his email down so you can send him Gina's story. You send it to Neil too, so we can get exposure in other areas as well. Now, let's get you home."

Chapter Twenty-Five

"Hey, Gary, I'm bringing Jessie to the house. You'll need to keep an eye on her, and I'm going to send Kip to act as backup. Make sure she stays down with her foot elevated. Don't let her get up unless it's necessary. Her foot is swollen. I can tell you right now she'll probably fight you, but you hang tough. We're almost there. Would you open the door?" He could see her giving him the look in his mirror.

Once there, Matt parked and carried her into the house, put her down on the couch, went back out and got her crutches, then set them where they were easy for her to reach. "Stay where you're put." He grinned at her and walked into the room with Gary.

About fifteen minutes later, Kip was coming in the door, and Matt was running out the door. "They're on the move. I'll let you know about it later."

****

Matt headed out of Blue Cove, following Dylan's directions. The command post was on a hill across from the site where the Harvest Club was gathering. At the fork in the road, he was to bear to the right. The club members would continue straight.

This was the perfect spot, nestled in the trees and underbrush, where they could watch undetected. Joe had a camera with a telephoto lens. He was getting close up shots of each of them as they arrived. Matt crouched low with his binoculars and watched.

"Who is that guy? I don't remember seeing him before." He tapped Joe. "Be sure you get a close up of him."

"I don't remember him, either." Dylan squinted. "There's Jason Cummings and Ed. We'll have to see if we can get a hit on the other guy's photo, through the system. I doubt if he'll be in there. I'm sure he has no record, if he's like the rest of them."

"Wouldn't you like to be a fly on the wall and hear what's going on in that room? I'm sure they're worried about what Rick put in that suicide note. I've always said they made a big mistake when they killed Gina. They overplayed their hand, and we're going to get them." Matt stood up and leaned on against the open door of his car.

The Harvest Club's meeting lasted a couple of hours. One by one, they emerged giving Joe a perfect full-face photo shot. The officers left only after the club members had all left, and they waited ten minutes beyond that.

Joe hurried back to the station and loaded all the photos into the computer. By the time Matt got there, he was able to see the entire series of close-up shots of the men in attendance. One of the other detectives from the county recognized the new man.

"I know that guy. He's Gordon Stockton, the mayor of Rocky Pointe."

Matt took a closer look at the picture of the mayor. "Let's find out what we can about this guy." He pointed at a tall man that stood in the background. There was no frontal shot of him.

"The Harvest Club has a recruiting site and a bank

account. From the looks of it, there are some pretty high rollers backing the actual cost of the organization. Gordon Stockton seems to be paid by the club itself." Dylan showed them a printed spreadsheet with figures on it.

"It looks like Stockton is paid pretty well for whatever it is he does. Look at those deposits." Matt reached for his calculator and added them. "Well over a million in deposits in the past six months." Matt pointed out the number totals to them.

Joe let out a low whistle. "A nice tidy little sum. I think I could live pretty well on that, thank you very much."

"The question is, is he the head of the club? Does he have the muscle to make these other guys dance to his tune? Joe and Dylan, find me everything you can on this guy."

Matt worked in his office for the next hour putting together his thoughts and observations. To him, Gordon Stockton was just the sort of nondescript person who could be the head of the club. He could use Buddy as one of his muscle men, and there probably was a hit man somewhere, too.

He contacted the Philly police and LA to see if they had any knowledge of Harvest Club operations in their area. If the club had been operating there, it was under the radar, and so began an exchange of information.

His thoughts were interrupted by his phone. "Hi, this is Matt."

"Matt, Jeremy here. Jessie told me I should call you with this information."

"What's up, Jeremy?"

"It took me a while, but I found the name of one of the key players. His name is Gordon Stockton. He's being paid pretty damn well, a whole lot more than the rest. He's the mayor of Rocky Pointe, but that's not the interesting thing. He has the smarts to run the operations. He walked out of a specialized medical program he'd gone into after medical school. Do you want to know what his specialty was?"

"Let me guess," Matt said. "A surgeon."

"Not just any old surgeon, but one specializing in kidney transplants. His transcript said he was a brilliant and skilled surgeon, but couldn't handle the stress of waiting for donors. He saw too many people die while waiting for their donor organs. He gave it up. Not too long before he would have been the lead doctor on a team, he simply walked away."

"We've been looking for someone to show up who had a medical background and a good reason to start the Harvest Club. Great work, Jeremy. My gut tells me this is the guy we need to be watching." Matt told Jeremy about what he had learned earlier in the day and their plans to flush them out.

"Be careful. In an operation this big, there has to be a massive protective structure in place. A lot of money is involved and some pretty high profile people as well. It seems the only way out for these guys, once they're in the club, is death. If Gordon sees you're getting close, he'll disappear, leaving the buyers, sellers, and brokers to take the fall. There's something else."

"What's that?" Matt asked.

"A percentage of money is being paid to someone they call the Grimm Reaper. I don't know who that is."

"I read about the Grimm Reaper in Rick's journal,

but he didn't give a name. I got the feeling they were all afraid of him, though." Matt's brows creased. "Thanks, Jeremy. Stay in touch."

Matt told Gary to have everyone come in for an early morning meeting the next morning. Some things needed to be settled before they headed into next week. Jessie was right. Nothing should be done until after the funeral. He wanted the freedom to observe the Harvest Club without them knowing anyone was on to them.

Dylan checked the flight manifestos every day to see if Buddy was headed back into town. Matt didn't think they would see him back until after the funeral.

He felt he was covering all of his bases. He needed to check on unsolved or unusual murders in the area, also in Philly and LA. What was this hit man's calling card? They all seemed to have one—that little bit of flair that fed their ego and made others aware that this was their job. Matt needed to go over all the notes and Gina's file with this in mind—see if anything stood out, something exclusive to him.

Dylan knocked on his door. "Are you done for the day?"

"I was just getting ready to relieve Kip. The ladies bring food for Jessie at 6:30, and believe me when I say I don't want to miss dinner. There are some great cooks in that church."

"Do you mind if I show up? I wanted to check in on her. I haven't seen her yet, today."

"If she doesn't mind, you'll get no argument from me. Plus, if you time it right, you'll get a great meal." Matt stood up, shut off his light, closed his door, and walked out with Dylan.

It only took Matt about ten minutes to get to

Jessie's. Beth turned on to Blue Iris Lane right after him. He couldn't have timed it better. He called Kip and told him to unlock the door, and that he was there.

Matt helped the ladies carry in the food. The aroma was very inviting.

"It seems you timed showing up here to the minute, Mr. Parker." Beth smiled at him.

"Yes, ma'am, to tell you the truth, the last meal was so good, I didn't want to miss this one." He held the door open for her.

"Did you make her elevate her foot today?"

"I brought her home and told her to. You'll have to ask her to see if she actually did it." He grinned.

When Matt saw Jessie, she was on the couch, her foot elevated, working on her computer, and Kip was sitting across from her with a besotted look on his face. Another one of his officers had fallen to her charms. He was pretty sure Dylan was somewhat besotted and Gary had expressed interest. He knew the feeling. What amazed him was she seemed totally unaware and unaffected by it. She treated them all the same. She was pretty cool to just about everyone.

****

She looked up from her computer and smiled. "Hi, Beth."

Beth looked at Kip. "Young man, did she stay down today, elevating that foot?"

"Yes, she did. We made sure of it." He smiled at Jessie. "She is a hard patient to handle, but we hung tough." Kip walked with Matt into the other room to see Gary.

Beth sat at the other end of the couch and pulled Jessie's foot into her lap. She unwrapped the ace bandage to take a better look at her ankle. "It's still pretty swollen and bruised, but it's looking better. I'll rewrap this, and you need to put ice on it for fifteen minutes at a time for the next few hours. It should help to take the swelling down."

"Beth is a nurse. She'll get you back on your feet in no time, Blondie."

"I thought that was you, Red." Jessie saved her work and shut her computer down. "How are you all holding up?"

"We're all busy trying to help John prepare the church for Sunday, help you, and get ready for a funeral, as well as wondering who the new pastor will be." Beth paused and added. "It's been an awful few months."

"I'm sure it has been."

"All this ruminating won't change a darn thing." Beth stood up and walked into the kitchen. "Here comes another one. You'd think these young men never get to eat."

"I'm sure they haven't had food like you ladies make since they were young boys at home."

"You know what my reply to that would be?" Beth laughed. "They need to get married. You seem to be a gathering place for a lot of the town's single guys."

"Only the police, who feel the need to look after me," she replied.

"Jessie, I think they enjoy the job."

"Sure, especially yesterday and today with the great food calling to them."

Dylan came through the door. "Hi, Jessie. Wow, that smells good." He headed to the guest room and the sound of Matt's voice.

"Now do you see what I mean?" Jessie laughed. "It's a guy thing, food and telling me what to do."

Beth brought Jessie her tray. It smelled heavenly. Lasagna was one of her favorites. Garlic bread, a green salad, iced tea, and strawberry shortcake for dessert were equally tempting. She would have to do a lot of running once her ankle could support it.

"Enjoy the attention and make sure you make those boys serve you." Beth patted her shoulder and then called to Matt and told him dinner was on. They all came quickly at her call and filled their plates.

"Thanks, Beth. I appreciate you and all of the ladies making meals for me. I can't tell you how nice this has been." Jessie thanked each of the women.

"You still have a few more days to be pampered, so enjoy. You boys need to serve this girl if she wants anything. That's my condition for you eating here every night."

"We'll take good care of her." Dylan grinned.

"Just see that you do." She winked at him.

Chapter Twenty-Six

He had to admit he was somewhat concerned about his control of the club members. They were all anxious since Rick's suicide. He hadn't seen that one coming, or he would have had the job done first. Rick's kidneys could have been put to good use. Now he had to watch for changes in Brad. He hadn't been right since Gina was killed. The only one who had held him together was Rick. He couldn't blame Brad. Gina had been a pretty, sweet little woman, a lot like his own sweet wife.

Damn, but he hated funerals. He would have to go, he supposed. Rick after all had made him a lot of money over the last few years. He didn't care much for being in church, either. It made him squirm. All of the club members would have to be there. They owed Rick that much. Besides they were, after all, civic leaders and exemplary human beings. He snickered.

He felt sure the club was still undetected. If there was even a hint of exposure, he would be gone, underground, and would resurface somewhere else down the road. The others would have to fend for themselves.

****

The next few days flew by with people in and out of her house. Jessie had a follow-up doctor's appointment and had been fitted for a boot so she could start putting weight on her foot. She was happy she no longer needed the crutches.

Katie had been with her on Saturday night, and was in her glory with all the males in the house. Jessie had more fun watching Katie flirting than she had had in a long time. Katie made no bones about the fact she was interested in anyone who showed interest in her. It made for a comical weekend. Katie chased and the guys retreated to the other room under the guise of monitoring the incoming calls.

Jessie was so ready to be back at work today. She dressed with care, knowing people from the district conference would be there along with guests coming for Rick's funeral. She opted for her pink floral sundress, one black sandal, and the black boot.

She got to drive herself to work, feeling a wonderful sense of freedom she hadn't felt in a while. Matt decided to let her move about on her own during the day. Gary would be at the house when she got home, and he would be there at night. Without Buddy in town, he felt it would be safe for Jessie. His excuse was that he didn't want to tip off the Harvest Club.

When Jessie opened her door to her office, she found a welcome back banner, a bouquet of flowers, and a group of ladies waiting inside.

"We are so happy you're back," Beth said.

"Yeah, Blondie, we all missed seeing your happy smiling face."

"Thanks, everyone, it is great to be here." She cleared her throat and wiped her eyes. "It's time for me to get to work. I need a schedule for the next few days, so I can answer the incoming calls about Rick's service."

"I put it right by the phone. Several of us will be around the church for the next few days getting things ready. One reason is we want to do all we can to help Pastor John, and we don't want you in the building alone, either." Beth smiled and walked out the office door. "I'll be in the fellowship hall and kitchen if you need me."

"It does my heart good to see you looking so much better, Jessie. This has been an awfully hard few weeks on you. You've managed to stand your ground, and I hope you'll be staying on here indefinitely." Reba sat down in one of the office chairs.

"I have no plans to leave." Jessie made it emphatic.

"Sightings of Gina have increased. I think she is agitated because of everything that has happened. I believe this whole mess will wrap up soon and our dear Gina will finally find rest." Reba paused and stared for a moment into the hall. "Just so you know, I think her murderer will be among the mourners on Wednesday, so you need to be on guard. I wouldn't be surprised if some strange things happen on that day. Rick's grave will be a few sites down from Gina's."

"I think he'll be there, too," Jessie commented.

"Gina will point him out in some way so that you'll know who he is. He'll be watching you, Jessie. I'm not trying to scare you, but you have to be aware. You are the one that must solve this case. You are the one she chose to do it."

Jessie felt the familiar cold chill run down her spine. She knew Reba was right. Before she gave way to all the unsettling questions in her mind, she turned to Reba. "Why me, I keep asking myself. Gina didn't know me. I don't understand why she chose me."

"Who knows all the answers?" Reba smiled. "You have the sight even if it's undeveloped, and she recognized that you would be able to understand. As a writer, you must learn to read between the lines. This, simply put, is just a bigger picture. I don't remember when I recognized my ability. I would find myself knowing when something was about to happen. I try not to make a big deal about it. It's just a part of who I am and who you are." Her expression was kind but earnest. "Why do you think you are so great at what you do? Isn't it because you have intuition, an edge, a third eye so to say?"

"I never thought of it that way." Jessie frowned thoughtfully. "I know one thing. This has changed me forever. There is no such thing as an ordinary murder. Each one is unique and changes everyone around it. Gina was virtually unknown to me, but I feel like I've known her forever. Her story has changed me."

"Some people would say we are all connected. You know, the whole circle of life idea." Reba smiled at her. "You stay on guard, and I'll tell that handsome Matt Parker to keep his eye on you, as if he ever takes them off of you." She laughed.

"I think he would rather strangle me. You might have to ask Dylan."

"Oh, Jessie, you need to wake up. There's a fine line between love and hate, my dear." Reba walked out the door humming a catchy tune.

The rest of the day and Tuesday flew by. There were lots of calls about the service and flower deliveries and ladies bringing in food for after the service. The fellowship hall had tables set up in it, with the cloths already on, and everything that could be done the day before, accomplished. Jessie was kept busy with little time to worry about the funeral and all the possible things that could happen. Secretly, she was happy that it was almost over.

On Thursday, there was a big concert in the park with a fireworks show after it, and she was looking forward to being there with Katie. All she had to do was get through the funeral.

Her first story about Gina had been sent to Max at the paper. She had heard back from him. Max told her the story was a winner, she could write for him any time, and he would pay her something. It wouldn't be much, but enough to make it worth her while. He set up a meeting Tuesday, during the lunch hour, and Jessie confirmed she would be there. It might be the ideal time to give him the article on the Harvest Club activities without naming the players. She also sent the story to Neil who said he would use it and was eagerly waiting for the conclusion.

Jessie helped wherever she could. Happy that next week the boot would be off, and if her foot had continued to heal, she would be running again.

Chapter Twenty-Seven

By 11:00 the church was packed with mourners and enough hidden firepower to take more than half of them out. Matt Parker wasn't about to take any chances today. He had warned Jessie in every possible way to keep her eyes open and be on guard.

He sat in the last pew in the back of the sanctuary where he could see her sitting next to Katie near the front of the church. In between them were church members and the now infamous Harvest Club. Somewhere in the group was Gina's murderer, of that Matt was sure, if not the hit man, then the one who had hired it to be done. His gut told him the small weasel Gordon was the one calling all the shots.

He was the one who had removed Gina's eyes and kidneys for sure. He wondered at what point they had been removed. Gordon was one sick bastard.

Matt had received information from Philly and LA this morning of a couple strange unsolved cases. One was a prominent lawyer and the other was a missing district attorney. The Philly police thought it was probably a homicide. The lawyer in LA had had his eyes and kidneys removed, and a note had been left by his body, like Gina. Both men could now be traced to having connections to the Harvest Club. The FBI had become involved when the Harvest Club's real activities came to light with their illegal international black market ties.

As the service drew to a close, Matt stood at the back of the church. The congregation prepared to follow the casket out to the cemetery beside the church.

Matt watched as each row was released. Jessie walked down the aisle, and Gordon Stockton never took his eyes off of her. Matt couldn't believe how bold he was. There was something familiar about the tall man next to him. What was it? Suddenly it came to Matt where he knew him from.

****

As they walked outside, Katie whispered, "That was sad. I can't believe he killed himself at my inn. My guests were traumatized by all of it. I wonder if any of them will ever come back."

Leave it to Katie to make it about something else. "It's crazy for sure. I feel so bad for John. He loved his son." Jessie gently reminded Katie of what was really lost.

Jessie kept thinking about Matt's warning earlier. "*Nothing is as it seems. Don't trust anyone.*" She also had Reba's words in her mind about Gina showing her something today and that she had been chosen to solve the case.

Jessie made her way into the cemetery, going automatically to the bench across from Gina's grave as others filled in around the new grave area. Jessie found her eyes drawn to the edge of the woods. There stood Gina in her floral dress, watching the scene in front of her. She crossed the ground in a blur. She hovered over Rick's grave with sad eyes watching everyone, and she reached out and stroked John's shoulders.

Suddenly her eyes sharpened like daggers and

locked in on Gordon Stockton and a tall handsome man not far from Jessie.

Jessie's heart began to beat faster. She knew Gina was trying to tell her something about those two men. Gina glared at them, moving jerkily back and forth between them. Jessie felt cold chills and wondered if anyone else did. She looked up to see Reba staring directly at her.

"Hello." His deep voice startled her.

Jessie looked into the tall man's smoldering gray eyes. "Hi," she said back to him.

"I'm Zach Johnson, and you must be Jessie. Rick talked about you all the time. Now I can see why." He looked her over.

He was giving her the creeps. "I'm Katie." Katie jumped in before Jessie could stop her. "I'm her best friend." She stuck her hand out, and he took it.

Jessie wanted to yank Katie's hand out of his. She had no idea who he was. Katie just thought of him as another handsome guy to conquer. Jessie was frantic inside. The man dropped Katie's hand, looked seductively at Jessie, and turned around as the minister started talking.

Jessie wondered if he was Gina's killer. He was smooth, handsome. Any woman would be flattered by his attention. She watched as he interacted with Gordon. In her heart of hearts she wasn't sure that it was him. Gordon was a different matter. She knew he was guilty of removing Gina's eyes and kidneys.

"Gina, what are you telling me? How will I ever be able to prove it?" she whispered.

Katie was staring at Zach and practically drooling. A familiar face came into her line of vision, their eyes made contact, and his smile brought a sense of relief to her.

As the minister prayed the final prayer, Dylan was taking Katie's hand and hers. He walked with them both back to the church before Zach and Gordon got hold of them. He sat beside them during the reception, not letting them get far from him.

"A penny for your thoughts." Matt stood beside her.

"It would cost you a whole lot more than a penny."

"I need to talk to you for a minute." He walked away from Dylan and Katie. "The tall guy, Zach, is under cover with the FBI. He wanted you to know so you wouldn't be offended by how he acted toward you. By the way, what did he do?"

"You know, guy stuff."

"No, I'm not sure what you're talking about. Could you be more specific?" He nudged her.

"He looked at me like a piece of meat. You know what I mean." She saw the amusement in his eyes and wanted to hit him.

"I don't believe I've ever looked at a piece of meat the way you're describing."

"You are really a piece of work. You knew all along, and you just wanted to embarrass me." She turned her back on him.

"It didn't cost me one cent, and you spilled it. You make it too easy, Jess."

One by one the club members came up to Jessie telling her some special memory of Rick. She almost felt bad because she hardly knew Rick and her only real honest glimpse of the man had come moments before he killed himself. But then she remembered who these men were and what they were involved in. They needed to polish and maintain a perfect image.

The last two to approach her were Gordon and Brad. Chief Anderson stood behind them. Jessie felt the all too familiar chills run up her spine and knew Gina's piercing eyes were homed in on them. Gordon boldly grabbed her hand and wouldn't let it go. His beady eyes leered at her with a thinly veiled anger. "I hear you are doing a story about Gina? What brought this about?" His lips thinned, and he obviously fought to control his anger.

"People in the church held her in such high regard and wanted to talk to someone about their love for her. Being the new kid on the block, they talked to me." She gave him a carefully sweet and sad smile. "I wrote a personal interest piece on Gina, the daughter, mother, and pastor. You'll be able to read it on Friday. It comes out in the local paper. If you'll excuse me, I need to give my regards to John before he leaves." She freed her hand and turned her back on the creepy little man and walked away.

****

His eyes narrowed, and he followed her retreat. Anger seethed in him, and he clenched his fist until his fingernails drew blood. How dare she. She thought she could turn her back on him. He'd kill the bitch, and he had the perfect time already in mind. The decision made, the tension left his body, his hands relaxed, and he talked with Brad as though nothing out of the ordinary had taken place.

Chapter Twenty-Eight

The day had come to a close and she was grateful. The people at church were weary. Frankly, Jessie was happy nothing too strange had happened at the funeral. It was weird to her that she no longer thought seeing Gina was strange, but her life had taken so many twists and turns in the last few weeks that Gina seemed to no longer be big news. Most people would think she had lost her mind. She was just thankful they would never know her personal thoughts.

Gordon was strange. He was a small man trying to play the part of a big shot. She wondered who the real murderer was. True, he had performed the surgeries, but who did the rest? There would be time to think of it later. All she wanted to do right now this minute was get home and spend a nice quiet evening.

The church was closed Thursday and Friday, so she had two days off, and she was looking forward to kicking back, a little sun, beach time, fireworks, and the concert in the park. It sounded great. She only had to wear the boot until Friday, and then she could try walking without it. Her foot was much stronger than it had been just a few days ago.

She left Beth and James to lock up. Kip walked with her to the car, she put the top down, and headed for Blue Cove Drive. Jessie went to the one place that always gave her perspective. Kip tagged along and they parked at the marina. Silent, they watched the waves lapping the shore. A family was playing Frisbee on the grassy area, and people strolled by them. Lost in thought, she had no idea how long they had sat there. Her phone started vibrating in her purse.

She pulled it out. "This is Jessie," she answered.

"Where in the hell are you? I've been calling and waiting for you to get back to your house. Jess, now is not the time to let your guard down."

"I'm at the marina watching the sailboats and people. I guess I lost track of time."

"I suppose you're sitting there with the top down on your car, a perfect target. Am I right?"

"Maybe, but Kip is with me." Jessie turned her engine on. "We're on our way back now." She hung up before he could say another word. Leave it to Matt to destroy a perfectly good moment.

It was too hard to maintain the pace she had been on. She needed a break. But of course, until this was over, there would be no break.

"Is he upset?" Kip looked over at her.

"A little. I didn't think to call him and let him know where we were."

He was waiting for her when she pulled her car into her parking space. He nodded at Kip as he walked past him toward her house. She didn't want to hear one more lecture from him, and she could feel the tension rising in her. If he opened his mouth, she would let him have it.

"I'm sorry, Jessie. I didn't mean to get on you. I was worried when I called the church and they said you had left a while ago. Sometimes I get like a bear during the waiting process."

Now why did he have to go and be nice? It messed her whole thought process up. "It's okay." She walked toward the house. "It's too pretty to be inside. I feel like I've been trapped for days. What I need is a good ten mile run."

"Is there such a thing as a good ten mile run? My philosophy is why run when you can walk, why walk when you can sit, and why sit when you can lie down." He grinned.

"Don't give me that. You run too." She laughed.

"Sure, but I'm not like you. I don't like it." He emphasized every word. "Were you aware that Gordon was so angry at you when you yanked your hand away from him and turned your back on him he could hardly control himself? I thought he was going to hit you right then and there." He watched her face for a reaction.

"He was creepy, and he wouldn't let go of my hand. Brad was hanging by him like some kind of zombie." She thought about it for a minute. "The thing that bothers me is that all of them let that man rule them, and why is that? What does he have on them that keeps them dancing to his tune? He certainly isn't the strongest male in the group."

"When we know the answer to that question, we might just have solved the case." They both sat down on a bench in the gardens. "There is something we're overlooking. It's been lingering at the back of my mind, but I can't seem to bring it into focus."

"You'll put it together. I have faith in you. When Zach was playing like he was hitting on me, Gina was there. It was strange. I saw her first at the edge of the woods, and she came forward in a blur. Her eyes were so sad when she looked at John, and she stroked his shoulder." Her voice softened at the memory.

"Doesn't that freak you just a little, dead people interacting with the living?"

"After the past few weeks, it doesn't seem like such big news now. I know, weird, huh?" She laughed at his expression. "Anyway, Gina's manner became agitated when she caught sight of Gordon and Zach. Her eyes could have burnt a hole in their shirts. She rocked back and forth between them. I was tempted to believe Zach was the one until you told me who he was. I didn't know the FBI was involved or that they had anyone undercover."

Matt stood up abruptly. "Oh, hell, what have I been thinking?" He grabbed his phone and called a few people. All of whom said they would check and get back to him.

"What's wrong?"

"Something you said got me to thinking. Once I have a confirmation, I'll let you know."

They walked together into the house, and Jessie went immediately into her room and changed into some casual clothes. When she came out, she could hear Matt and Gary's voices in the back room and decided to make dinner. She would have to thank Kip for letting her go to the marina the next time she saw him since he had already left.

Jessie browned some ground beef adding black beans to it when the meat was done. She cut up lettuce, tomatoes, and onions. Making a salad she layered it with the meat and beans mixture, cheese and tortilla chips. Fresh rolls and a German chocolate cake that Beth had sent home from the funeral topped it off. Jessie made a dressing of thousand island and mild salsa. When she was done, she set the table and called the two guys in for dinner.

Matt took two beers out of the fridge, handing one to Gary. They filled their plates and went back into the other room. Jessie picked up a magazine to browse through as she ate. She couldn't concentrate. and she wondered what Matt had thought about earlier. He would tell her when he was ready she supposed.

"Not bad, Jess, I could eat more." He walked passed her to fill his plate again. "You know what would be good with that cake? A cup of coffee. Do you have some I can make? The real stuff, not the unleaded kind."

"I have the real stuff. I keep both on hand." She got up and got him what he needed. "Won't it keep you up if you drink it now?"

"Yep, I need to be awake for a while." He took his plate in the other room and ate while he waited for the coffee to finish.

Gary filled his plate, and she cleaned up the kitchen. Jessie cut a slice of the cake, got a glass of milk, and sat down at her computer. She worked on her article about the dark world of black market organ selling. She was so involved in what she was doing that she paid the guys little attention as they rinsed their plates and put them in the dishwasher. They took cake and coffee to the back room on their return trip.

The night progressed with very little conversation. She was just finishing up the article when Matt came in and sat down on the couch.

"Will it bother you?" He held up the remote.

"No, I'm done. Would you like to read it?" She printed the several pages.

Matt began reading. When he finished he looked at her with admiration. "Wow, you sure can put words together. This is a great article. It will get people to sit up and take notice, including the Harvest Club. Max has never had articles like this in his little town newspaper."

"I forgot to tell you Max liked my story about Gina so well, he wants me to write for the paper for pay. He asked me to come in Tuesday and talk. I thought I could take this one in to him then. I won't tell him to run it until you say." She beamed. "I forgot how much I loved writing something besides a church bulletin."

"It's good, Jess, really good." He held the remote up again and grinned at her.

"Okay, I know you're a man of very few words, enjoy." She laughed.

"One more thing. Tomorrow you can have a free day with Katie and Dylan without me tagging along. In the evening, you will have to wear a vest for protection. It will fit under a loose sweatshirt or tee."

"Why do I need it?"

"Call me crazy, but I saw the look on Gordon's face, and I wouldn't put anything past him. For my peace of mind, I want it on you."

He turned on the sports channel. She answered emails and decided to do a little checking on something that was nagging at the back of her mind. Her last message was to Jeremy. She needed to know how to get around something, and he would know how to do it.

Chapter Twenty-Nine

July Fourth dawned as a picture perfect day. Jessie was looking forward to the activities and events around town. A free day. Time to do whatever she wanted. Of course, Dylan had to tag along, but he was laid back and she enjoyed him. At six they would meet Joe, his wife, and baby girl in the park for the concert and fireworks. Jessie had picked up a gift for the baby several weeks before, and this would be her first chance to give it to her.

Dressed in white walking shorts and a red top, she pulled her hair into a ponytail and tied it with a blue ribbon. She added red sunglasses, a blue sun visor, and armed with plenty of sunscreen, she was ready when Dylan arrived. Jessie was excited to escape what seemed like captivity to her.

"See you, Gary," she called out to him.

"Okay, Jessie. Hey, if you see something that looks really good like one of those funnel cake things or something else, bring me one. I would be happy to give you the money." He walked in the room.

"Will you get to see any of the fireworks tonight?" She had opened the door and was poised to leave.

"You actually have a perfect view out your front window, so if things are quiet, which I'm sure they will be, I'll sit on one of the chairs out there, watch, and wait patiently for the treat you bring back to me."

"I wish you could join us for the day. Please feel free to eat whatever you see in the fridge. There is some leftover cake." She grinned. "Please, please eat that too."

Dylan had his truck, and Katie had scooted over into the middle. Right where she wanted to be, Jessie thought. Dylan opened the door for Jessie, helping her in so she didn't have to put all her weight on her foot.

"Wow, you look patriotic." Katie eyed her outfit.

"It is the fourth after all, and I'm celebrating a few hours of freedom." She threw her hands up in the air.

The two of them chattered back and forth, forgetting Dylan was even in the truck. "Where to, ladies?" He recalled their attention.

"To the Seaside Village shops," they chorused together and laughed.

"Great minds think alike," Katie proclaimed.

"I'm sorry, Dylan, this likely to be a drag for you following after the two of us as we shop. Something most men detest with a passion." Jessie acted melodramatic. "But I'm determined to take full advantage of my day out, and shop to my heart's content. At some point, I do have to buy Gary something and bring it back to him since he has to remain on the job today."

"He'll survive." Dylan sounded surly.

"I would do the same for you or anyone who had to work on such a glorious day." Jessie smiled sweetly at him.

"I'm sure you would." Dylan smiled back at her.

"You must really be happy to be out of the house. I don't believe I've seen you this animated since you moved here." Katie nudged her.

"It's like this, just for the day I'm pretending my life is normal. I'm free to roam about without someone watching over me, and I'm spending the day with friends for the sake of having a great time. Reality will close in again soon enough."

"I hope your foot will hold up for you do everything you want," Dylan said.

A few hours later, Dylan was the one racing to keep up with her, Katie was complaining, and Jessie was shopping, visiting with everyone that she knew, and looking at all the artist's stands. She had bought something for her parents, her grandmother, and something more for Joe's little girl. She found a special treat for Gary and a little statue for Matt. It was a great day.

"Would you two like to sit down and get something to drink? You both looked frazzled," she asked innocently.

"Are you kidding me? I've been saying that for the past thirty minutes. Are you on speed or something?" Katie pushed damp hair back from her face.

"I did warn you both before we got here that I was going to pack whatever I could into this day of freedom."

They refreshed themselves with iced tea. Jessie's ankle was giving her fits, but she was determined to keep going. She popped a couple of Advil and waited for them to finish their drinks.

"Do we have to time to take this to Gary before we meet Joe and his wife in the park? That way I could drop off my packages and get a sweater for tonight."

"I need to get the picnic basket and make sure all the guests who wanted a box dinner got theirs."

"We have plenty of time." Dylan nodded.

Jessie got Gary a grilled Rueben sandwich, a funnel cake and, to complete his July Fourth experience, some kettle corn.

She walked in the house calling for Gary and saw Matt sitting on the couch. "What are you doing here today? I thought you had the day off."

"I do. I came by to check up on you and to see how Gary is doing. You look festive." He held up the vest he wanted her to wear. "And you've got a nice, healthy glow."

"I've had a great day, but I think Katie and Dylan are ready to strangle me." She carried her packages into her room. "I think I wore them both out following after me."

Gary came around the corner. "Matt, you need to hear this. Hi, sunshine…" He smiled at her.

Jessie followed him into the guest room. "Here, Gary, I brought you a little something so you could have your own little taste of the Fourth, from me to you."

"How did you know these are all my favorites? Thanks, doll." Gary took the food bags and kissed her cheek.

Jessie went to change her clothes for the night and put on the vest under a loose sweatshirt. She waited for Dylan to come back from helping Katie get their picnic dinner and the blankets.

Matt walked into the living room. "Did you put the vest on?"

"Can't you tell?" She grimaced. "It looks like I gained many pounds in my midsection. How do you guys stand wearing these?" She patted her stomach area.

"Believe me it beats the alternative. You probably won't need it at all, but it makes me feel better knowing you have it on. Let Dylan know I'll be at the station tonight. If he needs anything, he can call."

"I will. Try to enjoy some of your day off. You know the old saying, all work and no play."

She didn't have to wait long before she was out the door and on to the next event. She felt almost compelled to cram everything that she could into this day. She didn't want to stop to reason why she was feeling so driven.

"Why's Matt here? I thought today was his day off," Dylan asked.

"I just asked him that very question." Jessie shrugged. "He said he came to check up on Gary and me. I didn't get to ask him much. Gary called him in to hear something." She paused and then added, "I'm sure he'll be glad when this case is solved and he can have a somewhat normal life again."

They made it to the town square just as the music was starting. Joe and his wife were already there with their reserved spot.

Joe's wife, Sarah, was a pretty petite brunette with a beautiful smile and the sweetest personality. Jessie had a feeling that they would become kindred spirits. Abigail, their baby daughter, was precious. Abby had dimples and dark curly hair. Jessie was in love with her. Every chance Jessie got during the evening she held Abigail, walked her, cuddled her, and talked to her. Jessie was a sucker for Abigail's little smile.

This day had brought a contentment she hadn't felt in a long time. She was here with new and old friends, people who had worked hard to keep her safe. She looked at Dylan and smiled. The only one missing was Matt, the one who had worked the hardest to keep her safe. She could think of him as her friend, finally, and maybe a little bit more.

As the evening wore on and darkness settled over the park, Jessie started feeling a little nervous. She had the impression she was being watched. She tried to push the sensation away, but it kept rearing its ugly head.

Everyone else seemed relaxed enough, but she couldn't shake her reaction to what she was feeling. She started looking around the crowd, for what she wasn't sure. The hair stood up on her neck and chills ran up and down her spine. Her heart raced, and she began to wonder if she was having an anxiety attack. She quickly handed Abigail to Joe and started to get up.

She forced herself to sit back down, but it was a struggle. She tried following the conversation, but couldn't seem to focus on what they were saying. Jessie remembered Reba's words about the third eye and knowing when something was about to happen. She suddenly stood up, and she had to stop herself from running in a panic.

Dylan got up at the same time and stood beside her. "Jessie, are you all right?" He looked concerned.

"I don't know what's happening to me, "she whispered. "I feel a sensation of being watched, but I can't see anyone. Maybe it's an anxiety attack, but I feel myself starting to freak."

"Let's go with what you're feeling. You're pretty intuitive. Let's start by walking away from everyone here." He stood up and took her hand. "We'll be right back," he said in a normal tone. "I'm going to walk with Jessie to the restroom." The first of the fireworks went off with a loud bang, to the crowd's pleasure.

Dylan and Jessie had made their way to the edge of the crowd toward the police station when the first shot rang out. The bullet hit Jessie with enough velocity to knock her off her feet. The second round hit the tree beside them. Dylan fell on top of her to keep her from being hit again. He was scanning the area around him and radioed for help. The police were there within seconds. The crowd continued to watch the fireworks, not realizing anything had happened.

"Are you okay, Jessie?"

"Could you get off of me? I can't breathe," she gasped. "It hurts, and I can't breathe."

Dylan jumped up and was on the phone with Matt. "Shots were fired at her, Matt. Jessie's been hit. Did you hear me? She's down."

"Where are you two?" Matt asked

"I was leading her toward the police station."

"Can you see anything?"

"No, I'm thinking he had a rifle with some kind of night vision scope. He only hit her."

"Damn, did it pierce the vest? I'll be right there and the ambulance is on its way."

"She said it hurts, and she's having a hard time breathing."

"Thank God I made her put on a vest, but you know what a bullet still can do and the force it hits with. Is anyone aware of what happened?"

"A few police I radioed for help. Most people are watching the fireworks and still don't know anything happened."

Jessie listened, but didn't say anything. She couldn't catch her breath; it hurt like the devil to take a deep breath. She felt herself starting to panic when suddenly Matt was there.

"Jessie, look at me. Take it easy, just take nice short easy breaths. That a girl. You're doing good sweetheart, real good. I'm sorry to say you're probably going to have one nasty bruise, but at least no bullet tore up your insides." His smile belied his concern as an ambulance made its way through the crowd, lights flashing.

****

Matt met the ambulance at the hospital, followed closely by Dylan and Katie where they waited for the doctor to come talk to them.

"Weren't we just here, waiting to find out what happened just a short few days ago?" Katie was pacing the room.

"Katie, sit down you're driving me crazy." Dylan stretched his legs out. "Pacing isn't going to bring the doctor here any sooner."

"Officer Parker, I'm Dr. Morgan." A doctor wearing green scrubs pushed through the swinging doors. They shook hands. "I have Miss Reynolds stabilized, and she will soon be resting comfortably. She suffered a blunt force trauma at the point of the bullet's impact. It broke three of her ribs." He showed them the x-ray. "This is the reason for her difficulty breathing and her pain. She is bruised, and the bullet's impact cut her skin, but didn't penetrate. It could have been much worse." He smiled. "Someone must have been looking after her. We'll keep her overnight and maybe longer to monitor her breathing and pain. She is being taken to her room now. The nurse at the desk will have the information once she's settled."

"Thanks, doctor. Obviously someone tried to kill her, so we will have someone watching her around the clock. Please instruct the nurse's station not to give out her condition or room number to anyone."

"Will do." Doctor Morgan shook his hand again and walked back through the doors in the ER.

They were given the room number about twenty minutes later and took the elevator up to the third floor. Matt had already called and set up the first watch, with someone to take over in the morning.

Katie flew into the room and immediately wanted to know if Jessie wanted her pillow fluffed, if she needed water, if there was anything at all she could do to make her more comfortable.

"Yes." Jessie winced. "Please sit down, you're making my head spin, and I want to look at you."

"Are you in pain?" Katie looked at Jessie, her eyes moist with tears.

"It hurts like the dickens. They keep saying it will be under control soon. You know what that means for me. I'll either be loopy or asleep." She looked at Matt. "Thanks, by the way, for following your instinct and making me wear the vest. I'm alive because of it."

"Do you want me to call your parents?" Katie asked her.

"Are you kidding me? They would be on the first plane here and moving me to their house in a few days. I'll let them know when everything is over."

"Jess, I need to ask Dylan and you some questions before you get too sleepy. Katie, Kip should be out in the hall. Why don't you go talk to him, and then Dylan can take you home after we wrap up here?" He waited for Katie to walk out and close the door. "What happened? The police are searching the area now, but other than maybe finding a bullet casing if we're lucky, I doubt they'll find anything."

"I observed a change come over Jessie. She told me she had the sensation of someone watching her. I told her we would go with her feelings, and we excused ourselves and went toward the police station. We were nearing the back of the building when the shot knocked her off her feet. The fireworks covered the sound of the shot. I fell on top of her to cover her so she couldn't be hit again in case there was a second shot which came on the heels of the first. I didn't know she had a vest on. I thought it might have killed her." He smiled. "Until she told me to get off of her because she couldn't breathe."

Jessie frowned. "It's strange when I think about it now. I wanted to do everything I could do today. It was like I was driven. I wanted to see everything and talk to everybody. I know I pushed Dylan and Katie to the point of wanting to hit me." Dylan smiled at her. "Tonight I was almost philosophic holding Abigail, Joe's baby, like I would never hold my own. When the lights in the park went down and the fireworks started, I was a mess. I thought maybe I was having an anxiety attack. I felt I had to get away from the people, and now I know why. If that bullet had hit one of my friends, I don't know what I would have done." She shivered and began to shake.

Matt pushed the call button, and the nurse came in. She took one look at Jessie and left. When she came back in, she injected some medication into Jessie's IV drip.

"An adrenaline rush after a traumatic event is normal." She smiled soothingly. "This should take effect pretty quickly. You'll be just fine in a few minutes, and probably asleep. So get any questions in quick." She smiled again and patted Jessie's hand as she left the room.

"After that I felt something slam into me and knock me off my feet. It hurt like the devil, and I felt like I couldn't catch my breath." Her words began to slur.

"I'll talk to Dylan. You can let me know if you think of anything else." Matt became quiet as he read the text just sent to him. "They dug a .223 out of the tree."

****

They talked quietly, and before long her twitching stopped, and she was sound asleep. "I think everything we can do here tonight is done. You can take Katie home," he told Dylan. "I'll hang around here for a while and make some calls."

"Do you want me to check in on Gary? I'll be right by there," Dylan called back as he started out of the room.

"Sure, let him know what happened here and that Jessie will be okay."

Matt didn't know why he had felt so strongly about putting the vest on her other than the fact he had seen Gordon's hate for her written on his face and body language. And the fireworks made a perfect cover for a sniper shot with night vision equipment. In this case he used an AR-15 assault rifle with a night vision scope, but the shooter was a tad too far away. He didn't want Jessie to know, but a high powered rifle's bullet could and often did penetrate a vest.

Matt was happy she hadn't been killed. He had wanted her to have this day without him hanging over her, living a normal life. It had almost cost her, her life.

It didn't make any sense; it didn't follow the normal pattern. Gina was probably taken, her organs removed while she was alive, and then it was made to look like an execution-style killing. This was a sloppy attempt, firing into a crowd where there was a high police profile. He couldn't believe Gordon would put everything in jeopardy to appease his anger.

They had found the rooftop where the suspect had been, and there was, Matt hoped, with any luck, a fiber, or shoe print that might lead to the identity of a suspect. A CSI team from Freeport was combing the area now.

Matt walked over to the bed and looked down at her beautiful face as she slept. He pulled his chair up close so he could watch her. He hadn't expected to fall so fast or so hard. She had blindsided him. "You're one strong woman. Anyone else would be hysterical by now. But you've taken one blow after another and bounced back somehow. New York was a piece of cake compared to Blue Cove." He was angry. He had to keep her safe and find the bastard that had hurt her.

A night duty nurse came in to take her blood pressure and check her vitals. She slept through the whole thing. "She's doing well. Someone was watching out for her." She nodded at Matt as she walked out of the room.

Matt answered a few of his text messages totally unaware of the presence of a woman in the room watching over Jessie. Her pretty floral dress rustled as she moved back and forth, stroking Jessie's cheek. Never once did she take her sad eyes from Jessie's face.

Chapter Thirty

Jessie had been awake for a while. Her eyes kept returning to the face of her sleeping protector who looked very uncomfortable. The changing shift of nurses had awakened her earlier, and Matt didn't stir as an aide got her up to sit on the side of the bed for a few minutes. The pain nearly took her breath away.

"It'll be like that for a few days, honey." The woman gave her a sympathetic smile. "Unlike a broken leg or arm we can't put your ribs in a cast. They heal naturally on their own, but as you have found out, it can be very painful. They no longer wrap them because it tends to restrict your lung expansion and the result can be pneumonia. We'll be listening to your lungs today and making you take deep breaths. You're going to hate us before the day is over. Breakfast will be here in a minute, and then we'll be in to take you for a little walk."

"Thank you." She ran her fingers through her tangled hair.

"You just call us if you need anything. Don't let your pain get out of control. Would you like to have a shower this morning?"

"Yes, that would be nice."

The nurse helped her swing her feet back on the bed and left the room. Her breakfast tray was brought in shortly afterward. She was happy to be alone with her thoughts. She had made a decision in the night, and when Matt woke up she wanted to talk with him.

Jessie looked over at him and found that he was looking at her with a puzzled expression.

"What?"

"How is that you can go through a miserable night like you've just had, nurses poking you, waking you, and making you sit up when it had to have hurt like hell and still be such a pretty sight?"

"Were you were awake all this time?" She glared at him.

"Sure, who can sleep in a hospital? I didn't want to disturb you, so I kept my eyes closed. I thought you looked like you might pass out when they made you sit up, though. I peeked then. How are you doing?"

"To tell you the truth, I'm mad. I didn't do anything to any of these people. I'm new to this town. I'm not going to be anyone's sitting duck anymore. If I'm going down, it'll only be after I put up one big fight and take a few with me." Her eyebrows furrowed. "How do you like that, Mr. Parker?"

"The girl is sassy too. Let's get you on your feet first. I think we can keep you safe and take a few out."

"Here." She pushed her tray toward him. "You can help me eat this. I'm not that hungry. What I would really like is Java Joe's coffee and one of their great scones."

Matt exited the room when the doctor came in to examine her. He listened to her heart and made her take several deep breaths. She wanted to punch him by the time he was through.

"The nurses will get you up to walk this morning. I think you need to keep that boot on for a little longer. I don't want you falling on top of everything else." He smiled at her.

"When can I go home?" she asked him.

"The first question I'm usually asked. I want to keep you one more night. You'll still be hurting at home for several days and will need some help and something to manage pain. Broken ribs are no fun." He patted her hand. "Laughing, sneezing and coughing can hurt like crazy."

Katie came in next, carrying her overnight case with all her necessities. She brushed Jessie's hair, and wanted to help her into her nightgown, but when she moved her arm, Jessie turned gray, and Katie called the nurse for help.

"It's okay, honey. Every little movement is going to hurt her for a while," she told Katie. "You didn't hurt her." She nodded at Jessie. "I have your pain meds for you, and we'll wait an hour or so and then get you up for your shower and walk. You can put on your clean clothes then."

When the nurses came in later they helped her shower and get dressed. Every movement hurt. Next it was down the hall and back with Katie talking incessantly and the nurse encouraging her every few minutes. What she wanted to do was yell at all of them but she wouldn't, it wasn't their fault. It was a tough twenty minutes. It took everything she had to walk down the hall and back. Katie took one look at Jessie's white face and kissed her on the cheek, saying she'd be back later.

Settled in her bed Jessie tried not to move at all. "How long will it hurt like this?" she asked the nurse.

"I'm not going to lie to you, it takes a little while,

but the severity will diminish over the next few days. I see your muscles are quivering again, I'll get you a little something for that."

"Thank you."

"You did real well for your first time up. I hate to tell you this, but we have to get you up this afternoon for another walk. At least this time it will be another pair of nurses, so we aren't the only ones causing you pain. You'll be doing this on your own at home so we have to get you ready." The nurse looked around the room. "My, oh my, would you look at all your pretty flowers; why don't I bring you the cards to read."

"That would be nice." Jessie smiled at her.

"Conserve your strength and rest, you'll need it later on." She closed the door when she left the room. She came back a few minutes later to give Jessie new pills to take.

Thirty minutes later Matt walked into her room as she stared off into space with the unopened cards in her lap, feeling completely done in.

"Do you want some help opening all of your cards?" Matt startled her. "I'm sorry," he said when she jumped.

"Sure, why don't you pull the chair over here."

"I brought you something you might like." He handed her a decaf coffee with cream the way she liked it, and a bag with a lemon blueberry scone in it. "Molly said to tell you hello and she's ready to go to battle for you. Did you have a rough morning?"

"Let's put it this way. I've had better mornings." She thanked him for the coffee and scone. "I don't like how these pain pills make me feel, but I can't take the pain either." She felt defeated. "I don't want to even reach for the cup."

"How about I hand it to you when you want it?"

"No, I need to work through this, but boy oh boy, I don't want to."

"At least let me move the tray closer." He shifted the tray.

"Thank you, it's a little easier to reach now.

"I don't want to upset you, but I called your parents and explained the situation. They have a right to know." He raised his hands defensively. "They won't be coming because I asked them not to. I told them you are under police protection, and you didn't need to be worrying about their safety. You do need to call them and your grandma Sadie. I had a nice talk with her also."

"You're right. I'm not thinking straight right now, of course they should know. I'm going to need some help. I basically can't do anything. I may be fooling myself. Maybe I should just pack it in and move home."

"Only you can decide that, and I wouldn't blame you if you did. But you are one of the strongest women I've ever known, who is sweet to boot. What is it that Gary calls you? Sunshine, which seems about right to me."

For a while they opened the cards together. He opened the envelope and handed the card to her to read. The church sent flowers again and told her they would all take turns helping her. Grandma Sadie, the police officers, her parents, and Dylan had all sent her beautiful bouquets and cards with beautiful sentiments. The last card simply said in bold letters "Strike Three You're Out!"

Jessie handed Matt the card to read. He was angry.

His gut was twisted in a knot. He knew Buddy wasn't back in town. They had been watching, but someone was using his MO. Jessie didn't react at all; Matt was a little concerned by her apathy. While Jessie slept the nurse explained it was the medicine they had given her after her hard morning. She promised that Jessie would be a little more alert at lunchtime.

Jessie's process of healing began surrounded by Katie and many new friends, daily conversations with her parents and Sadie, all of whom wrapped her in love and well wishes. People were there to support her and help her until she was back on her feet.

As for the case, it was the time they needed to get all their ducks in a row and be ready for the next stage. Jessie and Jeremy used her down time to get more information on members of the Harvest Club. There were thirty people involved in their area who could be identified as active participants in the club. They were able to distinguish the buyers from the brokers through their deposits into their account. Jessie was positive Gordon was the head man or a leader in the group, but there was still someone whom they couldn't identify who might be the actual killer.

She was finally certified to carry a gun and wrote an amazing article about those who participated in the buying and selling of organs on the black market. Max was happy to run the story, and it became one of the most responded to articles in the history of his paper. Neil told her it was one of the best pieces she had ever written. He took the time to offer her a job, back where she had been safe.

It all came down to today. This was the day. It had been put off several weeks, but she was going with

Matt to Mayor Cummings' office. They were about to plant the seeds that they knew about the Harvest Club. At the same time, Dylan was bringing in Brad and Ed in for questioning.

One could only hope they would want to cop a plea by becoming witnesses for the state. But the hold Gordon had on them made it difficult to believe it could happen.

Matt and Jessie walked into the mayor's office five minutes before their appointment.

"I was surprised to see your name on my schedule today, Matt." He looked up, confident and smooth as ever. "It's good to see you."

"Jason, this is Jessie Reynolds, a good friend."

"It's nice to see you again, Jessie. I remember meeting you at Rick's funeral." He motioned to the chairs. "Please have a seat, both of you. Can I have my secretary bring you anything?"

"No, we're good." Matt answered for them both. "Something has come to Jessie's attention, and I thought she should make you aware."

"As you know I wrote a piece for the local newspaper about black market dealings with organs from India and Africa." She waited for his nod. "In my research I have found a group operating in this area known as the Harvest Club. I haven't been able to identify all of its members to date, but I have found out the names of a few of them."

"As a matter of fact, one of my officers is bringing in two for questioning right now," Matt added. "This is a major ongoing investigation with county and FBI participation."

Jessie took up the story. "My sources tell me there

are somewhere in the neighborhood of thirty active members, so we are trying to identify them as we speak. Matt thought it was important that as mayor you be made aware of what's going on in the investigation."

Both Jessie and Matt watched Jason to see his reaction. He remained calm, his expression one of expected concern. "I appreciate you briefing me. What would you like my office to do? Is there any way I can help?"

"Not at this time, but I'm sure in the future we'll be calling on you. We appreciate your support in this matter." Matt stood up to leave. "We know you're a busy man so we don't want to take up any more of your time." Jessie stood up too, and they both walked out together closing the office door.

"I imagine about now our honorable mayor is on the phone, alerting club members." Matt sounded confident.

"Do you think? It didn't seem like he reacted at all." She pushed the strap of her purse that had slipped down her arm back to her shoulder.

"Jason was a picture of composure except for his fisted hands and the look of steel in his eyes. He's calling them all right. Now all we have to do is be on guard and sit tight."

Matt opened the car door for her, got in on the driver's side, and started the engine. He paused to check his messages as Jessie listened to a message from Jeremy.

"Hi sweet thing, do you remember asking how to get around that firewall? I figured it out, and I've sent the directions in the email. Have fun and keep yourself from harm. If you

*need me to do anything, get back with me. Talk
to you later."*

"What was that all about?" Matt asked.

"I asked Jeremy to help me get around a firewall. I
have a theory, and I was checking it out, but I couldn't
get in. He figured it out and sent me the instructions."

"What are you thinking?"

"The Club has a lot of lawyers and politicians. I
figure they've built in a lot of protection. Once they're
in, the only way out is death. I have a feeling there is a
dirty cop in there somewhere, and that's what they're
scared of. There may be one undercover, but I think
there is one who's benefited by keeping quiet. You
know what I mean."

"I do. I've been checking out some things, too. I've
been waiting for someone to get back to me. I'm
impressed with your hunch here."

Chapter Thirty-One

"I can't believe that bitch survived being shot. She had a vest on, but still the bullet should have penetrated and caused a fatal wound. Why did she have a vest on? Did someone leak information? Someone had to be looking out for her." Gordon slammed his fist down on the table top in front of him.

"What's that supposed to mean? I told you not to do anything. You let your desire for revenge push you to do something stupid. Stupidity is what catches most criminals. I'm trying to figure out what to do next, now that you botched it."

"You had better hurry. They're closing in on the club. The article she wrote has created a stir, and the two of them were in Jason's office as big as you please this morning, telling him they knew about the club and some of its members. They mentioned they had taken two in for questioning. I haven't been able to find out who they are yet, but I will."

"If you remember I told you to keep your temper in check. I also told you to let Gina move away, but no, you wanted her dead. Instead of her being lost somewhere you left her body at the church to be found. You're just plain stupid if you ask me. I believe Gina was your first mistake, and Jessie was your second. Neither of them knew anything about the Harvest Club. Without Gina's death, no one would have been the wiser."

"You just do what you need to do and forgo the lecture."

"You may think you're calling the shots, but without me there isn't any way you could have controlled these guys, and you know it. I refuse to go down because of your petty revenge. I have a plan, and I'm doing it my way. You'll hear back when you need to know. For right now you sit tight and keep your damn mouth shut. I hear they've heard about you in Philly and LA, too, and they know you by the name Gordon or should I call you Mr. Mayor? I can sing and put you all behind bars." He chuckled.

****

It had been a couple of days since they had questioned Brad and Ed. They had already been released. At this time it was about letting them know they were aware of the group's activities, psyching them out, and hoping they would turn on each other. The evidence was mounting against them, especially from the international side, where more than a few people were willing to sell the Americans out.

Jessie arrived early to work. Kip was in the parking lot to watch her when she left the building. This was the day that John was back on the job as the pastor and a new associate pastor was also moving into the office. He was a year older than Jessie and unmarried. Already the women in the church were planning to set Jessie up with him, unbeknown to her.

Kevin Delaney was an energetic young man full of innovative ideas, primed and ready to try them out on a hurting congregation. John was the more seasoned, tenderhearted one, willing to carry them along for as long as it took.

Several of the ladies were there to welcome them and make sure the offices, which had been completely done over after the vandalism, were clean. Coffee was made, and some homemade baked goods were arranged nicely in the small kitchen area. Jessie was happy to be well, in one piece, and back full time at work.

Pastor John walked in the door, and Jessie stood up to greet him. "Good morning, Pastor, it is so nice to see you, and I'm so happy you're my new boss."

"Thank you, Jessie, I'm glad you are no worse for the wear and you have chosen to remain with us after all that has happened to you. I want you to meet the new pastor." He turned around to look for Kevin. "I thought he was right behind me. The ladies all had to talk to him, a single man you know. Here he comes now." He motioned to Kevin. "This lovely young lady is our secretary, Jessie Reynolds. Jessie, this is Kevin Delaney."

"Jessie." The brown haired young man strolled through the door, his green eyes bright above a wide smile. "I heard about all that you've endured to be the secretary in the church; I for one and I know Pastor John as well, are glad that you are here.

"Thank you. I enjoy my job and the congregation." She smiled at him.

Kevin was just a head taller than she, with a nice face, not drop dead handsome, but there was a kindness in his expression. Every time he walked through her office to get something he smiled, his eyes lit up, and two dimples appeared in his cheeks, putting a double emphasis on his great smile.

He was talkative and attentive to anyone who

stopped him to chat, which was so different than Rick. Her mind instantly seized on the idea that Katie would take to him right away and would probably become an active church member. Katie could do worse, because Kevin was a really nice man. Jessie was more impressed with him as the day went on.

Placing books on the shelves, Jessie helped John in his office, answered the phone when it rang, and stopped to talk to all the ladies coming and going in the office. The morning flew by.

She was growing accustomed to the ever-changing landscape of her life. She had no idea what her life in Blue Cove might end up looking like. Who knew what would happen next?

She carried a gun, and she didn't even like guns. Her rib cage was still a little sore, her ankle and toe were healed, but she couldn't run outside alone anymore, she had to have a constant shadow. She worked as a secretary and was aiding in a major sting operation with investigative research. The blissful, peaceful life that had enticed her here in the first place had never materialized, not since the moment Gina had entered it.

Her cell phone's vibration startled her. "Hi, this is Jessie."

"Jessie, Zach Johnson called, and he wants to talk with us at lunch. Do you have time to go today?" Matt asked.

"Let me check." She turned to Pastor John. "Is it okay if I take some time for lunch today, or do you need me to stay around?"

"Of course you can go, Jessie. You got here early and have been working all morning. Go take a break."

He smiled and waved her on with his hand.

"I can. Where and what time?"

"Noon at Patterson's, and by the way, I checked up on our friend Zach and he is legit. According to the FBI he is working under cover for them."

"Even if it's not him, I still believe there is a dirty cop in the equation. All my research shows someone had to have looked the other way and was getting paid to do it."

"Jessie, between you and me, we will be starting to make some arrests beginning in the next few days. I would like you to think about the next aspects of the story, Gina's, the Harvest Club's, and all the evil these guys have done in the name of good. I've been reading some of the stories coming out of India's poor villages where they did some of their greatest business. I'll give you a copy. Their stories need to be told."

"Okay." As soon as the words were out of Jessie's mouth, the cold chills went down her spine. She looked out into the hall and saw Gina standing there staring at here her. Gina's eyes never wavered from Jessie's face, her lips curled into a slight smile, and then she was gone. "Actually, I've written quite a bit and was waiting for the names of those arrested to be filled in."

At noon she crossed the street to Patterson's under the watchful eye of Kip. He went to get something for lunch at Java Joe's and took it back to his car to eat. Matt and Zach were seated at a table already. They watched as Patterson grabbed her hands and talked with her. He was smiling, and she threw back her head and laughed at something he had said.

"People really seem to like her." Zach vocalized his observation.

"She's terrific that way and one hell of a writer. She's the reason we found out about the Harvest Club. Someday you'll have to ask her how it all came about. It's quite a story." Matt was scowling.

"Hi, Mr. Parker. What has you looking so surly? Maybe I should go back to work early."

"I'm not angry. That's my impressed look." He grinned at her.

She faked a shudder. "Remind me never to make you angry then."

After they ordered, Zach got down to business. "I don't have much time, and I don't want to be seen in public with you two for long. The club members are getting nervous as the noose is tightening around them. I'm a little concerned the big boys are going to go underground and leave the others to take the fall. I know you're close to making all the arrests.

"I want to add one more crime to a lengthy rap sheet for these guys. I believe Gordon Stockton killed his wife. I base that on a few things he has said to me over the past several weeks. Her body may need to exhumed. There was no love lost when she died. His position made people believe him when he said it was a heart attack. No one questioned her death at all."

"What do you want me to do? That's out of my jurisdiction, but I know the police chief at Rocky Pointe. I could put a bug in Carter's ear." Matt leaned back in his chair placing his folded arms behind his head.

Zach turned his smoldering gray eyes on Jessie. "Gordon is blaming you for everything. He wants you gone. I think his thirst for revenge is what got you shot at to begin with. He has been talking to me again about it, but I talked him out of it, I think. You're never sure with Gordon. He's unstable. I'm going underground for a while. I think the big guys are getting ready to do something, and I want to know what it is. I'll watch out for you."

Matt was frowning and didn't say much for the rest of the meal. She and Matt walked out together.

"Keep your guard up, Jessie. I'm not going to be around much in the next several days. Kip will keep an eye on you and call for back up if he's concerned."

"It's been pretty quiet." She brushed her blowing hair out of her face with her hand.

"Quiet always bothers me. It doesn't mean things aren't taking place just because you can't hear or see them. It may be nothing, but I'm bothered by Zach."

"Me, too. I wonder why he would risk his cover to be seen in public with us." She looked sideways at him and touched his hand. "I'll be careful and Matt, you do the same." She hurried up the steps and into the church.

****

There was no way in hell he would let Gordon screw this gravy train up. He had a plan that would take care of the weak link and get rid of Gordon at the same time.

He might have been late to the party, but he was going to get his share and be done. He was already on his way to being a very wealthy man and could go underground if need be and resurface later, but there was no way in hell he would let Gordon do the same.

He called Buddy and told him to get back because Gordon wanted him. He knew he would be arrested, but it was one less person he would have to worry about. He would keep the cops so busy the next several days they wouldn't have time to think about anyone else.

He after all was an upstanding citizen. No one knew he was even near the Harvest Club. He had made sure of that, and Zach was becoming the convenient target. Zach was no choir boy, and he had gotten his hands dirty in the club, which the records would show. Matt was halfway to suspecting him already. He would keep them real busy, and they would never know he was in.

Chapter Thirty-Two

"Dylan, I was checking in for any updates you have." Matt called Dylan from his office.

"I was just getting ready to call you. I haven't seen Brad stir. His house is still closed up, shades drawn, car hasn't been moved, and that's unusual for him. Do you think I should check on him?'

"When was your last visual?"

"Yesterday. It was about six when he returned from work."

"It won't break any cover. They know we've been watching them off and on. Go check. If he doesn't answer, let me know."

Matt drummed his fingers on the desk and waited for the phone to ring. It didn't take long. "No reply. What's next?" Dylan asked.

"Canvas a few of the neighbors, and ask if anyone has seen him since the last visual. Check his job, and see if he was expected in and didn't show. If you establish that no one has seen him, go in."

"I'll let you know what I find out." Dylan hung up, and Matt studied Rick's computer, looking for something which would feed his building suspicion.

Rick kept referring to someone as the Grim Reaper.

Twenty minutes later the phone rang again. "Matt, we're going in. Brad didn't show up for work, and someone thought they heard arguing at the house last night."

"I'm on my way. You know the protocol. I'm sending back-up."

Matt arrived at Brad's with the kits, the bags, and the gloves. Dylan kicked open the door open, gun drawn. Brad was tied to a chair, his house had been ransacked, and a good portion of his face and head were missing.

"Geez, what a mess." Dylan snapped his rubber gloves on.

Crime tape went up, the coroner was called, photos, and sketches made of the victim and how he was found. Samples were taken for the lab. It was a long afternoon.

Matt now had two murders on his hands and an attempted murder. He was also trying to figure out why Zach would risk breaking his cover to be seen with them at Patterson's. Matt's suspicion was growing. This crime scene was too messy. Not the normal HC MO.

Matt unplugged the computer in Brad's office, rifled through his desk and personal papers. He saw a tablet where Brad had written the word *Gina* over and over again. He put both of them in bags and tagged them into evidence. He collected some sleeping pills, a gun, and few other personal items.

Matt sent out a couple of officers to canvas the neighbors and talked to the coroner about the time of death so he could establish a time line.

"Did you learn anything?" Matt asked the officers on their return.

"A little of this and a little of that; mostly we were told Brad hadn't been the same since his wife died. The guy right next door heard arguing about 1:30 a.m. He was sure of the time because he looked at the clock. He also thought he heard a gunshot or fireworks about ten or fifteen minutes later."

"Put it in your report, make sure you have his name, address, and phone numbers where he can be reached. His time fits in the approximate time of death established by the coroner."

This job was messy, and unlike Gina's murder site, there was plenty for forensics. Gina's corpse had been clean, no semen, fingerprints, shoe prints, or even tire tracks. No DNA under her nails, no sign of a struggle. This was a sloppy job, and who knew what they would find on the tape across Brad's mouth and the ropes holding his body to the chair? Matt thought maybe someone was being set up. He'd know more if he got a hit on the prints.

Matt went outside to make a call. "Carter, this Matt Parker. I need someone to go over to Don and Pam Bradley and let them know Brad Martin has been murdered. See if they know any of his next of kin. They will know best what to tell the children."

"Consider it done. What's going on in our county? Hardly a murder in years, mostly petty crime. Seems we have graduated to the big league now. Anything else we can take care of?"

"I'll get back to you on that, but I'll need any information on next of kin."

"Okay."

Matt would let them finish processing the scene. He asked for a rush on the fingerprints. DNA would take longer.

Kip was watching over Jessie. She was in safe hands. He went back to the office to make sure all the arrest warrants were in order. They had enough admissible evidence from Rick's computer and now maybe Brad's, all done by the book. He knew he was missing an important detail. It was driving him nuts. He pored over files and notes.

Matt had the results and a hit on the prints in a few hours. It was Gordon Stockton. It didn't make sense to him. Gordon was too careful to be so dumb. He hadn't kept the club off the radar by being dumb. Matt explained to Anderson what he was thinking, and he was told to go ahead with his plan. He picked up his office phone and pressed the numbers.

"Hey, Carter, Matt here…Look, the homicide I called you about earlier has Gordon Stockton's fingerprints all over it. Can you pick him up and hold him for questioning?"

"You mean the mayor? Are you screwing with me?"

"That's exactly who I mean. His fingerprints were the only ones found on the victim, almost too easy. I think it could be a set-up. The scene was a messy job unlike anything we've seen out of the club to this point. They've been careful to maintain spotless records, but the pressure could be getting to them."

"This will rock this community for sure."

"That's a ditto for several communities. We're going start making arrests."

"We'll send over a car to pick him up and hold him for you."

"Thanks, Carter. Let me know when he's in custody."

Matt had just hung up and his phone started beeping again. "This is Matt."

"Matt, you told me to call if I saw anyone pull into the church that shouldn't be there."

"Who do you see?" Matt's thought processes revved into full gear.

"The FBI guy Zach. Is he okay, or should I be concerned?"

"My gut tells me to keep an eye on him. Something seems a little off with him."

"He's just sitting in the parking lot and not getting out of his car."

"Don't let him approach Jessie alone. I'm sending some back up."

Matt walked out to get a bottle of water. Joe came around the corner and grabbed him.

"Hey, Matt, you're wanted on line two. It's an emergency."

He picked the phone up in the waiting area. "This is Matt."

"We've got Gordon, but you're not going to be able to question him unless you can get a corpse to talk. They're processing it now."

"Gunshot or what?"

"Nothing visible, but I'm not willing to write it off as natural causes. Our honorable mayor had some powerful and exotic drugs on hand. His body was lying on the couch, eyes wide open like he recognized who killed him and was stunned."

"Tell the coroner to look for a needle mark and any trace of a drug, one that might not show up in a routine toxicology exam. Traces were found in Gina's body of a strong muscle relaxant, Pavulon, a drug sometimes used in combination with others during surgery. Paralysis and a systemic shut down is just a couple of the symptoms. The person is aware, but can't do anything about it. They usually come out of it in an hour to two; if too much is given it's lights out."

They talked for a few more minutes and then Matt called Kip.

"Is Zach still there?"

"No, he left a while ago."

"Let me know if he comes back and don't let him anywhere near Jessie, you hear?"

"Got it."

Chapter Thirty-Three

Jessie hadn't seen Matt for a few days. She had heard about Brad Martin and Gary Stockton and the arrests of the Harvest Club members; to say Matt was busy was an understatement. Jessie knew he'd be around when things settled down a little to fill her in.

She had left a message earlier on Pam's phone. She wanted to make sure the kids were doing okay. When Jessie's phone rang, caller ID showed it was Pam returning her call.

"Hi, Pam, how are all of you doing?"

"We're hanging in there." She sniffed. "Don and I are wondering though, was Brad a part of Gina's death or not? It has been convenient to blame him so we could make sense out of what happened to our Gina. For the kids' sakes, I almost hope he wasn't."

"I think when all the dust settles, you'll learn he was culpable because of his dealings with the Harvest Club, but he didn't murder her and never recovered from her death."

"Do you really think that? For the kids, I want to believe you."

"It's my opinion, and I believe the facts will back it up."

"Rocky Pointe is in a state of shock over Gordon Stockton and his involvement in the club and all his shady dealings. I can't believe all the arrests that have been made; the mayor of Blue Cove too. I've known Jason's mother for years. She was shocked by her son's dealing and didn't have a clue what he had gotten into. It's a strange world in which we live."

"I hear you. When we can start justifying taking organs from the poor and selling them to save the rich who can afford it, something has gone terribly wrong." Jessie stood up and walked with her phone in hand. "I don't want to get on a soap box. I'll save it for my article. It bothers me how these guys were all taken in and controlled by Gordon."

"Will you be at Brad's memorial tomorrow? Don and I would love to see you."

"I'll be there," Jessie said. Something told her Gina would, too.

Jessie sat at her computer writing her article. Gary was taking the surveillance equipment out of the house. This part of the operation was coming to a close now that all the arrests had been made.

"I'm going to miss you being here every day, Gary." She looked up at him smiled.

"Don't think you'll get rid of me so easy, doll." He grinned. "I'll still need you to give me a decent meal from time to time. You'll have the Kipper to keep you company until Matt thinks the threat is over."

"I hope his job will soon be done. Not that I don't like him, but it will be nice to get back to my life without someone shadowing me. I believe Kip and a couple of the other guys would prefer not to have to run with me in the morning."

"It's been good for them." Gary smirked. "Besides, I think Kip likes being around you and will be happy to come see you even when he doesn't have to." He walked back into the room to get more equipment.

Gary came back through and opened the door with another box. "Well, well, look what we have here." He motioned for Matt to come in. He was carrying a couple of pizzas and a six pack of beer. "Boy, I'm glad to see you've come bearing food. I'll be right back."

Matt looked at Jessie. "How are you doing?" He placed the pizzas on the counter. "Let's eat while it's still hot."

"I'm well." She glanced sideways at him and smiled. "I'm finishing up the next article, but I have some holes in my information that need to be filled in. So is it over with? Can I resume my life?"

"Not so fast. I still have a few unanswered questions."

"Like?"

"Like who really murdered Brad and Gordon Stockton? Why has Zach been hanging around your job? Is he the big guy? I'm not sure, although I think his hands are dirty; he's only dabbled from his undercover position. I don't like him or trust him, but there is someone else that I don't think any of us suspect yet."

"I've never seen Zach at work."

"I know, but Kip has. We're getting close, but we're not home free yet. I think Zach came to us because he wanted to ruin his cover. Someone holds something over him and requested him from the FBI to work undercover on this."

"Did you come to fill in some of the blanks for me?" She went into the kitchen to get the plates, napkins, and glasses ready.

"Sure. What you just said, and I just wanted to see

you. I haven't had a good argument for a few days and I need someone to keep me on my toes." He grinned, his eyes flashed with something else. "Besides I needed to celebrate putting the club out of business." He followed her into the kitchen, filled his plate with several slices of pizza, and took a beer.

Jessie watched him and knew something was bothering him. He needed to talk something out. She walked into the room carrying her plate and sat down in the chair across from him.

"Okay, let's have it." She tucked her legs underneath her.

"What do you mean?"

"Something is bothering you, so out with it. You didn't come here because you missed me."

"I sort of did, but you're right, I do have something on my mind." His eyebrows furrowed, and his back straightened. "If anyone knew what I was thinking, well I can't even begin to imagine."

Gary popped back in and grabbed a slice of pizza. "Don't eat it all. I'll be right back. I have to take this first load to the station." He walked out the door with keys in his hand and pizza in his mouth.

"Don't tell me who you're thinking about, but what makes you think this person might be guilty." She watched his face for a reaction.

"There doesn't appear to be any connection to the Harvest Club, he has an exemplary life, above the fray. This person is a leader, could lead strongly behind the scene. No one would ever suspect him."

"Why do you?"

"Because he seemed to know things I never told him. He's a little too good and throws around a little too much money. Something I read in Rick's diary makes me wonder. What can I say? I have no strong evidence, but a gut feeling. It makes me feel guilty that I even suspect him."

"Dylan told me to go with my feeling the night I was shot, and I think I should say the same to you. Don't overanalyze it."

"But this is someone I've always respected."

"Remember what you told me. In this case, nothing is as it seems. We have a mayor, a city councilman involved, clergy, and lawyers. When it comes to the big three, power, money, and sex, I'm not sure anyone is immune." She watched him wrestle with his thoughts. "Greed, money, and being able to live the good life could draw in someone who was tired of the struggle. I know you just exchange one set of troubles for another, but you know your mind doesn't always play fair."

"You've got that right. How come you're so smart?" He gave her a half-hearted attempt at a smile.

"I was trained by one of the best." She smiled and nodded at him. "The question is, what are you going to do about it?"

"I'm going to set a trap and use you as the bait."

"What makes you think I would be party to being used as bait?"

"Because you're game, and even I've started to believe that Gina wants you to help solve this one."

He stood up to leave, and she walked him to the door. He turned around to look at her. His gaze moved down her face, lingering at her lips before returning to her eyes. Time stood still. He stretched out his hand, letting his finger follow the path his eyes had taken. "Goodnight."

Chapter Thirty-Four

Matt left Jessie's place in no better shape than when he had arrived. Seeing her had helped, yet he still felt a pent-up nervous energy; he lifted weights, ran on the treadmill, and nearly beat his punching bag to death all to no avail. Jessie had told him to *go with his gut.* She was right, of course, but she had no clue who he suspected, and neither did anyone else. Matt was still searching for evidence that wasn't just circumstantial. Anyone who knew the man would find it next to impossible to believe he could be involved. Hell, he found it hard to believe. He wiped the sweat from his brow tallying the evidence up in his mind. Matt's suspicion grew every time he was with the man; maybe he couldn't wait for the evidence to present itself; he would have to go with his gut.

Zach Johnson was a different matter entirely. Zach was guilty, and Matt had enough evidence to put Zach away for a long time. His fingerprints and DNA were found at the scene of Brad's murder even though Gordon was the one who had been framed for it. A money trail led to Zach. He was taking money under the table, kickbacks and payoffs for keeping the club looking like saints and leading the FBI away from them.

Matt had skirted the department and went to his friend Tom at the FBI, and Hamilton, the prosecutor, to see if the case he had built was strong enough to issue a warrant. It was a formality because he knew it was air tight. Matt didn't want to bounce anything off the chief right now. He wasn't sure where the leak in the department was, but he knew someone was giving out privileged information.

He walked outside. The evening air was cool and he could hear the sound of the waves lapping the shoreline. It was a clear night, stars filled the sky, and the crescent moon gave off just enough light to make the trees cast eerie shadows as they danced in the slight breeze. Matt pushed Dylan's number on speed dial, pacing impatiently as he waited. "Hey, Dylan, this is Matt. I'm waiting on the final okay to issue the warrant on Zach. I'm not sure if it will come through before the funeral tomorrow. So I want you and Kip there to keep him under surveillance just in case I'm late. We'll arrest him after the funeral once I have the warrant." Matt sat down on the retaining wall.

"Consider it done. You must be damn happy to see this winding down. Zach's arrest will be the end to a very brutal, time-consuming case."

"I wish I could believe that. I keep thinking there's still someone out there; someone more ruthless, who called all the shots. He's the one who killed Gordon, I'm convinced. I just don't have the evidence to prove it or a suspect yet." Matt's foot tapped restlessly against the wall.

"I think you should just accept that you've done a damn fine job, and it's almost over."

"I will when I've turned over every rock, and I no longer find one of these bastards crawling out from under it. I owe that much to all the people who were affected by these guys here and overseas."

"You can count me in, until you say it's done."

"Thanks, man. I'm going to need you. See you tomorrow."

Matt's night didn't get any better. Jessie filled his dreams, all of which started out innocently enough, but quickly turned into a nightmare. She was drowning, but there was no water, only a murky darkness that consumed her. She looked directly at him never calling out, but with a look of sheer terror in her eyes. He awakened with a start, afraid to shut his eyes again and risk seeing hers. He threw off his covers. His body was soaked with sweat. He was spooked, which was a sensation he hadn't felt in years.

He stacked his hands behind his head, stared up at the dark ceiling, and tried to calm his racing heart. "What the hell," he spoke into the darkness. He picked up his phone to call and see if she was all right. The dream had been too real. Of course, it went directly to her voice mail since it was 2:00 a.m. and she was probably sound asleep. Jessie was still in danger and he knew it.

Early in the morning, Matt called Joe Collins and asked him to attend Brad's service and watch over Jessie. Anxious, he still felt the lingering effects of a rough night.

"Make sure Zach Johnson doesn't go anywhere near her. Oh, and Joe, if you see anything strange or out of the ordinary when it comes to her, no matter who or what it is, call me."

"Are you expecting trouble?"

"I don't know. I'm just trying to cover all my bases."

"I'll have to get Gary to cover the desk because Fred isn't coming in this morning and they called me to take his place. Is that okay?"

"Sure, do whatever. You can ask your wife for all I care or leave the desk unattended, but make sure you're on the job."

"I'll be there."

****

Jessie arrived at the church early. She felt uneasy even though Matt had assured he was just joking about using her as bait. Jessie felt anxious so she got to work and tried not to think at all. It was almost as if she was flying blind, and she didn't like the not knowing.

Restless, Jessie found herself headed, for the umpteenth time, to the sanctuary to check on—she had no idea what. Out of the corner of her eyes, she caught sight of a familiar movement near the stage at the front of the church. Gina's floral dress floated about her as she paced back and forth, her desolate eyes fixed on the entrance to the sanctuary.

Jessie knew the moment the Bradleys walked in. Gina drifted up the aisle toward them, watching their every move; she hovered between her children. Jessie could no longer describe how Gina looked. Her throat tightened, tears formed in her eyes, and Jessie turned away not wanting to intrude on the private and poignant moment which only she could see.

Jessie hugged Pam and shook hands with Don. "How are they doing, Pam?" Jessie whispered.

"Okay, so far. This place is sure to bring back memories from not so long ago. It has only been five months since they lost their mother." Pam placed her arms protectively around her grandchildren. Gina wrapped her arms around her mom's and proceeded with them as Jessie walked the family back into a small reception area where Pastor Kevin was waiting. After seeing to everyone's comfort, she went back to helping the ladies and James in the foyer.

Ten minutes before the start of the service, Zach Johnson walked in next to Chief Anderson. Jessie handed them both a bulletin and forced herself to smile at Zach.

"How are you today?" Anderson grabbed a hold of her hand. "Sometime after the service I have something I need to give you for the church. It's in my car. Do you mind helping me out?"

"Not at all. Just let me know, and I'll go with you." Jessie felt a sudden discomfort as she watched them walk down the aisle a few rows and sit down. She didn't trust Zach. His innocence was still a question to her. She turned to give a bulletin to Melinda.

How strange this day was compared to Rick's funeral. No one from the Harvest Club would be attending. They were either dead or in jail awaiting trial. It had been a strange few months, but the sight of her two friends Dylan and Kip walking in the church doors lightened her mood and banished her troubling thoughts.

"Hey, sunshine, how are you holding up?" Dylan gave her a hug.

"Fine, and I'm sure happy to see the two of you." She regarded them with a smile. "Where's Matt?" She looked past them.

"He's on his way here, at least he was the last time I talked to him." Kip grabbed the bulletin from her hand.

"We definitely have to stop meeting like this." She winked at them. "I'll see you guys after the service." Jessie turned around to hand out another bulletin. Matt rushed by, grabbed it out of her hand, and nodded as he passed her to catch up with Dylan. They all sat down by Zach and the chief.

As the music began, Jessie slipped into an open seat at the back of the church. Her eyes were on Gina whose attention was riveted on her children as she hovered around them. Jessie thought about all the lives that had been impacted by the Harvest Club and the greed of a few men. The Bradleys' loss was great, a daughter, a mother, a son-in-law, and stepfather. How much could one family take?

"I tried to reach you earlier, but you didn't answer," Reba whispered as she slipped into the seat beside Jessie. "Today is the day, I can feel it. It will all stop as it began."

"I know. I'm not sure how, but it will be over soon." Jessie turned to face Reba. "Gina is by her children."

"She's here because he's here. You know, the one who could have put a stop to this years ago, but didn't." She motioned with her hands. "His handprint is on everything that has happened. He will face his accuser alone. Be careful today."

"I will." She still felt as though they were missing something.

****

This was his last funeral, and he was damn happy about that. All this mourning gave him the creeps. No one should have died. It was all Rick's fault. One little detail remained, and then he could slip out of the country unhindered. His wife was due to get the divorce papers sometime later today. He had settled a large sum of money on her as well as the house. He hated to embarrass her this way. She had been good to him. It was all he could think to do to spare her.

Life would have continued on as it had for the last several years if it hadn't been for Jessie and her damn articles. She was going to have to pay. It was too bad really. She was a pretty young thing, but her nose was always where it didn't belong. He would make her squirm the way she had made him. She had taken down the empire he had spent years building, and he wanted her to pay.

He wasn't a bad man really. He had tried to talk Gordon out of killing Gina, but Gordon was a stupid man. He never listened, at least not until the end, and then that was all he could do. He was happy he had thought to grab some of Gordon's exotic drugs just in case. The reason for them had just presented itself. With a little help from a grateful stooge, it would all be over before the lunch was finished here at the church.

When the final notes of the last hymn were sung, the family rose to follow the pastors out to the graveside followed by all the mourners as their row was dismissed. He would watch for his moment. He was always the one with the plan, and his great mind hadn't failed him this time either.

"Why don't you go with everyone to the graveside, and I'll catch up with you at the reception. I need to take care of some business," he informed the others beside him.

"Is it anything I can help you with?" Zach stood up with everyone in his row to walk out.

"No, Fred will help me. He's waiting in the car. He had a headache when we arrived earlier, and he's out there sleeping. Probably just a hangover. You know how these young men can be." Anderson grinned at Zach hoping he bought his explanation. "To tell you the truth, I never like graveside services. I always feel there is a grave waiting for me." He snickered.

Just as he suspected, his top three officers followed Zach out. He would be arrested, which gave him the time he needed. Matt was too smart to be hoodwinked for long. It was good he leave the country sooner rather than later.

Fred had parked the car under a tree on Main Street. Anderson stood outside the cemetery and observed. He was feeling a little edgy, everything had to be precise, or he would never get to the airport on time. So he waited. He would know when the moment was right. He would relish it.

He watched as the three of them edged Zach away from the rest of the people who were filing back toward the church. Yep, now was the time. They already had him in handcuffs with no fight. The three of them were too busy to be concerned with him, and there she was with no one to watch after her. He waited until the three of them had Zach in the cruiser and had pulled out of the parking lot. He motioned to Fred who pulled the car up a little closer to the church.

He looked around and didn't see anyone else from the department watching. He went inside to get her.

"Jessie, you want to come with me? I need to leave a little early. Matt just arrested Zach so I need to get back to the station." He nodded at Joe standing by the wall.

Relief filled her when she heard Zach had been arrested. "I'll be right with you." She couldn't help but smile as she walked toward Anderson. "You must be happy to see this case coming to a successful close."

"That I am little lady, that I am. There are only a few minor things left to clean up, and it will all be done." He held the door open for her.

She followed him to the car and was surprised to see Fred get out of the car and open the trunk. "How are you, Fred?" She walked around to the back of the car.

"Better than you're going to be." He gave her a hard shove into Anderson who jabbed her with a needle.

She cried out, but her body went limp so quickly, she slipped toward the pavement. Anderson caught her before she hit, but she could feel nothing, nothing but fear.

"Hurry, someone is coming; get her in the trunk and shut it."

They pushed her into the murky, smothering darkness of the trunk. She knew now who the Grimm Reaper from Rick's journal was, but it was too late; Jessie knew she was going to die.

Chapter Thirty-Five

Joe looked everywhere for her, but she was nowhere to be found in the church. He had seen her go outside with Anderson. Fred was waiting by the car for them, which was strange because he had called in sick earlier. Jessie had never come back in. Remembering Matt's words, he pulled out his phone.

"Hey, Matt, this is Joe. It may be nothing, but Jessie went outside with Anderson a while ago and never came back in. I can't find her anywhere. Should I be worried? Fred was with him, which I thought was odd." Joe walked back outside once again to look for her.

"What the hell was I thinking? I didn't think he would try anything at the funeral." Matt's voice made Joe wince. "How long has she been gone?"

"Anderson? Crap! Probably ten minutes maybe more."

"Anderson is going to kill her, and Fred's involved in this somehow. I'm on my way to Fred's. He'll take her there."

"Are you sure?" Joe asked. "Why not Anderson's?"

"His wife is there. Fred lives alone." Matt yelled at Dylan and Kip to get to the car and drive. "Joe, call an ambulance, and tell them a drug may have been used that shuts down the system. It could be Pavulon or something similar, so if they have something to counteract it, bring it. Hurry and meet us there. No sirens. Tell them no sirens."

"I'm on my way, Matt. Crap, I didn't know Anderson was in on it." Joe ran to his car, jumped in, and tore out of the church parking lot.

"That's my fault. No one was told, I couldn't believe it myself." Matt held on as Dylan peeled out of the parking lot.

Speeding with lights only from two sections of town, both cruisers pulled up in front of Fred's house within minutes of each other. Anderson's car was parked out front with the trunk partially open. Inside was one of Jessie's shoes. Dylan muttered an expletive when he saw it.

Matt motioned for them to be quiet as they entered the house. He was tense, every nerve on edge as he followed the sound of the mumbling voices to the basement. His .40 caliber Glock at the ready, he slowly inched his way down the stairs trying not to alert Anderson.

****

"I hope you're comfortable, Jessie. Of course I'm joking. You can't possibly feel anything. The only way you know you're breathing and are alive is you can hear me and see me." He patted her hand as he snickered. "I'm sorry for the plastic you're lying on but, it gets messy when you remove someone's kidneys. Which I'm about to do to you." Anderson took out a scalpel and a couple of knives. "I'm no skilled surgeon like Gordon was, so there won't be any tiny incisions, but it won't matter. You messed up my life with all your damn meddling, now I'm going to mess up yours." He laughed as he reached for the scalpel.

"Chief, do you mind if I leave? I don't want to be around to see what you're doing. I get sick at the sight of blood." Fred stood up and walked past him.

"Sure, get the hell out of here. I don't need you anymore. I bailed you out, you've helped me today, and now we're even." He watched him retreat toward the stairs. "Where were we before we were so rudely interrupted? I'm sorry you can't talk to me, but you understand it was the only way. I must admit I would have loved to hear your screams. It would have been music to my ears. Instead all I get is the terror in your eyes."

Out of the corner of Jessie's eye she saw a floral dress float by and heard a sound coming from the stairs.

Anderson had heard it too. "It would seem we have visitors. Matt, I know you're there. You may as well join us. I knew you would figure it out eventually, but I had hoped to get away before you did." Invincible, Anderson in one fluid motion pulled out his automatic, his finger caressing the trigger, and whirled around to face Matt, but it was Gina who stepped between them, suddenly solid, suddenly very real. Wild-eyed, Anderson fired several rounds at her, one missing Matt by inches. Matt didn't miss. He hit the mark with deadly accuracy. Anderson was dead before he hit the ground, his eyes wide open.

****

Anderson had to have seen Gina was her last coherent thought. Everything was in slow motion, and it was becoming hard for her to focus. People's faces were blurred, and their words sounded jumbled. A needle was inserted into her arm, and an oxygen mask was put over her nose and mouth. She could feel the panic, but she was trapped. She couldn't scream or even move. They were free to do whatever they pleased to her. She felt herself slipping away, but she didn't want to; she wanted to live. Gina was by her side looking with love and peace-filled eyes at her. Why could she see her and not anyone else? Gina bent down and kissed Jessie's cheek. Gina's transformation was beautiful. She hovered above Jessie slowly fading into a bright light never taking her eyes from Jessie's face. Was this what it felt like to die? Mercifully, Jessie passed out.

****

From a distance Matt had watched as Jessie's eyes, which had been filled with terror, suddenly looked serene. He had seen something hovering next to her until she passed out, something he wouldn't even try to explain.

Matt knew Anderson had seen something also that had frightened him. When he had first come around the corner, Anderson was terrified and shot wildly, but not at him. He looked through him with a shocked look on his face. One bullet flew within inches of Matt's head, and he didn't give Anderson a chance to get off another shot. He killed him, one bullet, one shot.

"Is she going to be okay?" Matt walked over to where they worked on her, holding his breath.

Neither of them looked up. "She's stable," one said tersely. "We'll know in a little while if the reversal agent is working." They lifted her on to the stretcher. Within minutes she was en route to the hospital.

Matt and Dylan went through the motions of processing the crime scene. Anderson had been his mentor. More importantly, he'd been a friend.

"Are you going to be okay, Matt?" Dylan walked up beside him.

"We could have lost her and still may for that matter." Matt turned away. "The only way I could prevent it was to kill a friend. Sometimes I wonder if the job is worth it."

"The team is here to take over. You need to get out of here, Matt. The town council has been notified, and they said you're on paid leave of absence until the investigation is done." Dylan put a hand on Matt's shoulder. "It's a formality. You know the routine. Joe and I both were witnesses to what happened."

"I know how it goes." He handed his gun and badge to Kip.

"Let's go to the hospital and see how she's doing." Dylan jerked his chin at the door. "You won't be good until you know, and neither will I."

Chapter Thirty-Six

It was over.

There were no more shadows following her. She was running alone again, enjoying her life, but waiting. Waiting for what, she didn't know. She put her gun inside a shoe box in her closet. She was glad she hadn't had to use it. Jessie relished the idea of giving life to people through words more than the thought of having to take away someone's life with a bullet. And still she waited for him to come by. She hadn't seen him since she left the hospital.

Her phone beeped, and she answered. "This is Jessie."

"I'm in the neighborhood. Do you mind if I stop by for a few minutes?" Matt's voice came over the phone.

Finally. Her heart raced. "Sure, I'm not doing anything, and I have something I wanted to give you."

"I'll be there in a few." Matt clicked off his phone.

He knocked on the door, and when she answered she thought he looked really good, but a little tired. "It's been a while. Come in." She motioned him into the room.

"How are you? I'm sorry I haven't been to see you sooner." He fidgeted with his hands and paced, looking uncomfortable.

"It's been three weeks since the last time I saw you, but who's counting?" She grinned at him, hoping to put him at ease. "Would you like something cold to drink?"

"If you have a beer, that would be great. Otherwise I'll have a glass of water." He sat down in one of the chairs and stretched out his long legs with his arms folded behind his head. He closed his eyes and sighed.

She handed him a beer, and she sat down on the couch with a glass of iced tea. "How are you?" She tucked her legs under her. "The last several days must have been crazy."

"They have been." He took a long swallow of his beer. "Everyone is still in shock over the chief. I knew all along I was overlooking something important, but not until the end could I have imagined it would be him pulling the strings. Nor would I have ever believed he would hurt you." He looked thoughtfully at the bottle in his hand. "I'm sorry, Jessie, God, I'm so sorry you came so close to dying. That's hard for me to live with." He folded his hands and unfolded them.

"Matt, there's no way you could have known what he would do when he was cornered. I don't blame you. I ignored my own warnings in my head because I couldn't believe he was guilty." She grabbed his hand. "I'm going to be okay. I have someone helping me through the fear I sometimes still have."

"I've been seeing someone too."

"How is his wife?" Jessie changed the subject trying to put him at ease.

"His wife is in shock, and so is the family."

"When did you first suspect him?"

"His reaction to you was one. How he stayed as far away as possible from the Harvest Club, was another. He let me handle it when he should have been the one. I also found out that he had requested Zach personally as the FBI's undercover man, which made me wonder if he had something on Zach and could control him." He scratched his head. "Why I didn't just go with my instinct right off, I will never know."

"Anderson always seemed like such a nice guy to me." She sipped her tea.

He took a swig of his beer and closed his eyes again. "Four people are dead, and twenty-eight behind bars in this area. Who knows what will happen in Philly and on the West Coast? This was big, Jessie, really big."

"At least the club is shut down, for now." She sighed. "With the kind of money they were making, you never know if someone else will come along and take up where they left off."

"I talked to Grandma Sadie today." He rubbed his temples and smiled at her expression.

"Why?" She frowned at him.

"I wanted to. I told her what great articles you had written and how you played the part to the end so well."

"You do know Anderson saw Gina?"

"I think I knew that when I saw his terrified expression before I shot him. He was looking through me, not at me."

"I know I'll never see her again. She's been a part of me for three months."

"I still don't get it." He sat forward in the chair.

"I don't either. It just was. I can't explain, but I no longer doubt or fear it."

"You're something, you know it? You had a run in with a ghost who became a part of your life; you were chased, and nearly killed. Still, somehow, you manage to be nice. You blow all my theories on big city girls."

"Someday we might have to have a little discussion about your stereotypes, and just how wrong they are." She smiled. "So who is going to be the new chief?"

"You're looking at him." He grinned.

"I should have known." She matched his grin. "Who else could they give it to after you took down the Harvest Club? Now I want to hear about everything that happened. I have a news article to write. So start at the beginning of the arrests."

"After Brad and Gordon were murdered, we started arresting all of the club members. I really think they were in a state of shock. At first no one was talking, and they all had the club's lawyers scrambling back and forth between them all."

"That must have been a sight to see. Did any of them show any remorse for what they had done?" She took another sip of her tea.

"I think they were all a little sorry they got caught. They were making big bucks and justified what they were doing."

"Why did they kill Gina? Without her death, they probably would still be a hidden group." She stretched her legs out. They were going to sleep.

"I've asked that same question over and over again. Here's what I've learned so far. The club has been active in this area for about five years. It started on the West Coast after Gordon left the transplant team he was interning on. Then he started a group in Philly and here of all places." He paused as he went into the kitchen to get a glass of water. "He did all his recruiting by the web site. It sounded like some kind of civic organization, but once the guys realized what the group was actually about, they couldn't get out. If they did, they were permanently silenced.

"Early on, Anderson found out about the club. He went to Gordon Stockton and threatened to turn him over to the FBI, but Gordon offered him a thirty-five percent cut of every penny the club made to turn his head and let them work. Gordon recruited him with the same line he had used to everyone else—the good they were doing, how many lives were saved by the transplants, and how many good people died waiting, because there were not enough donors. So everyone had to pay the chief thirty-five percent. He was the Grim Reaper and Gordon was the Harvest Master; both of them were very wealthy men."

"Not anymore." Her lips tightened.

"True. Anyway, Gina found out about the money. Like you said, she knew what they made and that they didn't have the money they were throwing around, and she got suspicious. She found the bank statements on Brad's computer and asked about them.

"They used scare tactics to begin with. Buddy followed her and pulled some things, like he did with you. Brad would never let her report it. He kept trying to keep her quiet, promising the club to keep her in line. I believe he probably loved her."

"He certainly wasn't the same after her death or at least for the months that I knew him." Jessie sighed and shook her head. "Who called for her murder?"

"Gordon wanted her dead. Anderson didn't want it, he thought they should let it go. When they heard she was leaving, Anderson was even more adamant about letting her leave. But Brad didn't want her to go, and Gordon thought they could control the men even more if they realized they had to keep their families in line or else.

"It was then Anderson requested Zach Johnson specifically from the FBI. He knew Zach wasn't opposed to looking the other way if money was in play. All he had to do was act the part of an undercover cop. So as the police started looking into the murder, Anderson, Gordon, and Zach could cover their bases and the other guys could take the fall."

"Sounds simple enough, but what went wrong with their plan?"

"Simply put, you did." He grinned at her. "Anderson was furious when Rick brought you here to work at the church. Zach did a search on you and knew your reputation as a reporter. They didn't have a clue that you knew nothing about the murder. They thought you took the job to do the story. So enter Buddy again to try to scare you off. After the night Buddy chased you, they thought for sure you would quit. They didn't count on you staying and writing the article about Gina."

"It was a simple human interest story. There was no threat in it."

"True, but it brought Gina to the minds of people. It reminded Anderson how angry he was at Gordon for having her killed. She was kidnapped, given a drug that caused paralysis, her kidneys were removed and her eyes, and then Zach shot her and dumped her at the church."

"It was brutal. I can't believe what they did to her." Jessie shivered. "What's worse was putting her in front of the church to be found by people who cared about her."

"Anderson told Gordon he was stupid and sloppy. It was an ongoing war. He was determined not to be taken down by Gordon's stupidity. He wanted you left alone, too. He didn't believe you had knowledge of the Harvest Club. So Gordon took it into his hands and shot you, but you didn't die. You did the article about the black market, and we went to see Jason. That's when Anderson and Zach decided to get rid of Brad and Gordon at the same time. Brad was killed by Zach, and Gordon's fingerprints were planted, and Gordon was injected with the drug he gave to Gina by Anderson." He stood up stretched and sat back down.

"I guess I'll never understand the why's of it, but at least Gina can rest in peace. She got to confront her murderer." She leaned forward and rested her head on her hands.

"You were the one thing they hadn't accounted for. Everyone liked you, you had a stellar reputation as a writer, they couldn't control you, they couldn't scare you, and they couldn't kill you. Plus, you had Gina on your side. We owe you a lot for a job well done."

Jessie got up and walked into the bedroom and brought out the gift she had picked up over the Fourth. She handed it to him to open. "This is a little something to say thank you for keeping me alive. Your instincts saved me more than once."

Matt opened the box to find a handcrafted pewter knight sitting on his charger with lance drawn. Attached was a note. *To Blue Cove's own knight in shining armor, who rescued the damsel in distress and saved the town from evil. She humbly thanks you.*

He laughed a loud and hearty laugh. "I never saw any damsel in distress, only you who fought me every step of the way."

"I surrender. No more wars for now." She held her hands up. "So what's next for you?" she asked.

In one quick move, he took her hand and pulled her into his lap. "Thank you." He kissed her on the cheek. He looked into her eyes, draping his arm around her shoulder.

"My first official act as the new chief is to ask you to work with me, as a part of my team, on any cases in the future. I know we haven't always gotten along, but somewhere along the line I've come to respect your professionalism, the way you handle people, and I want you on my team. What do you think?"

She pursed her lips and tilted her head. "I could live a peaceful, quiet life as a church secretary, with my beautiful view. Or I can see ghosts, carry a gun, be a target for murder. Hmmm, let me think about this." She paused, trying to keep a straight face. "I choose the second." She jumped up quickly. The rakish look in his eyes made her nervous.

He stood, shook her hand, and headed for the door with her following him.

"You still need to work at the church and write your stories. It won't pay much and maybe there will be no action. There wasn't much before you come to town, but on the other hand you do have a nose for a good story."

"I love my job at the church, and I like writing for the paper, so I guess we're good to go."

"Okay, then." He opened the door and stepped out. He put his foot back in before she closed it. Leaning in he kissed her, one long, hot kiss that seemed to go on forever. "Damn, but I've wanted to do that since I first saw you. Since I'm not on the clock today, it seemed like a good time to me."

Jessie's jaw dropped open, and she stared at him. On impulse, she reached up pulling his head down and kissed him back. "See you around." She couldn't catch her breath.

He traced her cheek down to her full lips and kissed her again. He picked her up in his arms, carried her inside, and kicked the door closed. "Let's give Blue Cove something good to talk about, Jess." He laughed. She smiled.

A word about the author...

Iona lives in Colorado with her husband of many years. As speaker, teacher, and a secretary, she has shared and heard many wonderful stories. Her love for family and the colorful people she has met have fed her passion for writing.